Praise for *THE HE*

"Cassia and Nathan's passionate romance will captivate readers. This is a winner."

—*Publishers Weekly* (starred review)

"Caldwell, following *The Duke Alone*, continues the stories of the chatty and charming McQuoid sisters butting heads with reluctant members of the *ton*, with some added swashbuckling for good measure."

—*Library Journal*

"Caldwell creates a delightful Regency romp filled with crackling dialogue and steamy love scenes . . . A fun, fast read for those looking for a satisfying escape."

—*Historical Novels Review*

Praise for *THE DUKE ALONE*

"Caldwell's chaste, emotional romance will charm readers looking for a Christmas story that mixes melancholy with joy."

—*Library Journal*

"Caldwell's humor, which often toes the line into farce, lightens the gloom of loneliness around the characters, and she hits every beat of the romance formula with charm and clever pacing. Sheer fun for readers who adore *Pride and Prejudice*, Christmas, and dogs."

—*Historical Novels Review*

A SURE DUKE

A Lady's Guide to a Gentleman's Heart
A Matchmaker for a Marquess
His Duchess for a Day
Five Days With a Duke

Lords of Honor

Seduced by a Lady's Heart
Captivated by a Lady's Charm
Rescued by a Lady's Love
Tempted by a Lady's Smile
Courting Poppy Tidemore

Scandalous Seasons

Forever Betrothed, Never the Bride
Never Courted, Suddenly Wed
Always Proper, Suddenly Scandalous
Always a Rogue, Forever Her Love
A Marquess for Christmas
Once a Wallflower, at Last His Love

Sinful Brides

The Rogue's Wager
The Scoundrel's Honor
The Lady's Guard
The Heiress's Deception

The Wicked Wallflowers

The Hellion
The Vixen
The Governess
The Bluestocking
The Spitfire

A SURE DUKE

Text copyright © 2024 by Christi Caldwell Incorporated
All rights reserved.

Published by Montlake, Seattle

www.apub.com

Amazon, the Amazon logo, and Montlake are trademarks of Amazon.com, Inc., or its affiliates.

ISBN-13: 9781662503849 (paperback)
ISBN-13: 9781662503832 (digital)

Front cover design by Juliana Kolesova
Back and spine cover design by Ray Lundgren
Cover images: © Juliana Kolesova; © zef art / Shutterstock;
© WindOfHope / Shutterstock; © jocic / Shutterstock

Printed in the United States of America

Alison Dasho, Lindsey Faber, and my entire team at Montlake.
In more than eighty books, I've prided myself on having hit every deadline. But sometimes life puts up roadblocks. The end of 2022 and the beginning of 2023 saw several members of my family and me with a number of health challenges. Through it, my team at Montlake showed me only kindness and grace. They supported me every step of the way, urging me to put myself and my family first.
Dallin and Alexandra's story exists because my editorial team loved the idea of their romance, believed in me, and waited patiently while I completed this book.
From the bottom of my heart, thank you. A Sure Duke is for you!

Chapter 1

London, England
Winter 1814

Lady Alexandra Bradbury stood at the corner of her bedchamber windows and contemplated the dark limestone townhouse directly across from her rooms.

The nearly full moon cast portions of the seemingly empty residence in a pale light, while the night sky shrouded the remainder of the home in mysterious shadows as curious as the people who dwelled there during the London Season.

Over the course of her seventeen—nearly eighteen—years, Alexandra, the eldest daughter of the Marquess of Queensbury, had wondered about much.

As a small child, she'd wondered why girls must wear skirts while boys everywhere had the freedom and luxury of far more comfortable-looking breeches.

As a young woman just out of the nursery, with the answer to that ponderous question having been ingrained, she'd wondered why daughters must be the ones to make the ideal match.

However, the greatest source of her curiosity was a roof.

Not just any roof, either. More specifically, the roof belonging to their eccentric neighbors Lord and Lady Abington, parents of the big, noisy McQuoid brood.

Alexandra peered more closely.

If she looked just so, it seemed as if the builders had left a tall silver pole . . . along with several narrow wood scaffolds.

Her mother would say one would expect the unruly McQuoids to have sloppy contractors, and she'd declare the roof an eyesore. Or she would if she bothered to look out and up at their Mayfair neighbors' roof.

Her mother, however, had always had a way of only looking down on the McQuoids.

Though loving parents, Alexandra's mother and father insisted on maintaining connections with the most respected and distinguished aristocratic families. As such, her mother hadn't ever been discreet in her opinions of that family with both Scottish ancestry and ties to mere merchants and those who worked for a living.

Alexandra would no sooner admit it aloud than speak the truth to her mother, but those exchanges she'd overheard between her parents had only further fueled her fascination with their neighbors.

A figure joined her at the window.

The crystal pane reflected back the image of her younger sister Cora. "What do you think they do up there?" she murmured.

"How should I know?" Alexandra directed that response to their reflection in the glass.

She didn't know what work had been done by the men hired to see to the repairs of the earl and countess's household. Just as she hadn't known for the past seven years why the McQuoid brothers and cousins and uncle and father often gathered atop the roof.

She *wanted* to know.

"Do you want to know what I believe?" their youngest sister, eleven-year-old Daphne, piped in from her place over at the hearth.

Alexandra and Cora spoke as one. "No."

Apparently, there was one thing on which they could concur.

Their mischievous sister went on anyway. "*I* believe they are pagans who assemble every full moon and make sacrifices to their overlord."

This managed to call Cora's attention away from Alexandra. The middle Bradbury girl went wide-eyed. "They don't look evil. In fact, the gentlemen are quite . . . handsome. Particularly—" She instantly cut off from whatever else she'd intended to say.

Alexandra sharpened her gaze briefly on Cora.

"Ah, yes," Daphne drawled. Pulling her knees up close to her chest, she looped her arms about them. "How could I forget that pagans have strict rules when it comes to the appearance of their members?"

Cora's eyes grew bigger. "Indeed."

"She is just jesting," Alexandra said, earning a laugh from Daphne. She favored the younger minx with a warning look, but her efforts where her youngest sibling was concerned proved in vain.

"I'm not," Daphne stated, and then whispered at their naiver sister, "Pagans, I tell you."

"What do you know about pagans, Daphne?" Alexandra asked impatiently.

"Loads." The girl gave a toss of her untamable ink-black curls. "I *am* one."

Even as Alexandra rolled her eyes, Cora clutched at her throat. "You mustn't let Mother find out, Daphne."

"There is nothing to find out," Alexandra said in a soothing way, even as a familiar worry filled her breast. "There are no pagans," she repeated.

Beautiful as the London Season was long, and innocent to the point of naive, Cora would find herself prey to all manner of unsavory sorts with wicked intentions when she made her Come Out.

Daphne opened her mouth to speak.

Alexandra sliced a warning glare—one she'd learned from her nasty governess—Daphne's way.

The younger girl seemed to think better of whatever yarn she'd intended to feed Cora.

Who'd have imagined there'd be uses for that frosty look, after all?

The moment her properly chastened sibling returned her focus to whatever outrageous book she'd secured from God knew where, Alexandra turned her attention back to their neighbors' townhouse.

"She isn't wrong," Cora murmured quietly, her words entirely too soft to reach the little figure they now spoke of. "I've seen several of them, you know, out there on that roof under the full moonlight."

That gave Alexandra pause. But then, if she had seen the McQuoids gathered on that roof, it would make sense that others—including her sisters—had as well.

"They *may* be pagans," Cora ventured, her voice trembling slightly.

God, when Cora got an idea into her head, she dug in like Lord Nelson at Trafalgar. "They *aren't*."

"But how do you know for *sure*, Alexandra?"

From where she sat, and with her nose now buried in her book, Daphne, not bothering to look their way, called out, "She *doesn't* know."

When Alexandra and Cora both ignored their youngest sister, the little girl let out a small *humph* and turned her page sharply enough to nearly tear it.

"Listen to me, Cora," Alexandra said, dropping her voice for good measure. "I just *know*." She tamped down the actual explanation of how she could speak with such certainty. To confess as much to Cora or *anyone*, for that matter, would reveal entirely too much.

Fortunately, her sister let the matter rest.

The truth was Alexandra had stared at that rooftop long enough to observe and know for certain the male McQuoids gathered at all manner of times: Under the fingernail moon. The half moon. The three-quarter one. The full. To say as much, however, would expose the fact that Alexandra had been staring at that household. And ladies did not stare—certainly not at gentlemen who gathered upon a rooftop like they were socializing in a parlor and not outside, high above the world below, in all kinds of weather.

Unfortunately, Alexandra's own pesky curiosity remained. What did the McQuoids do when they gathered there? What drew them to that apex of their household? What did the streets of London look like from that high vantage point?

And for all the ways in which her governess and mother had succeeded in schooling Alexandra, molding her into a perfectly proper lady, there remained that rebellious part, deep inside, that wondered about topics she oughtn't.

Cora wrapped her arms around Alexandra and rested her chin on Alexandra's right shoulder. "They're not coming back, you know."

From where they stood, eyeing that dark household, her younger sister dangled that tantalizing reminder.

"I don't know that, actually," Alexandra lied, keeping her gaze on that darkened townhouse on the opposite side of their Mayfair street.

And her sister saw right through it.

"That I'd find hard to believe, as you've been fixated on that window for the better part of a week."

Ten days, to be precise.

"You can go," Cora gently urged.

"Yes," Alexandra agreed, and looked to their youngest sister. "Cora is correct. It is late and long past time we sought out our beds." That was the first good thought any of them had had all night.

"That isn't what I meant," Cora murmured. "I meant . . . you can . . . go . . ." She angled her head and nodded several times at the windowpanes.

Alexandra puzzled her brow. What was she on about? Go? "Go . . . *where?*"

"Surely you aren't that thick." With a great exhalation, Daphne stormed to her feet and, book in hand, marched over, joining them beside the window. "Across the street, silly. She means across the street."

With wide, innocent eyes, Cora nodded. "That is correct . . . er . . . with the exception of you being thick."

Daphne waggled her thin black eyebrows. "Notice Cora did not disagree with my calling you silly."

Her pretty features stricken, Cora drew back. "Oh, no. I would never, ever call you—"

"Silly," Daphne supplied for her. "But you did think it."

"I'm the silly one?" Indignant, Alexandra crossed her arms at her chest. "This from the two of you, who are suggesting I steal across the street in the middle of the night and break into our neighbors' household?"

"Well, we couldn't very well suggest you do it in the middle of the *day*," Cora said with her usual guilelessness.

A laugh burst from Daphne's lips.

Refusing to let her sister's hilarity get a rise out of her, Alexandra gave both of them a hard look. "I'm not entering the McQuoid home uninvited." Or invited. Their mother would have looked at both those possibilities with a like horror.

"I'm sorry." Cora bowed her head. "I forgot."

Don't ask. Don't ask. "Forgot *what*, Cora?"

"That you are stuffy and proper," Cora said without inflection and with her usual complete lack of artifice.

Had it been uttered by absolutely anyone else, that pronouncement would have been an insult. Cora, however, remained incapable of cruelty.

"I'm not stuffy," Alexandra felt inclined to say anyway.

"Stuffy and proper," her younger sister reiterated, lifting two fingers. "Both of those together."

A noisy giggle interrupted their debate.

They looked over to their youngest sister, standing there, taking in the sisterly quarrel with the same attention she might have given a Punch and Judy show.

"I, for one, think it's a splendid idea," Daphne said.

Cora beamed, her face glowing with pride. "See?"

Drawing from a well of patience she'd built up just for such talks with her sisters, Alexandra spoke in a slow, even way. "It is a dangerous idea, Cora," she said gently, needing to know her sister understood at least that.

"Ah, but our doubts are traitors and make us lose the good we oft might win by fearing to attempt," Cora murmured.

"Never tell me?" Daphne called out. "Shakespeare."

Cora smiled widely and clapped her hands. "Yes!"

Of course it was Shakespeare. Because for all the lessons on proper social decorum Cora had failed hopelessly at through the years, she'd an uncanny ability to read and recall any quote—from the most famous to the most obscure—penned by the Great Bard.

"Yes, well, I say if Alexandra is too stuffy to visit the roof, then it must be either me or you, Cora."

Alexandra choked midswallow. "A-absolutely n-not," she strangled out through a strained breath.

"And why not?" Daphne persisted.

Why? her youngest sister asked. *Why?* "Because it's dangerous. Rash. Fraught."

"There she goes, making another one of her lists," Daphne said under her breath.

Yes, because making lists had always had a calming effect, and this time was no exception. *"And childish,"* Alexandra added, giving her a pointed look.

Daphne stuck her tongue out, and it was all Alexandra could do to keep from returning that gesture.

"Well, *one* of us has to go," Cora said matter-of-factly.

"No, we do n—"

Daphne interrupted the rest of Alexandra's denial. "I shall go."

"But I'm older," Cora argued.

"Yes, but I'm stealthier and you're often distracted and—"

As the girls broke out into a full-blown quarrel, Alexandra dug her fingers into her temples.

For all the ways in which Cora and Daphne were different—from their competing looks to the books they read to the state of their savviness—there was one way in which they were the same: they possessed the Bradbury obstinacy. Once one of them had an idea in their head, there was no shaking them free of it.

Alexandra let her arms fall to her sides. "I'll do it."

Her sisters continued their bickering.

"I said, I'll do it!" Alexandra shouted, effectively ending Cora and Daphne's argument midsentence.

"You shouted," Cora whispered with the same wonderment she might have shown reading a never-before-discovered Shakespearean text.

A blush slapped at Alexandra's cheeks. "I don't yell."

"*Or* sneak about." Daphne grinned. "It appears this is a night of firsts."

This was a night of madness, was what it was. Alexandra marched over to her wardrobe and plucked out a chemise and a dress. Exchanging her night skirts for a dark sapphire gown, she got herself dressed. "This is utterly ridiculous," she muttered as she slipped into the article.

"Here, let me help you," Cora said, rushing over.

It was a night of firsts in many ways, then. For Alexandra was and had long been the protector of her sisters. Now, in a great reversal of roles, Cora turned Alexandra about and buttoned up the back of her dress.

This was the absolute only reason Alexandra was doing something so outrageous. Because if she did not, it was a certainty one of her sisters would.

Daphne drew a black cloak from the wardrobe and tossed it around Alexandra's shoulders. "There we are! Splendid."

"Splendid," Alexandra mumbled, and a short while later, she found herself making her way down to the servants' entrance, into the now quiet kitchens, and outside to the darkened courtyard. The soles of her delicate satin slippers served her well in her furtiveness, but failed dismally when it came to protecting her from the frigid winter weather.

The night's chill ran all the way through her, and to keep her teeth from chattering, she gritted them hard.

Alexandra, however, *had* to get on top of that roof. She needed to see just what drew the McQuoid men there when they were in town.

Now, with their entire family having gone for the winter and their servants off while the property was being renovated, Alexandra found herself with an unprecedented opportunity to at last have an answer to her questions.

And yet, as she climbed that curious family's front steps, a dangerous thrill of anticipation rolled through her.

Alexandra was reaching for the handle when suddenly, her nape tingled, freezing her fingers on the bronze latch.

Stiffening, she stole a glance about at the surrounding residences. But for the handful of rooms still lit in her family's household, all the other townhouses remained shrouded in the same darkness they'd been in since their families had departed for their various estates scattered throughout the English countryside.

The Duke of Aragon's on the diagonal. The Duke of Stonehaven's adjacent. The Marquess of Merryweather's.

Alexandra slid her gaze back to the lavish timber moldings of the newly installed front doors of the McQuoids' townhouse. The wooden nailheads had been fashioned into an ornate design, and she peered at it for a long moment, more to make sense of whether the shape was a deliberate one than—

Another shiver raced up her back—an apprehensive shiver that came from a sense of being watched.

Tap Tap Tap Tap.

A gasp exploded from her lips, and she spun toward the staccato beat being drilled into the quiet. Her gaze collided with her family's home—more specifically, her noticeably illuminated bedchamber windows and her pair of sisters framed in those frosted panes.

Both girls waved excitedly back.

It is just Cora and Daphne.

Some of the tension slid from her frame, and she let her shoulders relax.

Of course it had been only her sisters watching her. On that score, there was nothing to fear.

Just then, there came the noisy creak of hinges in need of oiling.

Daphne threw the windows wide and leaned out. "Well, then, are you going to go in or *not?*" she called, and the winter still coupled with the nighttime quiet made the young girl's voice inordinately and damningly loud.

Alexandra slapped a finger against her lips. *"Shh!"*

Daphne merely giggled.

Cora snatched their sister by her arm and drew the troublesome girl back inside the room.

A moment later, Cora reappeared and smiled widely.

Alexandra smiled back. For all the ways in which Cora was so often without common sense, at least in this she'd exhibit some restr—

"I reminded her we must be quiet," Cora said, her voice several degrees louder than Daphne's.

Oh, bloody hell. At this rate, they may as well have been waving signs announcing their—her—turpitude to the entire world.

Grabbing for the bronze handle once more, Alexandra pressed down. The door gave with a surprising ease.

Before her sisters descended into any further jubilant celebrations, Alexandra rushed inside and brought the panel shut behind her.

Although infinitely warmer than being outside, a sharp chill hung over the vacant townhouse.

Bringing her palms together, Alexandra rubbed furiously in a bid to bring some warmth to her trembling digits.

"A McQuoid *would* leave the door open," she muttered to herself as she glanced about the spacious foyer with its parquet wood floor. Elaborate white, rectangular pillars framed the generous space; each column sported a silk taupe curtain, drawn as if warmly welcoming guests and visitors.

Her teeth chattering and yet the discomfort of the cold forgotten in place of ribald curiosity, Alexandra skimmed her gaze over the white, square pedestals built adjacent to them. Each sported unobtrusive lidded urns.

Absently, Alexandra trailed her fingertips along the gilded trim etched upon the white porcelain. Had they belonged to Alexandra's mother, the marchioness, the vases would have been ostentatious and overflowing with bright blooms.

Unlike her mother's taste, which favored the garish—like furniture dripping in gold—there was a surprising—and welcome—cleanliness to the lines and styling of the McQuoid residence.

Alexandra wandered past the pillars and looked up the long, dark wooden stairway adorned with a Prussian blue runner.

She didn't know what she'd anticipated the McQuoid home to look like, exactly.

Nay, that wasn't altogether true. On more occasions than she could recall, servants or the McQuoid men had carted peculiar-looking contraptions and statues and various other unidentifiable pieces through their double front doors. Given her neighbors' eccentricity, she'd expected the residence to be garish and as idiosyncratic as the family itself.

Only, it was none of those things.

Alexandra smoothed her fingertips over the wooden hand railing and climbed the steps, stopping only when she reached the first landing. A Venetian glass mirror the length of the landing had been fashioned into the wall; the angles of the octagonal piece had been painted in a soft shade of blue that complemented the carpet lining the staircase. A white console table on fluted conical legs sat tucked seamlessly against the staircase with an empty vase atop it.

And there, framed perfectly in that stunning mirror, was . . . Alexandra, her cheeks flushed red from the cold and her curls a hopeless tangle about her face.

Alexandra, the intruder.

Alexandra, who'd broken into her neighbors' residence.

And long overdue, much-deserved guilt swamped her.

She'd no right being here. Her family may have been lifelong neighbors of the McQuoids, but they may as well have resided on opposite ends of London for all the dealings and interactions they'd had over the years.

A brief moment of madness accounted for her presence here, even now. That was all there was to it.

Alexandra gathered her skirts; the muslin dress under her cloak crunched and crackled noisily.

She wrinkled her nose. With the carelessness she'd shown selecting the attire for her clandestine mission, she was decidedly not made for thievery.

Not that she was a thief.

She'd not taken anything.

Alexandra turned to go. Her foot touched the top step when she froze.

Yes, she'd no right coming inside the McQuoid residence, and yet, how common was it that members of Polite Society passing through the countryside stopped to visit and explore other lords and ladies' estates when there was no one in residence? Why, it was an English custom as old and true as tea and crumpets.

Surely, visiting a townhouse wasn't that different?

And she was already here. She may as well just climb the remainder of the way, at last have a look, and assuage her curiosity.

Reversing course once more, and before the part of her prone to logic and decorum could rear its head, Alexandra bolted upstairs, climbing and climbing and then reaching . . . a landing, which led to a different staircase, this one narrower but too central to be a servants' passage.

Her heart hammered with a breathless anticipation, and Alexandra raced the remaining way until she reached *it*—the doorway leading to the rooftop.

She let herself outside without hesitation. A blast of frigid air struck her cheeks and sucked the breath from her lungs. And yet, despite that cold, she couldn't care.

At last, she had a look at this roof that had so fascinated her. Only, as she ventured farther out, continuing her study, this place, with its stone benches and various oddities she'd witnessed from her window being transported into this very household, didn't resemble a roof so much as a veranda. Stone statues of great Greek gods and goddesses filled the space the same way they might a lord and lady's meticulously tended gardens.

She drew to a stop beside a lifelike metal statue. Armed with arrows and a sword, it could be nothing more than an ode to Apollo. Her breath formed a little cloud of white, and yet the cold was forgotten, replaced by a wonder of this rooftop playground.

She rested her fingertips upon Apollo's muscular stone-carved arm and gazed up.

High above the London landscape, the moon appeared closer from up here, the light cast by that orb in the sky brighter.

The McQuoid roof was everything she'd imagined and *more*. It was—

She tensed. That same apprehensive shiver that had traversed her spine on her journey to the McQuoid household ran along her back once more.

Click.

Alexandra's body recoiled.

"I know you are here," a low, deep voice as frosty as the winter night itself called into the quiet.

Her mouth dry with fear, Alexandra glanced frantically about, briefly contemplating the other side of the roof.

"I'd advise you to show yourself," the gentleman warned, his voice growing closer.

Dropping to the ground, she scrambled under the shelter offered by Apollo's sword, and positioned as the warrior's weapon was, Alexandra bent her body at an impossibly awkward angle and clung to part of Apollo's body to keep from tumbling headfirst and giving herself away.

She made herself stay absolutely motionless and focused on drawing slow, silent breaths.

She registered the soft tread of footfalls. Their approach grew closer, ever closer, and fear built rapidly in her breast, climbing into her throat.

Then those footsteps stopped, and only the thick, welcome quiet of the late hour greeted her.

Click.

And from just a handful of steps away came the distinctive sound of a pistol being primed.

"Step out slowly," the gentleman ordered. "That is, if you care to avoid a bullet in your hide or a cell at Newgate. Or better yet, both of those fates."

There was something very familiar about that voice. She'd heard it up close but once, and only years earlier.

She stilled, her fear replaced with an abject humiliation. Lord Dallin McQuoid, the future Earl of Abington.

Oh, hell.

Chapter 2

London, England

The McQuoid family's Mayfair residence had been broken into earlier this winter. That near robbery of familial relics accounted for this return journey he'd made to London. He'd decided to remain behind and keep the household secure, though his family had insisted there'd not be another break-in.

Dallin, however, had been the one proven correct.

Tonight would now mark the *second* time an intruder had entered the McQuoid townhouse.

But then, if there were thieves intent on stealing a fortune in rarities and oddities and antiques, this winter marked the ideal time.

With the London townhouse about to undergo renovations, Dallin McQuoid, Viscount Crichton, future Earl of Abington, along with his parents and many siblings, and his aunt, uncle, and numerous cousins, had departed some weeks before to celebrate the Christmastide season, and his relatives were remaining abroad while construction proceeded.

Dallin's family had been careless the first time, and it was a mistake he'd vowed they'd not repeat.

His sister Myrtle and their neighbor the Duke of Aragon—now her husband—had dispensed with two burly brutes who'd been attempting to rob the McQuoid household of their artifacts.

In contrast, this latest intruder, the one whom Dallin had come upon, was possessed of a smaller frame; were it not for the man's average height, he could have passed for a street waif.

Dallin narrowed his eyes on the hiding spot of the impressively silent but certainly not discreet trespasser, who'd entered through the recently installed front doors.

"The fabric of your cloak is sticking out," he said brusquely. "Clearer than a calling card."

For a moment, nothing happened. No words. No actions. No *anything*.

Then deft fingers sneaked from under the shield and swiped the material back out of sight.

"For the love of Satan on Sunday," he muttered impatiently. "Do you think I don't see you?"

By the answering silence, that was at the very least what the prowler hoped.

If he weren't so annoyed at having ridden all the way from Scotland, he'd have laughed at the fellow's sheer ludicrousness.

But Dallin *had* ridden nearly straight through, stopping along the route just long enough to swap out horses, steal a light repast, and an even lighter sleep.

Impatient with the impasse the fellow clearly had no intention of abandoning, Dallin raised his pistol, pointing it in the general direction of the still-silent thief crouching behind Apollo.

Taking a step forward, Dallin again cocked his weapon.

Click.

He approached the other side of the statue. "I'll not ask you a . . ." His words trailed off as he got his first full glimpse of the *bandit* clinging to the recently acquired Roman statue. The bandit, who proved to be very much . . . female.

"You're a woman," he blurted.

"Lord Dallin." She spoke crisply with a trifle of annoyance layered within his name.

The biggest, widest azure-blue eyes he'd ever seen met his. And those eyes were not ones a man forgot: Lady Alexandra Bradbury, of the infamously beautiful Bradbury sisters.

Curiously, she also recalled his name. It'd been years since they'd last exchanged words . . . and snowballs. Or rather, he'd sent one her way. She'd been as put out by that wintry missile as she now appeared to be at having been caught stealing about his household. The only thing she'd thrown that day had been a sharp rebuke for his childlike antics.

For the first time since he'd made the journey back from Scotland and witnessed a cloaked figure standing bold as you please on his front steps and then entering the McQuoid residence, Dallin grinned. "My, my, my. If it isn't Lady Alexandra."

"I'll have you know, it was an order," she said in crisp, clear tones Queen Charlotte herself couldn't have managed.

"Beg pardon?"

As casual as if crouching on the ground were a common occurrence for any member of Polite Society, the lady gave a toss of her big golden curls. "Since you arrived, you haven't once asked me anything. What you have done is go about issuing orders."

It was on the tip of his tongue to point out they were, in fact, arguing in his household.

Instead, curiosity prompted a different response. "And the two are so very different?" he asked, tucking his pistol inside the back of his trousers.

The lady followed his movements. Her eyes grew so big they threatened to swallow her face.

Her disquiet lasted all of a handful of seconds. "Oh, indeed. There is a vast difference between an ask and an order."

When it became clear she didn't intend to further elucidate without prodding from him, Dallin propped his hip against the nearby statue of a battle-weary Hercules leaning on his club. "This I really must hear."

"I'd say that's accurate," she said in perfectly arch tones.

Another grin twitched at the corners of his mouth. God, she was as proud and haughty as the papers proclaimed her family was, and that one long-ago interaction had proven.

He schooled his features into a suitably deferential mask. "You have my full attention."

"When you think you should like something, you may ask and it is only a question. *However*, if you believe you are *entitled* to something, and speak thusly, then you are making a demand."

He stretched out a hand to help her to her feet. "May I help you up, my lady?"

"Very good. *That* is a question."

They may as well have spoken over the tea table in his family's parlor.

"Let me help you." He leaned down. "That is an *order*." He softened his words with a wink.

The lady made no move to take that offering. She continued to warily eye his dusty riding glove.

Was she horrified by the state of that leather article or by the prospect of his touching her? He'd wager it was a blend of both.

"Unless, that is, you are content to keep your hand where it is . . . ahem"—he slid his gaze and gave a pointed look—"*anchored*."

The striking but quarrelsome minx blinked her confusion.

She followed his deliberate stare to where one of her hands firmly gripped the impressive length of Apollo's stone shaft betwixt his thighs.

The lady gasped and quickly wrenched her fingers back, in the process losing her phallic purchase and toppling onto her bottom in an inglorious heap.

Dallin burst out laughing.

Alexandra glowered. "You, sir, are no gentleman."

Only a Bradbury could appear graceful and elegant sprawled flat on her back.

"Burglarizing households and handling the male parts on a statue are ladylike behaviors, then?"

"I was not"—she dropped her voice to a whisper—"handling the male parts of a statue."

He leaned over her prone form. "But you were burglarizing my household?"

Her high, proud cheeks gave rise to another rush of color. "You are insufferable, Viscount Crichton."

"It occurs to me you did not answer my quest—"

"Of course I was not burglarizing your . . ." Her words trailed off, and she eyed him warily. "You are teasing me."

He flashed another wink. "I trust that's foreign to a young lady destined to be a future Diamond."

Nor were these particular words teasing. All of society well knew of the beauty of the Bradbury sisters, and that elegance coupled with their fortunes made them certain diamonds of the first waters.

It did not escape his notice that she hadn't denied his claims. But then, why should she or would she? Her splendor spoke for itself.

Something flitted across her eyes, some emotion so fleeting and quick he couldn't confidently identify it but that looked a good deal like panic. It came and went so fast he might have simply imagined the sentiment.

"Help me up?" Lady Alexandra asked pertly.

"A question."

She stared confusedly.

"Yours was a question and not an order."

Understanding flashed in her eyes, and in a flurry of skirts and annoyed mutterings, the lass got to her feet with a surprising grace and agility. She made a show of arranging and smoothing the skirts of her cloak.

"Given my edification this night, I would have thought you'd be impressed with my accurately identifying your inflection."

She lifted her chin and met his gaze with an impressive frankness. "It *wasn't* a question."

Liar. "Ah, you were ordering me about, then, because really, it *sounded* like a question."

And by her deepening blush, he was, in fact, right. The chit, however, was as proud as the day was long, which likely accounted for the enjoyment he found in teasing her.

He chuckled. "Of all the burglars I could have imagined raiding my household, Alexandra Bradbury, you were certainly not the one I'd have expected."

"As I said, I'm no burglar. My family has more than enough funds." She gave her head another little regal toss. "I merely thought I should pay a visit."

"The dead of night, when my family and I were away, seemed like the ideal time to do so?" he asked drolly.

"It was as good a time as any."

Lady Alexandra slipped her gaze away from his and over to various parts of the rooftop.

She'd now avoid looking at him, then. Dallin preferred her bold and meeting his eyes and challenges. Not that he'd given any prior thoughts to preferring her in any way. Their families were neighbors, and yet the notably prim, decorous lot of Bradburys couldn't be more different from the noisy, raucous McQuoids.

Still, oddly, he found himself wanting the haughty Lady Alexandra squaring off with him. He—

The lady's gaze stopped and lingered.

Dallin froze.

Why, the lady wasn't avoiding his eyes. Rather, her previously composed features now revealed a rapt fascination.

"It is an aerial telescope," he said.

She whipped her startled gaze back Dallin's way, and it was as if she'd forgotten his presence. "I . . . ?" She shook her head.

Dallin motioned to the twenty-foot-tall vertical pole positioned at the center of the terrace, and then walked over to the object in question.

"You hold the eyepiece like so," he said, picking up the connecting rod to demonstrate. "And you point it at various parts of the sky." Unable to resist, he stole a glance through the telescope at the starry night sky above, settling on the constellation Auriga.

The lady said nothing for a long while, and then Dallin detected the faint tread of her slippered feet as she moved closer.

When she reached his side, he straightened and motioned for her to have a look.

She hesitated a moment, then wordlessly slipped her fingers around the pole and pressed her eye against it. "What am I looking at?" she asked without inflection, and with a genuine perplexity. "It is just black?"

Moving closer, he lightly tapped her arm, and she relinquished her place.

Angling the telescope, Dallin repositioned the sphere until his gaze found it once more.

"Here," he urged, holding steady. "Careful."

With a surprising ease, she slipped under the fold made by his arms.

In the clear winter night air, the scent of rose water that clung to her skin filled his senses, like a field of flowers in the heart of summer. Dallin briefly closed his eyes, drawing deep of those fragrant blooms.

"They're . . . stars."

It took a moment for her words to register through that haze. "Is that a question, my lady?"

"No. It is . . ." She seemed to register the teasing quality of his query. "They're stars," she repeated, this time with greater conviction.

"Ah, but they aren't just any stars." Dallin took a moment to exchange places with her again so he might verify the accuracy of their location.

"That," he continued when she put her eye against the smooth glass, "is the constellation Auriga. If you look at the top, you can make out the distinct shape of a charioteer's helmet, and if you follow that point, it brings you to that larger, brighter star just over there."

"I don't s—" Lady Alexandra's pronouncement faded to a whispery gasp. "I *see* it!"

In her eager excitement to reposition the instrument, she knocked Dallin back, and perhaps, had he been a rogue or a rake or some manner of scoundrel, he'd have been offended at her being more captivated by the sky overhead than by Dallin himself.

But he never *had* been one of those wicked sorts. He'd been a fellow perfectly content with engaging in his interest in the very stars that now commanded all Lady Alexandra's focus.

And as he eyed the top of her head as she chatted away about the stars she was currently looking at, it occurred to him he couldn't name one woman who'd ever been so affected by the pursuit.

And he'd never been the romantic sort, either. But if he had been, he rather suspected this captivation was where that whole "love at first sight" bit came from.

"Would you know," Lady Alexandra was saying as she shifted the telescope a fraction, "I've looked up at the sky more times than I can surely count and never noted any of this? I wish I had one of these upon my r—"

She drew back, and the rest of her sentence withered on her lips. The eager light in her eyes dimmed, and it was like one of those stars that Dallin enjoyed gazing upon had flickered out.

"What?" she asked, fluttering her hand about her flawless face, which only drew his attention to its most perfectly kissable heart shape. "Have I done something?"

Her fingers dipped lower, and she touched those long, slender digits to her chest, and the press of that fabric only accentuated the full flesh underneath, and thoughts slipped in—scandalous ones. Of Dallin, removing that sapphire gown and baring her to his—

Hell. I'm going to hell.

He could only manage to shake his head.

The lady's inherently arched blonde eyebrows slipped a fraction, and then she dropped her gaze to the terrace floor.

"You must have taken my appreciation for envy," she murmured.

Lady Alexandra made to leave.

Get a hold of yourself, man.

"No," he said on a rush, freezing her where she stood. "It is not that." *I'm ogling you the way some rogue would.* "It is just . . ."

Lady Alexandra settled those enormous blues upon him, and all rational thought fled his head once more. Her irises . . . they were the same shade of blue as the distant oceans his younger brother Arran, the traveler, had regaled the McQuoids with tales of.

Before Dallin had longed to see those waters. Now, he wished to drown in them.

He cleared his throat, but still, when he spoke, his voice emerged embarrassingly thick. "In all my years with tutors and then at Eton and Oxford, I've never known another person . . ." *Who enchanted me so.*

Her cherry-red lips quivered slightly.

"With such an obvious appreciation for the constellations," he finished weakly.

Her features fell.

"Yes, well, this time I will not deny it," she said, hugging herself and rubbing vigorously at her arms. "I do envy you your studies.

Young ladies are schooled in embroidery and playing instruments. All the while, you gentlemen have a whole other world opened to you."

"I understand that," he murmured.

She snorted.

"I know it is not at all the same," he hurried to acknowledge. "Men have freedoms women do not. And yet"—he glanced up at the sky—"heirs are constrained in ways younger brothers are not."

"How so?" Lady Alexandra eyed him with a renewed seriousness.

"It's different in every way, really. My studies, of course, included the classics, but most of my lessons were dedicated to details about our estates and landholdings. Ledger after ledger," he said, slashing the air with his hand as he spoke, "filled with vital information about the overall health and well-being of crops and the villagers reliant on my handling of those records and the purchasing of equipment."

Suddenly, his frustration found a place to breathe, and as he spoke, he exhaled all those long-buried regrets.

"Then there's the lessons on all the previous earls, as though theirs is a history of accomplishment and not simply a study in good fortune."

She eyed him a long while. "You sound a bit like . . . a revolutionary, my lord. My mother would be scandalized."

He noticed she did not include herself in that pronouncement. "And you're not?"

Her eyes twinkled. "I don't scandalize easily."

"I understand it's incredibly churlish, resenting fortunes and lands that have come to me through no efforts or contributions of my own, and yet I'd find a greater sense of fulfillment and purpose making a future for myself. I don't believe I would have realized just how incredibly narrow my existence was, and how empty, until my younger brother took his first voyage."

Dallin would forever recall standing at that London wharf, watching until the ship his brother sailed upon had become a distant speck on the horizon, then disappeared from sight altogether.

"When he returned, he came back with stories of the people he'd met, and he talked about their lives and cultures. He just had this . . . expanded view of the world. It was then I saw just how very different our lives were," he murmured, "and when I realized . . ."

"Realized what?" she asked quietly.

"How much better I could be as a person and as an earl, how much more open-minded and compassionate I would be, if I were able to travel beyond our shores. But where heirs and noblemen are concerned, society doesn't see it that way. They'd tie us to this place. All the while, the second-born sons are free to explore the world with absolutely no obligations, *no* responsibilities, without anyone reliant upon them for security and well-being. He just had the sea and the stars and the sunsets to take in. Someday, I'll see it all," he quietly vowed, speaking more to himself.

Alexandra slipped her fingers into his, and he glanced down. "It appears we understood one another more than we think." She gave a light squeeze.

Dallin looked at their joined hands. How right it felt, talking with her. Holding hands. It was as though they'd known one another their entire lives.

"You needn't have a telescope to take all this in," he said quietly.

Lady Alexandra blinked slowly several times, as if hearing Dallin speak recalled her to their earlier discussion.

She released a little snort. "If *that* were in fact true, then you'd not have all of"—she drew her palm back and waved it at the terrace—"this up here."

She spoke with entirely too much cynicism and dryness for one of her seventeen or eighteen years.

"No, that is fair. The tools I've invested in over the years certainly make it easier to study the stars. But neither, however, are they the only way to appreciate them."

"What do you mean?"

Closing one eye, he pointed just over her shoulder to a particularly bright cluster.

"Look there," he urged.

She made to reach for the telescope.

"Uh-uh." Dallin rested his hands on her shoulders and directed her away. "You can see them well enough without the benefit of a telescope. There," he repeated, stretching an arm over her shoulder and pointing to the celestial body overhead. "Do you see them, Alexandra?"

Alexandra hesitated a moment. Was it his bold use of her familiar name? And yet, in this intimate moment they shared, it felt . . . somehow right.

"No . . . Dallin," she said softly. "I'm not sure which ones I'm looking at, which is why a peek through your telescope . . ." She made to dart over to the instrument.

Dallin laughed. "Uh-uh."

His amusement faded as the solemnity of the moment enveloped him once more.

He reached his hand out for hers, then stopped and turned his palm face up. "May I?" he murmured.

With an absolute trust, Alexandra rested the tops of her fingers in his.

Dallin lightly curled his fingers around hers, and damned if holding her hand so didn't feel *right* in some way.

Her breath grew slightly more ragged, as did his, and the soughs of their warm breaths mingled and kissed in the night air.

"There," he continued, his voice low and slightly rough. "That cluster there is the constellation Cassiopeia. Do you know the tale of Cassiopeia?"

Alexandra shook her head slightly, and her abundant golden curls bounced at her shoulders, tickling his cheek. He'd never known hair could be soft, like silk.

"Tell me," she pleaded.

He opened his mouth to tell her he was no poet, and yet he could now understand why those great wordsmiths penned odes to their ladies' hair.

Alexandra angled a glance over her shoulder. "Who is she?"

Who is . . . *who*?

Oh, hell. Embarrassed heat chased the cold from his face.

"Cassiopeia," he blurted, hastily getting control of his outrageously mixed-up thoughts. He looked to those stars in the sky and directed Alexandra's attention back their way, too.

"She was a vain queen who boasted that she and her daughter Andromeda were more beautiful than the Nereids."

"Who . . . ?"

"The Nereids were sea nymphs who attended to Poseidon, the god of the sea, and his wives. To avenge the Nereids, Poseidon flooded the kingdom belonging to Cassiopeia and her husband, King Cepheus, and contained within the waters he sent to ruin them was a sea monster."

At some point, Alexandra had ceased looking at the sky and now stared raptly at Dallin. No one had ever looked at him the way she did, as if he were the only person in the world, and certainly not for a story he shared about the stars.

Warming to his telling, Dallin continued. "King Cepheus consulted an oracle, who told him the only way to assuage Poseidon's wrath was to sacrifice his daughter Andromeda and feed her to the sea monsters."

Alexandra gasped. "Was she eat—"

"No. Legend has it that the hero Perseus saw Andromeda strapped to a rock and instantly fell in love. He struck an arrangement with her parents: he would slay the sea monster and save her if he could have her in marriage. Though she was already betrothed, they agreed, only to then ultimately break their promise. Perseus, however, went on to interrupt the wedding and save Andromeda once more. Poseidon cast Cassiopeia into the sky, and to punish her for her treachery, he strapped her to that throne to represent her daughter's ordeal."

Dallin gently folded down her middle, ring, and pinkie fingers, until he'd isolated her index one. Then, ever so slowly, he guided the tip of that long digit up to trace that place in the sky.

"Her name means 'Seated Queen,' and you can make out a *W* in the constellation," he said quietly. "The *W* represents the queen sitting on her throne."

"I see it," she said happily.

They remained that way a long while: Their hands interlocked. Her back against his chest. Their breaths melding.

And with her warm, slender form resting against him, not even the bite of the winter's cold could chill him.

Perhaps it was the intimacy of the two of them alone on this rooftop, high above the nearly vacant London townhouses. Or mayhap it was the forbiddance of their being alone when society didn't permit so much as a long look between a man and woman without censure.

But there was a rightness to . . . this. To them.

Alexandra stepped out of his arms, and the cold instantly returned.

Rubbing her palms together, she directed her gaze up to those heavens they studied.

Dallin's focus, however, was not on those mesmerizing lights flickering thousands and thousands of kilometers away, but on her— Alexandra Bradbury.

Her eyes glittered with more of that sadness.

"If that isn't the way of all societies, then," she murmured. "Sacrificing their daughters for their stability and security."

He startled. In all the times he'd read and studied that legend, he'd not once made the connection Alexandra now did. Perhaps because he'd been born into a family where his sisters were viewed as equally cherished members.

Studying a suddenly quiet Alexandra, he wondered at this neighbor for whom he'd spared hardly more than passing thoughts through the years. Were she and her sisters equally beloved and cherished? Had the earlier musing she'd spoken aloud been a general statement she made about all society? Or did she speak of her own experiences?

"And . . . what of Andromeda?" Alexandra asked.

Lost in his thoughts as he'd been, he struggled to follow Alexandra's jump in the discussion. "What of her?"

"Well, it is just you speak about Perseus falling hopelessly in love with Andromeda. Did *she* love him in return?"

Dallin paused. "I . . ." He searched his mind for everything he'd come across in his study of the classics about that particular detail. "Do you know, I . . . don't recall if there is mention of whether she did or did not."

Alexandra frowned. "It *seems* like a very important detail."

It did. So why had he not asked about it or thought of it before now? Because it didn't have any bearing on the science behind why the stars were in their existing formation.

He bowed his head. "I will continue my research and find that answer, and when I do, you have my word I shall share my findings with you."

Her eyes went soft, and she moved them slowly over his face. "Truly?"

"On one condition," he said.

"There's *always* a condition," she muttered, pulling a laugh from him.

Dallin tweaked her nose. "You must promise to look for the answer in your library, and whoever finds it first must report it directly to the other person."

A smile replaced her scowl, and with an eager nod, she placed her palm out.

He shook her hand, binding the two of them in that promise.

They remained that way a moment.

Alexandra, however, remained oblivious to Dallin and his fascination with her.

She wandered off, meandering over the rooftop terrace. During the slow circle she made, she'd pause on occasion to peel back the tarpaulin and peek at the telescopes shielded under those heavy cloth coverings.

"You have a good many telescopes," she remarked as she moved to inspect another.

"The outdoor elements are not suitable for a telescope, and yet, neither are five younger, mischievous siblings," he drawled.

Alexandra looked over.

"My brothers and sisters are so fascinated by them, but also curious, particularly when it is raining and they are confined to the house."

"Which, as we live in England, is a very good many days."

He pointed a finger her way. "Precisely."

Alexandra wandered back over to the opposite side of the aerial telescope and gripped the long pole.

"And you have such a problem sharing, do you, Dallin?" she teased.

Dallin matched her movements. "I wouldn't if they showed greater care in their handling of them," he explained. "In their exuberance they've damaged a good many of them, and as Homer aptly said in *The Odyssey*, out of sight, out of mind."

They shared a smile.

Then something palpable shifted in the air. As one, Alexandra and Dallin's mirth faded.

With their gazes they did a like search of one another's faces.

The moon's glow kissed the perfect planes of Alexandra's, casting a soft, ethereal light upon her skin, blemished only by the rosy hue wrought by the winter's cold.

God, she was exquisite, possessed of the manner of beauty that saw mothers boast and goddesses beat their chests in envy.

No wonder the papers all made predictions of the lady being a Diamond when she eventually made her Come Out.

Alexandra's long, curled lashes fluttered, and the moment he leaned closer, she did the same, their bodies swaying in a like harmony.

31

Thwack.

Somewhere in the distance a door slammed, breaking them apart.

His unlikely nighttime companion looked off in the direction from where that echo had come.

She is going to leave.

Which was for the best. She should leave. The two of them being up here, alone together, were it to be discovered, invited all manner of mayhem . . . and scandal.

So why, then, did he feel an overwhelming urge to keep her at his side?

"I insisted it be built," he blurted.

Confusion clouded Alexandra's eyes.

Dallin gestured to the aerial telescope. "My mother was adamant we not have anything so outlandish here for all to see. In the end, we compromised, and it was placed there, out of sight."

"It's not out of sight."

He stared at her.

"I can see it from my bedchamber," she clarified.

Which meant, at some point in time, mayhap several of them, the lady had watched this place that was so very special to him from her window. Knowing that they had been observing the same precious telescope from two different places brought more of that welcome warmness in his chest.

He—

Dallin stopped as suddenly it hit him . . . what she'd been doing here. Lady Alexandra had indeed been a thief this night. Only, a thief of a different sort. "You came tonight to steal a look, then."

"Looks are free."

She did not attempt to pretend she didn't know what he'd been talking about, or deny having observed his household, and she rose several notches in his estimation.

He grinned. "If one is invited inside, then yes, looking is free."

"We are neighbors," she pointed out. "In fact, one might argue, given our neighborly association, you might be a good deal more welcoming."

"Who would argue that?" he asked, gently teasing. "You?"

The lady gave an emphatic nod, and with all the sureness of one who owned the thing, Alexandra stole another look through the telescope at the stars overhead.

Had Dallin not been looking as close as he was, he could have easily attributed the flare of color in her cheeks to the cold and not to a blush. But he was staring, and he did mark that slight difference in the shade of crimson. And God help him, he found himself falling madly under the spell the Bradbury daughters were said to possess.

This was not good.

Chapter 3

Alexandra kept her gaze pressed to the glass of the telescope. Before, she had marveled at the majesty of the celestial bodies above her, but now she experienced a different type of wonderment—a wonderment she didn't know what to do with.

Dallin teased her.

Aside from her sisters, no one had ever teased Alexandra, and they did so only on the occasions they were alone and not in the company of stuffy, miserable governesses and instructors.

For the Marquess and Marchioness of Queensbury would have never allowed it. Their daughters were to be treated with only a deferential respect.

In other words, through the years, Alexandra, Daphne, and Cora had been placed upon a pedestal, and there they were expected to remain. It was a hard place. It was a lonely place.

This, being here with Dallin McQuoid . . . felt anything but.

It was why, even as reason reminded her that her departure was longer overdue, she found herself lingering, loath for this exchange to come to an end.

Being here alone with Dallin felt somehow normal and magical all at the same time, and Alexandra discovered in this instant with him that the line between both was very much blurred.

"You'd never know it," he murmured, and even with her gaze still affixed to the telescope, she registered his shifting nearer.

She drew back from the sight she'd not really been looking at. "Know what?"

"We are neighbors," he said. "You live there." He pointed to the sloped roofline of her family's home a short distance away. "And I, here." He gestured to the floor beneath them. "And yet, we may as well be strangers."

"Because we *are* strangers."

What if they hadn't been? What if they'd been the best of friends and visited one another's homes? How many other moments might she have shared with Dallin?

Dallin proved nothing if not persistent. "Yes, but *why?*"

"I don't know, Dallin," she said impatiently.

In truth, though, she did know. Though Alexandra's mother and father were faithful and loving to their daughters, they were also devoted to their power and position amongst Polite Society. They viewed Dallin's unconventional, unordinary mother and father as inferior and not ones to mingle with.

Too ashamed of her vainglorious parents, Alexandra couldn't say as much. Not when to do so would offend him.

"Mayhap because our parents keep different social circles," she finally said. "Mayhap it's reasons we don't know."

"Isn't that the way," he mused, echoing her earlier murmurings.

And it was the way: The way of Polite Society. The way of the world. Certain individuals decided others were inferior and erected barriers to ensure their two differing worlds didn't intersect, but if truth be told, those divides existed only to keep the superior lot from seeing that they really were no different.

Unable to meet his gaze, Alexandra wandered off, close enough so that she might see her window.

At some point her sisters had abandoned their places there, so that Alexandra and Dallin may truly have been the only two in London.

She felt him before she saw him, sliding into the spot beside her so that they stood arm to arm.

Eager to change the subject, to avoid the possibility of more of his prodding, she asked, "Why did you begin studying the stars?"

He was quiet a moment, and she thought he might not answer.

Alexandra glanced over.

Continuing to stare into the distance at a particular patch of stars, Dallin rocked forward on the balls of his feet, as if his toes twitched to find that freedom he now spoke of.

"When I was twelve or so, I'd look overhead at the stars and imagine an entire other world out there for me to explore," he murmured.

"And why can't you?"

Dallin briefly glanced her way with a question in his brown eyes.

"Explore the world, that is."

"As I said, there are expectations for the heir that prevent me from doing what I truly want," he said matter-of-factly.

"Yes, you are the heir. But you are also a man who enjoys freedom, should you seek to take it."

"I'm the one who has been schooled on every last detail about our familial holdings and properties. I know each part of the inner workings of the estates. I know the men, women, and children reliant upon my family for their existence. Not Arran, but *me*."

Unlike her, he could go. It was his honor and devotion to his family that kept his feet firmly in England.

Dallin continued. "If anything were to happen to my father, then I need to seamlessly step into that role. I expect it sounds ungrateful to be born into privilege and property and envy Arran for seeing the world and all it has to offer beyond the borders of our kingdom, while I . . ." Dallin trailed off, letting that sentence go unfinished.

He would remain behind. Like her.

It had never occurred to her that a man might feel the same sense of entrapment as women did. Of course, being considered chattel and without any of the rights afforded lords, it wasn't *entirely* the same, and yet in some ways, she knew what it was to be denied true autonomy of self and soul.

And mayhap that was why they'd found each other this night. Mayhap fate did have a future in store for them—maybe even a future together.

"And you?" she quietly urged.

Dallin breathed deep of the night air. "I have seen nothing."

She'd wager her soul on Sunday that he'd seen far more than she ever had or would. But she proved far more selfish, knowing that even though she'd never see the world, she'd find solace and even . . . joy in knowing he remained in London, as stuck as she.

He quashed those foolish yearnings with his very next breath.

"This isn't forever," he said, flexing his jaw. "I've already informed my parents that at some point when my brother is not abroad, I will set out on my own adventure."

And her heart sank a whole lot in her chest, not with sadness at her never seeing the sights he would, but in knowing he'd leave and these romantic musings that had entered her head were wholly one-sided.

Suddenly, Dallin turned, startling her with the speed of his movements. "Where would you go?"

Her heart lifted a fraction. "I . . . I'd go where the stars shine the brightest," she said softly.

Was he inviting her along? Either way, her studies had hardly consisted of distant peoples in far-off lands.

"My brother insists that he's never seen a more magnificent night sky than that of the Canary Islands," he said contemplatively. "That is where I shall go." He smiled.

How funny that she could mourn his eventual departure when she'd only just met him. "When will you go?" she asked, dreading that answer.

"That is as yet undecided. It all depends upon my younger brother's sailings."

And her heart broke a little. Which was preposterous. Though she did believe in the emotion called love, she couldn't imagine that one should fall so very hard, and so quickly, for a man.

His grin slipped. "What is it?"

"I was just hoping that . . . when the time came . . ." As she rambled, a question lit his eyes. "That is, the time when I have my Come Out . . . I'd find comfort knowing you were there." *And not on the other side of the world.*

She curled her toes so sharply the sole of her foot ached.

Dallin slid closer and cupped a palm about Alexandra's cheek.

Under the caress of his strong palm, her lashes fluttered.

"I'll be there." His murmuring was a promise, wrapped up in a vow.

"W-will you?" Except as soon as that question left her, reality reminded her: he couldn't. Their families moved in completely different social spheres.

"I will," Dallin vowed. He waggled a brow. "Eccentric family or not, it shouldn't be impossible for a viscount to wrangle an invitation to at least two of the same affairs."

When he said it like that, she believed him. She rather believed he could do anything.

He leaned in closer. "And do you know what else?" he whispered, as if he imparted the most intimate secret, one that would unite them.

Enthralled, Alexandra managed to shake her head.

"I'll even steal two sets from every event we both find ourselves attending."

That promise warmed her all the way through. Funny how the thought of his being there, this man who'd been almost a stranger to her at the start of this night, should bring her this vibrant joy and make it so that she not only didn't dread her debut but also . . . longed for it, because it would bring them together again.

"Will one of the sets be a . . . waltz?" She somehow found the daring to ask him for that forbidden dance.

The intensity of his gaze warmed her like a physical touch. "If that is what you wish for."

"I do." Bashful at that honest admission, Alexandra dampened her lips.

His gaze darkened.

As one, they glided closer, their bodies swaying in graceful harmony.

He is going to kiss me. She, Alexandra Bradbury, would finally have her first embrace. A thousand butterflies danced within her chest and belly as she leaned in, swaying toward Dallin, wanting not just her first kiss but for it to be with this man, in this moment. N—

Thwack.

Another panel slammed somewhere in the distance, putting yet another definitive and tragic end to an embrace before it even began.

Dallin immediately drew back, putting several steps between them. That rejection filled her with a disappointment, both bitterly keen and humiliating.

"I should go," she murmured.

"Yes."

The speed with which he concurred caused another pang, where before there'd been only elation.

She dipped a curtsy. "My lord."

He returned a short bow. "And here I'd thought that as we were strangers no longer, we'd dispensed with formalities."

No, they weren't strangers.

"Dallin, then."

"Alexandra."

He offered her his elbow.

Without hesitation, she placed her fingertips upon his well-formed arm and allowed him to escort her from this rooftop paradise and back along the path she'd traveled a short while ago.

For Alexandra's whole life, she'd been reminded that a lady in the presence of a gentleman didn't allow silence to flourish. She'd been schooled on all the appropriate topics that would demonstrate her pedigree: The weather. Watercolors. Floral arrangements.

As she walked in step with Dallin, she marveled at how very wrong all the governesses, instructors, and *ton* parents everywhere had been: there was a good deal to be said for a companionable, comfortable silence. Only, she rather feared it wasn't so much the silence as her unlikely companion for the night.

She expected there should be some unease at being alone here with a man she hardly knew.

Only, foolish or not, she trusted him implicitly.

"Here," he murmured as they arrived at the front door. "The neighbors have all gone, and the servants who've remained in those households have likely already long ago taken their beds."

"I know." If she were seen leaving the McQuoid household in the dead of night, her reputation would be destroyed. So why didn't that thought rouse the fear it should?

They both hesitated there at the doorway.

A wistful smile played on Dallin's lips. "Of all the intruders I could have discovered raiding my household, Alexandra Bradbury, you were the perfect one," he murmured.

She and Dallin shared another smile.

Alexandra drew her hood back into place, and the moment her face was completely concealed, Dallin opened the door.

The blast of cold air hit her with an equally cool blast of reality. Gathering her hems, she hurried off.

As Alexandra made her way back to her family's townhouse, those words played in her mind over and over, spoken in that deep, appealing baritone.

She should have been horrified at having been discovered, and by a McQuoid, no less.

Only, she could ideate on just one detail of this night: how much she'd enjoyed being with him.

Feeling eyes upon her, she slowed to a stop and turned.

Standing there in a window, Dallin stared back. He was making sure she arrived home safely. That realization sent a welcome heat through her.

Dallin gave a small wave, and reflexively, she lifted her fingers in a return wag.

Reluctantly, she forced her arm back to her side and made herself resume the short walk home.

Lost in thoughts of Dallin and their meeting together, it was a moment before Alexandra registered the sight before her.

She stumbled to a stop.

The townhouse she'd left silent and dark was no longer. Now, every window of every room was bathed in light, and Alexandra was met with the sight of servants frantically rushing back and forth amongst those panes.

Her stomach sank, and then turned.

Blast and double blast.

Hiking up her skirts, she went flying to the same servants' entrance she'd taken leave of a few minutes—an hour?—a lifetime ago.

Her heart knocked all the more.

Blast, how long had she been gone? Lost as she'd been in discourse with the more-affable-than-she'd-ever-credited McQuoid son, she'd failed to note the important detail of the passage of time. Really, she'd failed to note any detail aside from him.

Alexandra let herself inside.

The moment she slipped through the panel, a wretched sobbing from somewhere abovestairs and deep in the house reached her.

Oh, God.

Her mother.

Alexandra gathered up her skirts and sprinted toward that ghastly wailing, all the way to her father's office.

She staggered to a halt outside the ornate oak panel. It appeared she was to face both her mother and father. Quickly smoothing the front of her skirts and then patting her flushed cheeks, Alexandra entered the room.

She found her mother with her hands covering her face. Where she sat in the marquess's favorite chair, made of walnut and leather upholstery, her shoulders shook under the weight of her grief.

Alexandra's stomach churned.

Perhaps her parents would just be so relieved she'd returned unharmed they'd spare Alexandra the likely line of questioning as to where she'd gone off to.

Stepping farther into the room, Alexandra drew the door shut behind her.

That noticeable click went unheard over her mother's tears. Alexandra glanced about for her father.

Only, he wasn't here.

She'd be spared from facing both of them, then. At least for now. Welcoming even that brief reprieve, she cleared her throat.

However, her mother's sorrowing reached a frantic pitch.

"Mama," Alexandra called out, and when even her voice failed to penetrate, she raised it an octave and stated loudly, "I'm here, Mama."

At last, that managed to pierce her mother's grief.

The marchioness whipped her head up; her vacant eyes, swollen and red, stared sightlessly back at Alexandra.

"Alexandra," she whispered, and that ravaged sound brought Alexandra rushing over.

The moment she reached her side, her mother surged to her feet and wrapped her arms tight enough about Alexandra that she squeezed the air from Alexandra's lungs.

Where there'd previously been only breathless joy from her visit with Dallin, now there came guilt for the terror she'd brought her parents.

"It is all right, Mama," she said against the marchioness's still quaking shoulder. "I'm here. There is nothing to worry about."

Her mother drew back. "Nothing to worry about." Her face flushed from tears, the marchioness looked at Alexandra through dazed and grief-stricken eyes. "There is *everything* to worry about."

With most of London gone and the servants unaware, her reputation remained intact. None were the wiser as to what she'd been up to this night.

"It will be all right, Mama," she said imploringly. "You'll see."

"Your father is dead, Alexandra," she whispered, her voice ragged from tears and grief. "How can anything ever be right again?"

With that revelation, her mother broke down once more. The marchioness's legs went weak. Or were they Alexandra's? Mayhap both of theirs.

And as Alexandra's arms fell away from the hold she had upon her mother, the marchioness sank back into the folds of Papa's favorite chair and dissolved into agony-filled tears.

Her ears buzzing, Alexandra stood there, numb, until the task of keeping herself upright proved too much for her limbs, and she collapsed onto the edge of Papa's desk to keep from falling. To keep from dissolving into the same infinite bundle of grief that had pulled her mother under.

My father is dead.

Alexandra closed her eyes.

And nothing would ever be the same for their family again.

Chapter 4

One Year Later
London, England

Blue was the color of calm.

Or that was what Alexandra's mother had always claimed. It was the reason so many of the rooms in the Bradbury households had been wallpapered or decorated in that soothing hue.

Only, seated upon a powder-blue upholstered mahogany armchair within the dark-blue-painted room with a blue Eastern rug adorned in a floral design, Alexandra found the color proved little help in combating the dread that slipped slowly through her.

Her mother stared at her with tortured eyes.

Not a word passed between them . . . that was, aside from the last ones the marchioness had spoken.

There are no funds.

Alexandra gave her head a slow, clearing shake, and yet that utterance remained, dancing in the air and inside her mind.

"I don't understand," she said, her voice calm.

How was her voice so calm?

The marchioness wrung her hands together. "Your father was a good man."

"Yes, yes. I know that." He'd been the best of fathers. He'd never lamented over the fact that there'd been no sons—no all-important heir—and had always found pride in his daughters' accomplishments.

"But he was not the best with money," her mother murmured. "To afford us the luxuries he did, he was forced to take on creditors."

Creditors.

The panic built.

And amidst the shock, the horror of her mother's revelation, a memory of a long-ago night chose that inopportune minute to slip in.

It occurred to Alexandra that, during that rooftop exchange with Dallin, she'd lied to him, after all. She and her family didn't have more than enough funds; they didn't have any.

She drew a slow, uneven breath through her teeth.

It didn't help.

She took another.

And another.

Her mother hastily gathered Alexandra's forgotten teacup. "Tea?" She pressed the glass Alexandra's way. "It always helps."

Alexandra stared incredulously at the fragile scrap the marchioness somehow held in steady hands.

Tea? Her mother thought tea should help ease Alexandra's dread over the implications of what she'd learned.

Alexandra, however, had always been sensible. Composed. Possessed of impressive self-control and logic.

"Our dowries," she said, finding comfort in that reminder.

Because there was a dowry, there was the prospect of a future with the gentleman who'd occupied every thought she'd had of her future.

Her mother dipped her gaze.

But not before Alexandra caught the flash of sorrow in their revealing depths.

Her heart thudded in a sickening way against her ribs.

"Mama?" she somehow managed to ask.

Still avoiding her eyes, her mother returned the teacup Alexandra hadn't taken to the table. As she did, this time, the marchioness's hands trembled slightly, and the cup's contents pitched dangerously, sending droplets of the brew over the side.

The moment she'd relieved herself of that tiny burden in her palms, Alexandra's mother smoothed her skirts.

At last, she lifted her head and met Alexandra's gaze directly. "There are no dowries, Alexandra," she said quietly, calmly.

Apparently the color blue did have a calming effect on one of them. It must. For nothing else accounted for her poised demeanor.

Alexandra surged to her feet, and in a bid to release some of the restless tension, she began to pace.

Ladies were expected to come to a marriage with two things to their impeccable name: untouched virtue and a marriage portion. The absence of a dowry meant the absence of marriage, which meant . . .

"How could he do this?" she whispered, her strides growing more frantic.

"He took care of us," her mother chided.

Alexandra stopped abruptly; the angry flutter of her skirts blended with her ragged breathing and the pulse pounding away in her ears.

She glared at her mother. "Taking care of us would mean we weren't impoverished and reliant upon . . . upon . . ."

At the stricken look in her mother's eyes, Alexandra made herself stop.

Her mother was no more to blame for her father's wastefulness than Alexandra or Cora or Daphne.

What . . . or who . . . were they reliant upon? They were four women dependent upon the magnanimity of the new marquess, a distant relative who possessed a fortune, but who'd also come through the week after her father's passing to inventory the items and who'd visited often to remind them of his generous nature and solicit praise from the marchioness and her daughters over his altruism and—

Alexandra dug her fingers into her temples.

"I'd not have you worry, Alexandra."

"Not worry? *Not worry?*" Had she been capable of anything other than numb horror, she'd have laughed outright.

"I have spoken to your guardian," her mother continued.

Alexandra stilled, and in the far recesses of her mind, a place where panic had somehow not yet reached, warning bells clanged.

"My guardian," she repeated slowly.

Her mother gestured to the chair Alexandra had vacated. "Will you please sit with me?"

Which suggested whatever her mother intended to say merited she be seated when she heard the news. And because Alexandra didn't trust she could take another shock without being brought to her knees this time, she joined her mother.

As soon as she'd been seated, the marchioness spoke. "He is of the opinion . . . and I agree, that you marry."

Yes, that was the expectation for all young ladies. With her debut delayed by her father's passing, Alexandra was a year older on the Marriage Mart. But now, she entered it with nothing to her name, except her name.

"I've always known what my responsibilities are," she said without inflection.

The marchioness beamed with motherly pride. "You've always been a good daughter. Most dear. I am so lucky to be your mama."

With that, her mother picked up her tea and resumed sipping as if they discussed something as mundane as the weather and not the precarious state they now found themselves in.

Unmoving, Alexandra sat staring vacantly at her mother, who even a year after the marquess's death continued to wear mourning attire.

She'd called Alexandra a good daughter. Yet if that were the case, if she were, in fact, a good daughter, she'd not harbor the resentment building inside at discovering the true state of her family's circumstances.

Her mother returned her cup to its little saucer; glass touched glass with a delicate *clink*.

"Your uncle"—her mother's brother, Alexandra's guardian—"has been so good as to take it upon himself to arrange a match with a gentleman willing to overlook your situation."

Several seconds ticked on the gilded Louis XV mantel clock before Alexandra's mind registered that statement.

Through a thick fog of confusion, she managed to speak just one word. "What?"

"Yes, yes. Terry has been most generous in helping me sort through our situation. Well, he had the *wonderful* idea to coordinate a union for you so we needn't worry about spending funds we do not have on a Come Out, while also making it so that Cora may have her debut the same time as yours." The marchioness smiled widely. "Isn't that just splendid?"

Splendid? This was what classified as *splendid*? She'd always known how little power women had over their futures, but even the small amount most ladies were granted had been wrenched away from Alexandra. The unfairness of it all, the expectations placed upon daughters with derelict fathers, fed a fury within her, and she welcomed that fiery sentiment, for it was the only thing that kept her from breaking apart.

"No," Alexandra said, her voice garbled. Mayhap a lifetime of being a dutiful daughter made it so very hard to speak that word.

"No?" Her mother puzzled her otherwise unwrinkled brow. "I don't under—"

"I'll not do it. Marry . . . some man selected for me by some gentleman who knows me not at all."

"He is your uncle, Alexandra," the marchioness chided. "For that matter, I do not understand what has come over you. You are being unreasonable."

"I'm being unreasonable?" Alexandra asked, her voice rising.

"Yes, you are. Matches are made every day without a woman's input. It is the way of our society. You know this."

"Yes." Alexandra spoke with a calm from she didn't know where. "I know how the world works, Mother. What I did not know"—*until this exchange*—"was that my parents would rob me of choice."

Shock and disapproval rounded the marchioness's usually kindly brown eyes. "Your father is dead, Alexandra."

"His mishandling of our affairs and finances while he was alive is the reason for *all* of this."

Her mother reared back in her seat. "He provided us with every luxury and comfort a lady could wish for."

"I'd have rather had a say in who I'd marry than been dressed in the finest silks and satins all these years."

"Daughters make the matches their parents arrange," her mother said impatiently. "That has always been the way. It was the same for your father and me, and we went on to have a most joyous union."

"It's not what I wanted, Mama."

"And what do you want, Alexandra?"

Unbidden, her gaze slipped over to the partially open window that overlooked the London streets. A whispery, transparent curtain fluttered, taunting Alexandra with a glimpse of the neighboring townhouse and the memory of a long-ago time she'd spent with the gentleman who resided there.

Her mother asked what Alexandra wanted. She wanted a husband with whom she could speak freely on all matters. She wanted stolen terrace moments while the whole world slept, and talks about subjects she'd never before learned because her parents had believed ladies should not learn them.

"I cannot do this," she whispered. "I cannot marry a stranger chosen for me by an uncle who visits not even once a year."

Her mother recoiled. "*Alexandra. He is my brother.*"

"That doesn't take away from the fact that he's a terrible uncle."

The marchioness shifted closer on the bench. "What did you think would happen?" she whispered furiously, her tone sharper than Alexandra had ever recalled.

"Not this," she said quietly in return.

At that show of defiance, shock filled all the planes of her mother's unwrinkled face.

But then Alexandra had always been the dutiful daughter who'd not questioned her parents on anything. That was before, however. With the discovery that had been made this day, everything had changed.

Her mother asked what she'd thought would happen? In her mind, she'd imagined . . . something different. After her exchange with Dallin McQuoid on the terrace and his promise to be there when she made her Come Out, she'd allowed herself thoughts of love and marriage to a man who spoke with her as an equal, a man with whom she could discover interests that she didn't yet know because of the restraints which had always been placed upon her.

Only, new restraints were falling into place—manacles that would prove permanent. That would see her married, and to a man who was . . . not the man she wished he was.

Restless, unable to sit a moment more, Alexandra scrambled to her feet and headed for the door.

"Do you believe any of this gives me pleasure, Alexandra?" her mother called out, staying Alexandra in her tracks. "Because I assure you, it does not."

She caught the rustle of crinoline as her mother stood.

Slowly, reluctantly, Alexandra turned back.

Her mother stormed over.

"Do you think for an instant you are the only one who resents the circumstances we find ourselves in?" the marchioness demanded when she reached Alexandra's side.

The marchioness jabbed a finger at the floor as she spoke. "Because I assure you, having to seek funds and help from the new marquess as

if I'm some child without any control of its future or fate is not a state I enjoy, Alexandra. Having to rely upon a distant cousin for his charity. Having to fear what will happen to not just one daughter, not two, b-but three . . ." Tears pooled in her mother's eyes. "And one who is just a young girl without a father in a world where women desperately need a f-father."

At the sight of her mother's suffering, pain filled Alexandra's breast. She stretched a hand out, and her mother immediately placed her palm in it.

"But whether right or wrong . . ." The grieving marchioness gave Alexandra's fingers a light squeeze as she took in a shaky breath.

Wrong, it was so very wrong.

"This is a woman's lot, Alexandra," her mother finished quietly.

They stood there, the marchioness's words between them.

A woman's lot.

Her mother was the first to draw her arm back. "It is ironic, is it not?" she said tiredly. "Men have fashioned a world based on the idea women need looking after and they possess greater judgment. They make themselves our keepers and withhold power from us, and yet, women are also left attempting to sort out the messes men made of their . . . and subsequently *our* . . . lives."

It'd been so much easier to resent her mother for being unconcerned about Alexandra's future. It was one thing when her mother condoned and defended decisions that couldn't or shouldn't be.

Alexandra closed her eyes.

But this? This sad, quiet regret, which indicated her mother previously had only put on a brave, cheerful face. That all the while, she and Alexandra were sisters in this, alike in their enmity over the circumstances they found themselves in as women.

Alexandra wanted to rail and protest and reject entering a match with a man whose name she still didn't know. She wanted to curse her father, who'd left their female family in shambles, and think of only herself.

But she couldn't.

There wasn't just herself to worry after. There was her mother . . . and two younger sisters. For them, she would do anything.

Since they'd all been in the nursery, it had been Alexandra who'd looked after her sisters. When they had the meanest, sternest governesses, Alexandra had filled first Cora's and then, when Daphne came along, Daphne's *and* Cora's lives with warmth and love. When they scraped their knees, she'd nursed their hurts. When they got up to antics which would have seen them severely scolded, Alexandra had gone to lengths to conceal their naughty behaviors.

This time, however, it wasn't about soothing the tears of little girls with scraped knees.

It was about truly saving her sisters.

Why can't there be another way? Why can't there be a grand love with a sweetheart who sees me as a partner and friend?

For a sliver of a moment, Dallin's visage slipped in, and the contemplations he'd shared: *"But where heirs and noblemen are concerned, society doesn't see it that way. They'd tie us to this place. All the while, the second-born sons are free to explore the world with absolutely no obligations,* no *responsibilities, without anyone reliant upon them for security and well-being . . ."*

An anguished laugh, born of her own misery, roiled in her throat.

How ironic. She'd met just one gentleman in her life, and under the stars had fallen more than a little in love with him. She'd dreamed of a future for herself. One so very different from the one her mother now spoke of. Now, penniless and dowerless like her sisters, she'd become something Dallin would never want and certainly did not need—a burden.

Alexandra stared out blankly.

"I will do it."

Is that my voice? Surely not. For how could it be so steady when she was one breath away from breaking?

Her mother pressed her palms to her mouth. "Oh, Alexandra. As I said, you have always been the most wonderful of daughters."

"Who is he?" Alexandra made herself ask.

"The Duke of Talbert's heir."

The Marquess of Wingrave?

A hysterical little giggle spilled from Alexandra's lips. He possessed a perfectly villainous name, and it suited the gentleman, whom society had coined "The Devil," for the perpetual sinister scowl he donned at the rare societal functions he attended.

"Once you are wed," her mother was saying, "the duke offered to place a dowry upon your younger sister."

That brought Alexandra up short, killing off her panicky amusement. "Why?"

"He is being most generous."

"Yes, but *why?*"

The way her mother avoided her eyes didn't escape Alexandra's notice. "He approves of our bloodlines."

"Our *bloodlines,*" she echoed.

Only, why should that admission bring with it any shock? At the end of the day, ultimately, aristocratic families sought connections with equally aristocratic families. They were no different with their daughters than they were with their broodmares or finest hunting dogs.

"Why is the Duke of Talbert seeing to the arrangements?" Alexandra asked carefully.

"All parents take an active role in their child's future, you know that."

It didn't escape her notice the way in which her mother avoided her gaze.

Alexandra narrowed her eyes. "Does the duke intend to court me, as well?"

Her mother trilled a laugh. "Do not be silly. You know the Duchess of Talbert is in the best of health."

"Mother," she said warningly.

"The duke wishes to see the matter of a future heir be settled. Given the circumstances surrounding his daughter's failed union with the Duke of Roxburghe's son, he's keen to shore up matches for both his children."

Early on, Alexandra had learned her mother rambled when she sought to avoid a topic.

"As his only son and heir, Lord Wingrave is well aware of what his responsibilities are."

"Mother," Alexandra repeated.

"Lord Wingrave doesn't want to . . . go through the troubles of a courtship."

The troubles of a courtship?

A laugh burst from Alexandra's lips, earning a slight frown from the marchioness. "I do not find the current situation merits amusement."

"No, it most certainly does not," Alexandra said, uncaring about the bitterness that had seeped into her tone.

She brought her arms about her waist and hugged herself.

This was to be her future, then. Marrying a man who'd only chosen her in order to avoid finding another woman and having to learn about her interests and determine whether their dreams and hopes aligned.

Restless, needing to move, she headed to that translucent curtain still rippling with the breeze let in through the opening in the window.

Catching the filmy material in her fingers, she drew it back. This past year, she'd thought so much of Dallin. She'd searched the papers for some bit of information about him, anything indicating he'd set out on the journeys he'd longed to make. Unselfishly, she'd wanted him to experience all he'd longed for. Selfishly, she'd hoped he'd do so during her period of mourning so that he would be there when she made her Come Out.

Her gaze—as it had done hundreds of times since that night—
automatically went to the hint of that aerial telescope peeking out, and
to the last exchange she'd had with him.

"I'll be there."

"W-will you?"

*"I'll even steal two sets from every event we both find ourselves
attending."*

"Will one of the sets be a . . . waltz?"

How ironic. She'd dreaded her London Season and had looked
forward to only the prospect of reuniting with Dallin.

Only, there'd be no Season that saw her free and unattached. There'd
not even be the possibility of . . . more with Dallin.

There'd be no waltz.

Agony got a hold upon her throat, and Alexandra released the curtain so that the filmy silk fabric blurred the view of the household across
the way.

Alexandra's mother rested a hand upon her shoulder, and she
tensed.

"All men prove reluctant to marry . . . at first. But then after they
do, their eyes are opened," her mother murmured, mistaking the reason
for Alexandra's upset.

Alexandra bit the inside of her lower lip hard.

Then, as if she feared her daughter might withdraw her agreement,
the marchioness left Alexandra with the memory of a rooftop meeting
and regret at what might have been.

Chapter 5

Everyone who was anyone amongst the *haute ton* attended the Marquess and Marchioness of Brookhaven's distinguished ball, held annually at Culpepper House.

That was, everyone *except* the McQuoid family. Their failure to appear at one of the most distinguished affairs year in and year out hadn't been by any choice on the McQuoids' part. Rather, they'd failed to turn up for the simple reason that the marquess and marchioness hadn't bothered to put them on the guest list—that was, until now.

Because not unlike so many other members of Polite Society, Lord and Lady Brookhaven cared *very* much that the two eldest McQuoid daughters had married: one to a duke, the other to a marquess from one of the *ton*'s most eminent families.

Standing in the familial foyer, due nearly an hour ago at Lord and Lady Brookhaven's renowned ball, Dallin found himself in a state he'd never been where *ton* events were concerned: *impatient*. His impatience, however, had nothing to do with attending the marquess and marchioness's event . . . but rather, at having entry to one that *she* would also be attending.

The memory of her, Lady Alexandra Bradbury, and their stolen exchange on the rooftop had stayed with him, always.

His fingers went reflexively to the front of his jacket, where a scrap of paper rested, and the words he and Alexandra had shared just over a year ago whispered forward. A year. With the lady's family in mourning for the late Marquess of Queensbury and Alexandra's debut subsequently delayed, Dallin had waited a year for this reunion.

"I will continue my research and find that answer, and when I do, you have my word I shall share my findings with you."

"Truly?"

"On one condition . . ."

"There's always a condition."

"You must promise to look for the answer in your library, and whoever finds it first must report it directly to the other person."

A silly grin played on his lips.

All this was unlike him. As a young gentleman with two brothers and a healthy father, he'd absolutely no urgency to wed. He'd always been content to discreetly keep a mistress, but Dallin had never been the romantic fellow entertaining thoughts of respectable young ladies and a dull, mundane future marrying one of those respectable young ladies.

But there'd been nothing dull about Alexandra or that night, or about their time together. The anticipation of seeing her again was palpable.

For the dozenth time since he'd taken up a place at the double front doors, he tugged the gold timepiece from the inside pocket of his black wool tailcoat.

Where in blazes were they?

An hour. They were a bloody hour late.

With more than a little annoyance, he stuffed his fob back into place.

"Are you unwell?" A voice from overhead filled the foyer.

With a quiet curse, Dallin spun and found the owner of that mischievous tone.

His sister.

That was, his youngest sister . . . Fleur.

Fleur and Quillon, boy-girl twins, identical in every way but for their gender, sat shoulder to shoulder with their gangly legs dangling through the spindles.

She gave her fingers a waggle.

"I was perfectly well . . . until now." He added that last part under his breath. For one could rely on only certain things as being truly certain: The sun rose and fell. The tides came and went.

And the McQuoid twins brought with their every appearance double the trouble.

Fleur cupped a hand around her ear. "What was that?"

Dallin opened his mouth to speak, but his younger brother Quillon beat him to it. "He said he's not well."

"That isn't what I said."

Not that what Dallin actually said mattered in any way. At least, not to the pair above him.

"You've been patting your heart," Fleur pointed out.

Oh, bloody hell.

Dallin felt his cheeks flush with heat and gave small thanks for the sizable distance between him and his siblings which kept them from noting—

"Oh, dear," Fleur said in a not-so-quiet whisper. "Now his cheeks have gone all red."

"Don't you have anything to do other than spy on me, scamp?" he called up. "Some other trouble you and Quillon can find yourselves in?"

"Oh, certainly," Fleur called down. A wicked smile turned her lips up at the corners. "*This*, however, is a good deal more fun."

At her side, Quillon added an exuberant nod of agreement.

"Of course it is," Dallin muttered.

"Are you having chest pains?" Fleur asked.

"Chest . . . pains?" Dallin mouthed, completely flipped upside down, as he so often was by the whiplash that came in an exchange with the little rascals.

"An apoplexy, perhaps?"

Quillon gave his small head, in desperate need of a hair trim, another mighty shake, knocking big curls over the boy's eyes. "He's too young for an apoplexy."

"Don't be too certain of that," Dallin grumped. "You're both pushing me closer to one. If that's your intention."

Quillon scoffed. "Do not be ridiculous. That would leave just Arran between me and the title, and that is hardly enough space between me and the earldom."

Now, that was a sentiment Dallin understood all too well.

"You warm my heart, dear brother," he said dryly, pressing a hand to his chest.

It proved the absolute worst action on his part.

"Well, now?" Fleur scooted closer, pressing her forehead against those wood slats and putting a test to the renovations recently completed by Mr. Phippen, London's most esteemed master builder. "Go on with yourself. What are you hiding there?"

Dallin instantly dropped his arm to his side. "Nothing."

The pair of his most unruly, mettlesome siblings snorted.

"Who is hiding what?"

Dallin cursed again, as for a second time that night, the stealthy arrival of yet another sibling took him by surprise.

This time, none other than his world-traveling brother Arran, younger by a year, strolled into the foyer. He had exchanged the more casual attire he donned for his journeys for the fine garments that suited a *ton* function.

Arran and the bothersome twins spoke at the same time.

"Dallin."

"Nothing." Dallin turned a glare upon his youngest siblings.

Arran rested an elbow against a nearby pillar. "Now I'm intrigued."

"Or he's having an apoplexy," Quillon chimed in.

Arran caught his chin between his fingertips and rubbed in a patently false contemplation. "I'll say, now that you mention it, he does appear flushed."

"Who is flushed?"

The McQuoid siblings all glanced over as their parents, the Earl and Countess of Abington, appeared in their finery at the top of the stairway.

At last.

Never before had Dallin been so very eager to one, see his oft-prattling mama, and two, attend any societal function.

"No one is—"

Dallin's protestations were interrupted by a trio of points and contradictions from his siblings. "Dallin."

A worry that would have been a good deal better reserved for the youngest McQuoids, with their legs stuffed between the railings, filled his mother's eyes.

"This will not do. This will not do at all." She hastened down the stairs, while Dallin's father continued along at a much slower, ambling pace. "He does look quite flushed," she said the moment she reached Dallin.

He opened his mouth to dispel her of the notion he was anything other than annoyed.

"Do you see it, as well?" she asked the moment her portly husband made his way to them.

"Indeed, I do." Distracted as he always was, the earl's attention remained fixed not on Dallin—thank God for small measures—but on something in his gloveless palm. "Look at that. Just look at that," he said with a little laugh.

All eyes went to the earl, who'd long possessed an interest in antiquities.

"Baoding balls, they are." The earl proudly displayed the pair of silver spheres in his palm.

Clang. Clang.

"I have it on authority from Lord Chilton"—the gent who helped the earl procure his oddities—"that they date back to the Ming Dynasty."

Overhead, Fleur and Quillon giggled.

Their mother cast a swift—and ineffectual—glower at the youngest of her brood before turning her perturbed focus on her husband.

"I wasn't referring to your newest toys," the countess admonished, "but rather to your son, Harold."

The earl instantly snapped his attention upright to Quillon. "Uh . . ."

In return, the youngest of the McQuoid boys waved at their father.

"Not *that* one," Dallin's mother said impatiently.

The earl looked to an entirely too amused Arran.

"The other one, Harold. The other one."

"I've a name," Dallin felt inclined to point out. Though in truth, with the number of children they possessed, he'd wager the earl and countess would be hard-pressed to get it right on any given day.

"Dallin," Fleur called down helpfully.

"Yes, Dallin," the countess said, exasperation dripping from her voice. "He appears flushed, does he not?"

This time, she didn't bother to wait for an answer from her husband, who'd returned his attention to those silver balls.

She slapped the back of her hand against Dallin's forehead, and relief filled her eyes. "He is not feverish! We are still able to attend Lord and Lady Brookhaven's affair."

"At least Dallin will not have the bad form to ruin the evening with his ill health," Arran drawled.

Dallin shot him a look.

The countess gave her gloved palms three quick, sharp claps. "Gentlemen," she chided in the same tone she'd reserved for Dallin's and Arran's naughtiest days.

"I still say I'd like to know what had Dallin woolgathering like Cassia and Myrtle over their big, handsome dukes," Fleur said.

The countess turned to Dallin with a new interest. "*Was* he, now?" Dallin resisted the urge to squirm.

"Cassia's husband is not a duke," Arran pointed out, redirecting their mother's attention from her line of questioning, and over the top of her head, Dallin shot him a grateful look.

"Not yet." Their mother perked up. "But one day soon."

"Yes, and all it will take is Cassia's father-in-law turning his toes up," Arran added dryly.

Fortunately, four footmen came forward with cloaks and helped each McQuoid into the articles, ending any further discussion. As the butler drew the door open, Dallin and Arran fell back and followed at a more sedate pace behind the earl and countess.

Some twenty minutes later, with his mother filling the confines of the lacquer carriage with an endless litany of gossip and his father clanging those two silver balls together, Dallin readily acknowledged he'd been a tad too hasty in his earlier opinion.

Where Dallin's father comfortably closeted himself away, studying the many pieces he'd acquired over the years, Dallin's mother spent her days with an embroidery frame and entertaining. Their interests were separate and different, and Dallin had long ago come to expect that was just the way of married couples.

Until he'd stumbled upon Alexandra and they'd discussed the stars and she'd been equally as captivated by the topic as he.

With most guests having already made their appearances, the McQuoids arrived at a largely nonexistent receiving line.

While his parents exchanged brief words with their host and hostess, Dallin scoured the ballroom.

The very *crowded* ballroom.

Filled with more guests than any event he'd ever attended in the whole of his life, had the marquess and marchioness's affair been held in any other ballroom, there'd not have been a spare space for couples to complete the steps of a single respectable dance.

Dallin searched amongst the partners completing the steps of a quadrille on that parquet dance floor. Impatience filled him. Late as he and his family had been, every set on the lady's card had undoubtedly been claimed, and she was surely already on that floor.

His gaze wandered away, and then he froze as he locked on the graceful figure conversing with the older woman at her side.

Dallin's attention, however, remained focused on Alexandra, and he drank in the sight of her . . . the siren whom he'd caught only glimpses of over the years, and only in passing. The lady was draped in a white satin dress with a silver fabric overlay that glittered—actually glittered. The chandeliers cast her and that ethereal gown in a luminous light, and she was somehow even more magnificent than she'd been that not-so-distant day ago, atop his family's roof.

The folded sheet of paper inside the front of his jacket took on an almost lifelike force, and Dallin touched his spare hand to the place where his heartbeat had quickened.

As if she felt his eyes upon her, the lady tensed, then did a little sweep of the ballroom before the older woman at her side called her attention back.

"Ah," Arran murmured at his side.

Dallin stiffened.

"So *she* is the reason for your woolgathering." His younger brother clapped an arm around Dallin's shoulders and gave a supportive thump. "The lady is out of your league, big brother."

Dallin's annoyance redoubled. "You don't know that."

"I don't know much," Arran said modestly. "But *this*? This I know."

Dallin shrugged off his brother's touch. "You do not know her." No one in their family did. That was, no one except—

"And *you* do?" Arran quipped.

Not for the first time that evening, his neck went hot, and Dallin studiously avoided his bothersome sibling's gaze.

His bothersome sibling, who proved as relentless as Fleur when it came to nettling another McQuoid.

"Let me save you the trouble," Arran said. "What I do know about the family is this: one"—his younger brother shot a single digit up—"she's from one of the most illustrious families, and illustrious families only marry into equally or more illustrious families."

"We are hardly *small ton*," Dallin grumbled.

"Need I say it more clearly? The Marchioness of Queensbury is supercilious on a good day and imperious on every other. And families as high in the instep as the Bradburys are *never*, and I do mean *never*, going to let their precious daughters marry into *this*"—he gestured around the room—"eccentric family."

"We're not *that* eccentric," Dallin muttered.

Arran stared incredulously at him. "Do you know who our father is?"

Their father, who with his fascination with his antiquities collection, didn't know what day it was most times.

"He's an earl. That means something to most of Polite Society."

"Perhaps that alone would be overlooked if we didn't, say, forget our sister during the holidays, leaving her home alone here in London."

Yes, certainly a failure to properly look after one's daughter and sister would cause nearly all peers to decide the McQuoids weren't suitable in-law material.

"Should I continue?"

"I'd rather you didn't," Dallin muttered.

"Our younger sister ran off to sea without so much as the benefit of a companion and boarded a privateer's ship," his brother said, flat-out ignoring him. "Gossip claimed *one* privateer ruined her, while she ended up married to a different one, which left her reputation—and our family's—somewhat tarnished."

A lot tarnished.

Dallin brightened. "Not sullied enough for us to be excluded by Lord and Lady Brookhaven this evening."

A Sure Duke

His brother clapped an arm around his shoulders once again. "Get it out of your head. It is never going to happen. Lady Alexandra possesses the manner of pedigree *and* beauty most men can't even begin to dream of getting close to." He gave Dallin a pitying look. "The kind of perfection reserved for dukes . . . *or* future dukes."

Arran added that last part with an air of finality that only further stirred Dallin's irritation, when from the corner of his eye, his gaze snagged upon a very familiar figure on the dance floor—their cousin Brone with another, albeit less familiar, person.

Alexandra's sister Lady Cora stole shy peeks up at Dallin's cousin.

The pair looked at one another as if the entire room had melted away.

"Apparently," Dallin said for his brother's benefit, "our cousin did not receive the memorandum."

Arran glanced at the entranced couple. "It's hardly the same."

Wasn't it?

A crimson-clad servant bearing a tray on his shoulder stopped before them.

Taking advantage of the young man's timely intervention, Dallin, with a word of thanks, helped himself to a crystal flute of champagne. Even as his brother collected a glass for himself, Dallin made his excuses.

Arran's knowing laughter followed him.

The moment he'd placed a comfortable distance between them, he turned his sights back on Alexandra and the place where she'd been—which was now empty.

Dallin frowned.

Weaving between guests, he continued along the side of the dance floor. All the while he scanned the area for a glimpse of the lady.

And then he caught it: the shimmery flutter of fabric from just behind a pillar. And the sight of that material sticking out harkened back to another time when the lady had been bent on hiding.

Dallin's lips curved up in their first smile of the night as he approached Alexandra's hiding place. Only the moment he reached her, a frantic voice on the other side stilled him in his tracks.

"It is a disaster, Alexandra. A disaster."

The marchioness.

There came a flurry of whispers, these ones fainter and near impossible to make out.

Oh, hell. From the moment an invitation from Lord and Lady Brookhaven had arrived addressed to the McQuoids, Dallin had intended to seek her out. He'd imagined how their reunion would go. It'd be teasing. There'd be fond remembrances exchanged . . . and then answers to that long-ago question revealed.

But nowhere in the scheme of his meeting with Alexandra had he in any way included her mother being part of it.

He turned to go, leaving them to the privacy they'd sought out.

"What is she thinking, dancing with that man?" the marchioness said, fury giving her words a clear form.

Go. Do not stay. You do not want to either hear or know whom it is they're speaking of.

Only . . . he already knew.

Even before Alexandra's reply came. "Surely just one dance with a McQuoid is permitted."

Dallin froze.

Surely just one dance with a McQuoid is permitted . . .

That private exchange brought another long-ago one whispering forward.

"I'll even steal two sets from every event we both find ourselves attending . . ."

"Will one of the sets be a . . . waltz?"

"It isn't, Alexandra," the marchioness said earnestly. "You know how that family is viewed. We do not mingle with the McQuoids. Not then, and not now. *Especially* not now, with you girls having made your debut. Cora must not be seen with him, ever."

How smug. How full of conceit the lady's mother was, and yet, through the sting of resentment burning at his throat came the reminder: Alexandra wasn't to blame for her family's lofty—

"I will make it right, Mother," she was saying. "I'll speak to her the moment the set ends and make it clear she's not to partner with a McQuoid."

"You are a good girl, dearest. The very best daughter."

Ice filled him.

What a deuced fool he'd been.

Dallin tossed back the entire contents of his flute, welcoming the fiery trail down his throat.

Having heard more than enough, and empty glass in hand, Dallin made his way back on the same path he'd taken. With every step he took, his rage grew, and he welcomed it. He embraced it. For the fury was easier to take than the shock of discovering the woman he'd looked forward to being reunited with was nothing more than the shallow, smug, self-important person her mother was.

As he approached Arran, the orchestra's latest set drew to a close. Amidst the dancers' polite clapping, Dallin set his glass down harder than he intended on the tray of a nearby servant.

The moment he reached his younger brother's side, Arran gave him a single and sadly knowing look. "I take it the meeting did not go as intended?"

"It did not," he said tightly, not even pretending to misunderstand his brother.

The thing about the McQuoids was this: They may grate on one another's nerves. They may be vexing and outrageous. But that was not a courtesy that extended to outsiders. At the end of the day, a McQuoid could always rely upon another McQuoid. They were a loyal family.

Arran's expression grew serious. "As I said, ladies like her marry dukes. It is just the way it is."

Dallin hardened his jaw. "Well, unfortunately for them, there isn't a vast array of young dukes to go around."

Something in Arran's hesitation gave him pause. "What?"

"You didn't know."

Arran's was a statement. Even so, Dallin found himself asking impatiently, "Know what?"

"The lady is to marry the Duke of Talbert's son."

Dallin narrowed his eyes. "And with that, she'd still encourage Brone?"

Confusion glinted in Arran's gaze. "Not the younger Bradbury girl. I refer to her sister Lady Alexandra."

That revelation nearly bowled Dallin over, and he rocked back from shock.

Alexandra was . . . to marry.

Dallin's stare went to the otherworldly beauty who'd just stepped out from behind that pillar. With her mother at her side, the lady moved with a singular intent toward the path her sister now took.

The silly scrap of paper in Dallin's pocket, that note he'd jotted down, now mocked him for having been a fool, and for harboring romantic thoughts of a woman he knew not at all—that was, aside from an intimate night they'd stolen a year back. The lady's parents had proven snobbish and exclusionary where his family was concerned. Should it truly come as any surprise that she was the same?

Yes, because that night, you gave her the benefit of the doubt. Over the years, he'd heard his own mother lamenting the way they were treated by the Bradburys, but he'd merely attributed those grumblings to her usual ones. Dallin had formed his own opinion.

That opinion, however, had proven dead wrong.

"Oh, hell," Arran muttered.

"What?" Dallin gritted out. What could it possibly be now?

"The two of them are heading off in the same direction . . . alone."

His brother discreetly motioned to Brone and Lady Alexandra's sister, who were doing a comically bad job of escaping the room . . . together. The couple would be *that* careless?

Dallin silently cursed.

They didn't have a brain between them.

But then, Dallin, *too*, had fallen under the spell of a Bradbury. What had he gotten out of it? Nothing more than an understanding of the family's supercilious nature. The last thing Dallin intended was to let his cousin end up trapped in marriage to a cold, unfeeling Bradbury.

With that fueling him, Dallin set off in pursuit.

Chapter 6

The moment Alexandra escaped from the crowded ballroom and the eyes of the guests looking everywhere and anywhere for even some small scrap of gossip, she took off running down Lord and Lady Brookhaven's corridors.

Even her mother, who'd advised her daughters never to walk at anything more than a sedate pace, wouldn't find fault with Alexandra now.

She paused before an open doorway, assessed the empty, darkened room, and then sprinted on to the next.

What was her sister thinking? What was she *thinking*?

That question played over and over in Alexandra's mind as she peeked into yet another empty parlor.

Alexandra's steps slowed, and she stopped before another door. Nay, she knew precisely what madness had seized her sister.

There was something about the McQuoids. They possessed a je ne sais quoi that made a lady imagine something different, something more than the loveless, dull, emotionless unions daughters were expected to make.

She'd thought she'd come to terms with her future.

Then tall, black-clad Dallin McQuoid had entered the ballroom and proven Alexandra all kinds of a liar. And for an instant, as he'd swept his gaze purposefully over the assembled guests, she'd thought he looked for her.

Only, the minute the idea found a place to grow in her mind, she'd kicked rocks upon it.

Had he been as moved by their exchange as Alexandra had, surely he'd have made some attempt at seeing her. They were, after all, neighbors.

But he hadn't sought her out.

That reality, however, still didn't chase away the lump of familiar regret perpetually stuck in her throat at the possibility of something that would never be. Not the waltz. Not the further talk of stars. Not teasing exchanges.

Even knowing she couldn't have danced with him did nothing to diminish the hurt at his not having even asked.

Frozen on the threshold of another one of the marquess and marchioness's parlors, she felt panic beat like a slow, incessant drum in her chest.

Instead of a kind, affable man like Dallin, she'd have marriage to an obscenely wealthy, reportedly frosty fellow. And given the fact he couldn't be bothered to so much as attend a ball she also happened to be at, the gossips, wrong over much, were only right about the man Alexandra was to marry.

Her ragged breath came hard and fast, those frantic little gasps filling her ears and blending with the hum of the silence, deafening.

Stop it.

Alexandra gave her head a firm shake. It wouldn't do to focus on her own miseries.

Redirecting her attention, she resumed her quest, then stopped at the last, unsearched room.

Unlike all the others, which had stood open, this one's white-painted, carved panel had been drawn shut.

Alexandra hesitated a moment, then pressed her ear against the door and strained to hear.

She didn't have to wait long.

There came a small but familiar giggle, loud enough to penetrate the solid oak between the occupant of that room and Alexandra. On the other side of the door came another laugh, this one a quiet, low rumble.

Alexandra narrowed her eyes.

Nay, not an occupant. Rather, *occupants*.

Alexandra grabbed the door handle, but it gave nothing more than a jiggle.

The whispering came to an immediate stop.

At least when presented with the potential for discovery, her sister had the sense to go silent.

Alexandra glanced about, and after doing a search, she verified she was still, in fact, alone.

She gripped the handle and placed her mouth so close to the oak panel that when she spoke, her lips kissed the cold wood. "Open the door."

Alexandra waited a moment more, and then again pressed the handle.

Only resistance met her grip.

Resistance and silence.

Of course, her younger sister never managed to stay silent for long. As small girls who'd dashed about, playing hide-and-seek at their family's various different households, that weakness had proven advantageous for Alexandra. This time was no exception.

"Sister," Cora whispered. ". . . if . . . quiet . . . go away . . ."

What was *she* thinking? She'd be so careless with her reputation, risking being caught in a compromising position. For that matter, discovery wouldn't bring about just Cora's ruin—though that would be bad enough. Her irresponsibility put their entire *family* at risk.

Galvanized by anger, Alexandra opened her mouth to speak.

Suddenly, her nape tingled at the feeling of someone watching her.

Unnerved, Alexandra did another sweep of the hallway.

Silence served as her only company.

For now.

She leaned closer. "Yes, it is your sister," Alexandra spoke quietly. "And no, I won't go away."

A long, beleaguered sigh met Alexandra's pronouncement.

Tapping her slipper silently in an annoyed staccato, Alexandra folded her arms and waited for her dupable sibling to open the door.

And waited.

And continued waiting.

There came more of those whispers, then the distinguishable sound of lips smacking.

Alexandra's face went hot.

Then a single set of footfalls moved, coming closer, and stopped on the other side of the panel.

Cora didn't draw it open with any discretion, but rather pulled it wide and greeted Alexandra with exuberance.

Cora's pretty dulcet tones echoed in the empty halls. "Alexandra!" she exclaimed, like they were grown women paying one another a visit in their own homes and not their hostess's.

Sweeping inside the room, Alexandra instantly slapped a finger against her lips warningly. *"Shh,"* she mouthed.

Cora flared her eyes. *"Alexandra!"* she repeated, a touch more quietly.

Under any other circumstances Alexandra would have marveled at Cora having completed what she'd previously taken as an impossible feat for her sister.

Alexandra pushed the door shut and locked it.

Steeling her jaw, she proceeded to search the room for the dastard who'd lured her sister away. "Where is he?" she demanded in hushed tones.

"Where is who?"

Alexandra shot her a look. As a girl, her sister had always been as bad a liar as she'd been at playing hide-and-seek. Not much had changed on either score.

Cora strode over to the floor-to-ceiling windows, pulled the first set of embroidered curtains back, and then headed for the next.

"Oh, he wouldn't be there, silly. He's entirely too big to hide behind the curtain," her sister said happily, as if it were the most natural thing in the world to admit finding herself in a clandestine meeting.

Alexandra stopped her search and stared at Cora, and for the first time since she'd stormed inside, she took note of how she looked. Of how she truly looked.

Several strands had pulled loose of Cora's elaborate chignon, as if she'd been racing through the halls. Bright, cheery color filled her cream-white cheeks.

Alexandra's gaze settled on Cora's swollen, red lips.

Her younger sister had . . . kissed the McQuoid cousin, and in what was surely a testament of Alexandra's failings, she envied her sister for having claimed what Alexandra had previously only dreamed of with a different one of those McQuoid gentlemen.

Her throat worked. "Where is he?" She managed to get that question out again through a pathetic disappointment.

Cora remained mutinously silent.

Only there wasn't a shred of artifice to the girl. Alexandra knew her sister better than mayhap she knew herself.

She gave the younger girl a firm, sharp look.

Cora's gaze slipped reflexively, and Alexandra followed that accidental tell.

Alexandra narrowed her eyes and started across the room.

"No, Alex! Please," her sister implored, hastening after her.

Any other time, hearing that childhood nickname, that small, secret rebellion between two girls who'd chafed at the rules being ingrained into them by their tutors, would have tugged on Alexandra's heart and prevented her from feeling any real anger.

Not this time.

Not when some bounder had met her sister alone. Not when, with her reckless actions, Cora put not only her future but also their mother's and Daphne's in the greatest peril.

Firming her jaw, Alexandra pulled the door open and swept her stare around the library.

"He is not here," Cora said at her shoulder. "He merely made his escape through this door. We plan to meet elsewhere later."

Some of the tension eased from Alexandra's frame, and she closed her eyes, digging deep for patience, and when that sentiment didn't come so easily, she continued digging harder.

With her sister keeping pace at her side, Alexandra returned to the candlelit parlor and brought the door closed with a quiet but firm click.

"What are you thinking, Cora?" she pleaded the moment they were alone.

"I was thinking I love him and need to be with him." Cora shrugged. "And so I went."

"In love with him? *In love with him?*" Alexandra repeated.

Cora nodded. "Very much so."

Alexandra's temper flared. Yes, her sister had always been more than a little naive and trusting and innocent . . . but not . . . to this degree. That reminder managed to cool her ire.

"Cora," she murmured in the same warm, gentle way she'd adopted whenever her younger sister woke to a nightmare at night. "It is not possible to love a man you only just met."

Unbidden, a different gentleman's visage flashed to her mind's eye: His features, chiseled. His nose, aquiline. His uneven grin, charming.

"Alexandra, you're silly." Her sister smiled, and Alexandra's heart missed a beat. "Even I know that."

Her panicky mind processed those last four words uttered entirely too slowly.

Cora *knew*?

"I didn't just meet him."

It was a moment before her younger sister's words penetrated.

Alexandra blinked slowly. "What?" she asked carefully.

"I've seen him for a year."

Alexandra rocked back on her heels. "A *year?*"

Her sister gave a happy nod.

Through the shock of that admission, Alexandra attempted to process what, exactly, her sister was saying.

Cora's smile widened. "Whenever he visits his family—which is often—Brone and I see one another."

And here Alexandra, who'd believed she knew her sister so very well, turned out to not know the younger girl at all.

She could manage just one word. "How?"

"You see"—Alexandra didn't *see* anything and rather wondered if she truly ever had—"the McQuoids were doing renovations last year. You might remember that?"

A pang struck close to her heart.

Actually, she did. Alexandra recalled all too well. She'd never admit as much to her sister, or to anyone.

At Alexandra's answering silence, Cora cleared her throat. "Yes, well, you may *also* remember the news that their household had been burglarized." She paused in her telling and wrinkled her high brow. "Is that a word?"

"Cora," Alexandra said impatiently.

"Oh, yes. As I was saying, last winter, when . . . when . . . Papa died." Cora whispered that last part. Her expression grew stricken, and a pall hovered in the air between the two sisters.

Alexandra's earlier frustration over Cora's recklessness vanished. She slipped her fingers into Cora's, offering her a gentle support. The pain of losing their father would never not hurt.

Her younger sister's throat moved up and down. "There was so much crying and suffering, and I couldn't bear to be around it, and so one night, I bolted outside and ran and kept running."

A wave of fear gripped Alexandra. Her naive and too-trusting sister shouldn't have gone out alone. Any number of dangers could have befallen her.

"And I ran straight into him." The sorrow had lifted from Cora's telling, and in its place came a soft, joyous wonderment.

"Him?" Alexandra echoed.

Cora beamed. "Why, him, silly—Brone." Her eyes grew dreamy and far-off as she became lost in her memory. "He tossed his cloak around my shoulders"—she paused—"because I forgot to go outside with one and wandered off in my nightgown and wrapper."

Alexandra slid her eyes closed.

On a rush, Cora went on to reassure her. "Oh, you needn't worry, Alexandra. I was unharmed." She clasped her hands to her breast. "Because of Brone. I told him I'd just needed some time alone and explained . . . why. At that point, he offered to accompany me back, and we returned to the McQuoid stables, which were in the midst of renovations. There were no workers. There was no family. There was no one . . . but us." She spoke with a quiet amazement that Alexandra knew all too well.

How odd to know that nearly the exact night Alexandra's world had been turned upside down in the best way by Dallin McQuoid, Cora had experienced a like meeting with Brone Smith.

Alexandra found her voice. "How often have you seen him?"

"Oh, at least a dozen times."

Alexandra strangled on her swallow. "A . . . dozen," she managed to say.

Cora puzzled her brow. "Perhaps . . . *more?*"

More?

No, Alexandra had been wrong moments ago. Cora's meeting with a McQuoid relation hadn't been the same at all. For Alexandra had done so but once and lived with only the memory of that one time, whereas her sister continued to meet Dallin's cousin.

Alexandra finally found her voice. "Cora." She spoke in that gentling way she'd always reserved for her younger sister. "I understand it is very exciting to meet this gentleman, alone, away from the rest of the world."

And she did. For Alexandra had felt that same thrill. "But you cannot meet him like this any longer."

"But if we do not meet in secret, I will not be able to see him at all. Our family dislikes his family. You know that. Mama and Papa were forever saying that they are a shocking, peculiar, outrageous lot, and it is a wonder they're permitted attendance at any truly respectable function."

Alexandra started.

Her sister had managed to recall verbatim the disdainful words their parents had spoken about the McQuoids. But then, perhaps that was because Cora, like Alexandra, had heard them shared so many times.

Alexandra took her sister firmly by the shoulders. "Cora, I need you to listen to me. The duke and Lord Wingrave—"

Cora interrupted. "Lord *Wingrave*. Given the gentleman is your betrothed, I always find it strange that you never refer to him by his name, rather, only by his title."

"It is perfectly normal for husbands and wives to refer to one another so."

"That it is the norm does not mean that makes it right or good, Alexandra."

Alexandra bit down hard on the inside of her cheek. Of all the times for her sister to become insightful. Only, Alexandra couldn't tell Cora the truth. She couldn't explain the one and only time they'd met and would meet until their marriage, the marquess had looked her up and down as if she were some broodmare he sought for his stallion and then coldly ordered Alexandra to never call him by anything other than his title.

"The duke," Alexandra resumed, bypassing that unexpectedly keen observation on her sister's part. "He is an enemy of the McQuoids, and were it discovered that you, my sister of all people, are stealing off with one of them—"

"I don't care."

"Well, you should. If not for yourself, then you should think of Mother and Daphne."

Cora's big brown eyes went wide. "You would use our younger sister as a way to drive a wedge between Brone and me?" she whispered, a wealth of incredulity contained within that query.

"I'd remind you of our sister, and that her ability to make a match is strengthened by my marriage to the duke's son." And as Alexandra spoke, frustration and misery at her lot mounted. Frustration born of the fact that she'd make the ultimate sacrifice yet her sister would give no thought for either their mother or Daphne.

Alexandra tried again. "You are not thinking rationally—"

"Because there is nothing rational about love."

"You jeopardize *everything*, Cora. *Everything*."

Suddenly, Cora jerked away from Alexandra, knocking Alexandra's hands free in the process.

"Your match," Cora said furiously. "Isn't that what you *truly* mean when you say 'everything'?"

"Yes, that is what I mean," Alexandra cried, and her voice echoed damningly around the library. "Everything does rest upon my marrying the duke's son. My marriage will bring great wealth and—"

"I do not care about great wealth, Alexandra!"

"Well, you should." She opened her mouth to paint the grim future that awaited them all, should Alexandra fail to do this thing she had no wish to do. Only, Cora was the manner of romantic dreamer who'd believe love conquered all.

Instead, she opted to reason with her. "You should care very much about my marrying Lord Wingrave."

"You have become just like Mother."

Alexandra recoiled as that charge hovered in the air between her and this sister whom she loved with every fiber of her being. "This is what you'd say to me, Cora?" she whispered.

Stony-faced, Cora lifted one shoulder in a dismissive shrug.

And for the first time, Alexandra felt something she'd never felt where either of her sisters was concerned: resentment. Cora would paint Alexandra's actions as selfish, when in fact, in having agreed to wed the duke's son, she'd committed the greatest of sacrifices in the name of her family's security and future happiness.

Shoving aside the hurt and pain, Alexandra took a step closer. "You are not to see him again, Cora. At least, not until my marriage to His Grace." At that point, she'd be in a position to reason with him . . . if such a man could be reasoned with.

Cora cried out, "No!"

Alexandra pressed a finger to her lips. "*Shh.* And this isn't forever, Cora."

"I'll not be quiet."

"You may care about him."

"I don't just care about him, Alexandra. I—"

Alexandra shook her head. "No." *Don't. Please, don't say it.*

"I love him," her sister entreated, pressing a fist to her chest.

Alexandra had always been able to reason with Cora—until now. Because when love entered the proverbial equation, nothing aside from one's feelings and dreams added up.

"If Mr. Smith were in fact an honorable gentleman with honorable intentions," Alexandra said quietly, "then he'd not be meeting with you in secret, but would instead have openly courted you, making clear to the world his honorable intentions toward you."

Her sister's eyes darkened with an anger and resentment Alexandra had never seen there. That Alexandra hadn't even known the younger girl was capable of . . . until now. And because of her.

"Now," Alexandra continued, "once I am . . ." A familiar panic climbed up her throat, threatening to strangle her with thoughts of her prospective future.

"A marchioness?" Cora supplied.

Anger and resentment and outrage swirled and surged through her. Her sister would punish Alexandra for marrying so that she could save her and their family.

Drawing her shoulders back, Alexandra gave her sister a cool look, and when she managed to speak, she did so with a calm from she knew not where.

"That is right, Cora," she said in frosty tones that sent the younger girl's brows up. "When I'm a marchioness."

That hated title that would secure Cora's, their mother's, and Daphne's futures.

Her expression stricken, Cora stared at Alexandra. "I do not like what has happened to you since Papa died."

Yes, well, that made two of them.

Alexandra's throat worked painfully. Had her sister been coldly mocking or furious in that deliverance, it would have been easier to bear than this tragically regretful way with which Cora looked at Alexandra.

Alexandra, however, didn't have to ask her newly stubborn sister again. This time, without so much as a goodbye, Cora turned on her heel and quietly took her leave, closing the door with a faint, barely discernible click.

The moment she'd gone, Alexandra stood there motionless, staring at the place where her sister had last been. Her shoulders rose and fell quickly to match the rapid intake and exhale of her breath, and her toes twitched with the primitive urge to flee—to run and keep on running to a place back in time when her father was alive and Alexandra was oblivious to her family's circumstances and the late marquess was the one expected to clean up the mess he'd made of their finances.

Alexandra hitched her skirts, prepared to take flight.

Click.

That familiar tell of her sister's return echoed around the room like a shot in the night.

Alexandra gritted her teeth at this new, defiant version of Cora. Flattening her lips into a hard line, she turned. "I've already told . . . *you*." Whatever measured lecture she'd prepared to give froze on her brain, and all the thoughts flew straight from her head.

She stared at the tall figure lounging against that door panel like he was a gentleman who'd just arrived in Bath to partake of the soothing spas there.

The sight of him, this man who'd come to mean so much to her from just one secret exchange they'd stolen under the stars . . . For the first time since her father's death, the fear, fury, and bitterness all faded. Dallin McQuoid stood silent for so long she suspected she'd merely dreamed him up.

Until he spoke. "Hullo," he said in greeting, and her heart jumped at nothing more than that casual greeting.

She tried—and failed—to make her lips form words. Instead, she silently took in the sight of him before her.

Just like that, all the misery that had become ingrained in the fabric of Alexandra's life since Papa's passing lifted like the clouds parting after a storm. Dallin was here. How often had she longed to see him again? How long had she waited for this very reunion? Only, she well knew the answer to that. From the moment they'd waved to one another before she'd returned home, more than a year ago, she'd dreamed of seeing him again.

Dallin.

He pushed away from the door. As he straightened, the panel rattled lightly in its frame, and she couldn't care. She couldn't care if her mother, their host, or some other random passerby heard that sound.

Several long, languid steps brought him closer, and then he stopped less than a pace away.

"Alexandra," he said, laying bold claim to her name, and the sound of those four syllables wrapped in his low, unhurried baritone brought her eyes briefly shut. "Or would you rather I say 'future duchess'?"

It took a moment for that more than faintly mocking question to penetrate the dreamy haze left by his arrival.

Alexandra's eyes flew open, and through the initial and overwhelming joy at seeing him again, she noted the details that had previously escaped her: His once warm, tender gaze had gone hard. The firm line of his once relaxed mouth had gone even harder.

He was stoic and cold, and not for the first time that night, Alexandra wished to cry at one more change—this one to the warm, tenderly teasing gentleman she'd met alone on that rooftop terrace.

Chapter 7

God, what a fool Dallin had been.

He'd spent nearly a year thinking of the lady, even pining for her, and playing over and over in his head the whole of their stolen exchange, only to now realize he'd been so entirely wrong about her character.

Tamping down the acrid taste of bitterness that climbed his throat, Dallin forced himself to rest his right hip upon the back of the inlaid mahogany side table and feign nonchalance.

"Though," he drawled, "I expect being discovered alone with a McQuoid would be a sheer disaster."

Confusion briefly clouded the lady's eyes, and Dallin knew the very moment she registered those words. More specifically, what was familiar about his pronouncement.

"Being discovered alone with *any* man would be a disaster," she said in careful, measured tones.

"I suppose that much is true," he allowed, inclining his head in a slight acknowledgment.

He'd hand it to her. Based on her smug, self-important exchange with her mother, he'd not have thought her capable of humility. Nay, that sentiment far better suited the bright-eyed young woman he'd first met upon the rooftop.

"That is, with the exception of a future duke, perhaps?"

Color bloomed on her aristocratic cheeks. "There are no exceptions where a lady's reputation is concerned," she said pertly. "Now, if you'll—"

"Tell me . . ." He took a step closer. "Does your disapproval stem from the fact he's a McQuoid or the fact that your sister would be a mere 'Mrs.' were she to wed him?"

Her perfectly arched golden eyebrows went flying up. "You were s-spying on me," she sputtered, and Dallin took a perverse delight in the lady's righteous anger.

"If by 'spying,' you mean I happened to be in the adjoining room and was able to discern your voice as you spoke?" He paused. "Then *yes*."

That slight rosy hue of her cheeks deepened to a near vermilion, which almost made her appear human and not the profoundly haughty lady she'd proven to be.

"If you'd been a gentleman, you'd not have listened in on a private exchange between my sister and me."

"That is true," he allowed. "Given, however, that my family was the source of your discussion, I do believe it was fair for me to avail myself to your carelessness."

"Actually, there are no grounds with which eavesdropping is appropriate, my lord," she said acidly.

The impudence of this one. She'd continue to school him on politeness. In fact, had the circumstances been something—anything—other than what they were, he'd have laughed.

"And I trust it is polite for your family to speak of my family's supposed inferiority, and for you and yours to dictate your sister is too good for my cousin?"

"I didn't say that," she said between gritted teeth.

No, she hadn't. She may as well have.

Dallin felt like the world's worst sort of fool for having romanticized that long-ago meeting . . . and pined for the day when he and she would one day be reunited.

The lady tensed and marched over to the door.

Dallin clapped, the slow, rhythmic tap of his leather gloves freezing her with her fingers on the handle. "I must hand it to you."

The lady's spine grew several inches to an impossible erectness before she turned and eyed him warily. "My lord?"

"I daresay I've not heard so many honorifics strung together since Shakespeare penned *Julius Caesar*."

Fire flared in her eyes, and with a hiss, she gathered up her skirts to leave. Only, he should have known better from a proud, self-important woman.

Alexandra marched over in a fury and stopped with enough distance that she could meet his eyes. "I'll not let you make it as though I'm somehow wrong in any of this. Your *cousin*"—she jabbed a finger as she spoke, emphasizing Dallin's relationship—"has behaved in a dishonorable way. Were he a true gentleman, his courtship of my sister would not be made up of clandestine visits."

Dallin took an angry step forward. "You'd question his honor," he gritted out.

"There is no need for me to question it," she shot back. "With his surreptitious behavior, he's revealed his true colors in such a way he hardly requires any help from me to make him look any worse than he already looks."

He flattened his mouth into a firm line. She'd speak so disdainfully of his cousin Brone, who, with the time he and Dallin and their families spent together, was more of another brother to him.

"Let me be clear, madam," he began, adding a layer of steel to his words as he spoke. "There isn't a finer man than Brone Smith."

"I'd argue it wouldn't be hard to find any number of gentlemen more respectful and decent. In fact, her score of suitors who arrive during the appropriate hours and pay open court to her."

Damn her for being right.

"You don't know him—"

"No, I don't. That is precisely the point, my lord. He may be *your* cousin, but all I know about him is that he's been carrying on clandestine meetings with *my* sister. And I feel quite confident in saying that were our situations reversed and I had a brother who was sneaking off alone with one of your sisters, you'd be a good deal less forgiving."

He'd have called the bounder out at dawn . . . and the insolent glimmer in her eyes said she knew as much.

She wasn't done with him. "Are you telling me you're actually in *favor* of a match between them?"

He sputtered. "Absolutely *not.*"

As the son of a merchant, his cousin was building a fortune and future. While Dallin couldn't admire his cousin more for being a self-made man, the haughty Bradburys would never find Brone worthy.

Alexandra passed her gaze over his face, and then her eyebrows shot up. "You find my sister somehow wanting."

"I never said that," he said in a bid to keep some manner of peace between them.

"You didn't have to. You've made your opinion so clear that no words are necessary." Emotion flared in her eyes. "I cannot believe there was a time when I—"

When she what? "Yes?" he asked, filled with an inexplicable desire to have her complete the remainder of that.

Their chests moved quickly from the force of their breathing, and God forgive him for being a pathetic, pitiable man, without a scrap of pride, but his body cared naught for their families' quarrel or even her disdain.

With Alexandra's generous bosom rising and falling, a different kind of heat ran through him.

The air pulsed with a charged energy made up of their newly discovered dislike of one another . . . and desire.

The lady's mouth formed a small, perfect moue.

She wanted the kiss, too. He sensed it in her and saw it in the way her lashes fluttered and her body swayed nearer to his.

He lowered his head a fraction, and she angled her mouth up to meet his.

The rapid thump of Dallin's beating pulse filled his ears.

His gaze locked on lips as red as rubies and crimson apples, and on the supple flesh that visited him in his dreams . . . back when they weren't antagonizing one another, before he knew precisely what she and her family thought of him.

With but a hairbreadth between their lips, Dallin froze.

What in hell am I thinking?

Did he have so little pride that he'd stand here, lusting for a woman who so plainly spoke of his and his family's inferiority?

That reminder of her imperiousness kicked ash upon any and all embers of his desire, banking them and leaving Dallin properly cold.

He spoke quietly. "Let us be clear, madam," he said, and Alexandra's eyes flew open. "You and I . . . our families may be altogether different in every other way. But in this? We are like. I'd not have Brone wed your sister were she the last woman in London."

She gasped. "How dare you?"

"Quite easily," he drawled, attempting to get a further rise out of her.

If the lady's face turned any redder, she'd have set herself ablaze. "You are obnoxious and rude, and I cannot *believe* I actually thought I enjoyed that time I spent with you."

He lowered his head so he could better meet her eyes. "It appears we're able to come to a consensus on *two* things this night, for I can hardly believe I enjoyed it, either," he whispered tauntingly against her mouth.

"Alexandra . . ."

A tentative voice reached across the room.

As one, he and Alexandra whipped their focus to the front of the room.

They instantly broke apart.

The lady's sister stood with her head cocked, eyeing them with a peculiar look.

Alexandra turned a glare on Dallin. "You didn't lock the door."

"Nor did you."

"You were the last one to enter," she shot back.

"Yes, well, locking it implied I wished to be alone with you, which I decidedly did not."

She gasped. "Failure to lock it risked anyone entering and finding us here, and then we'd both be trapped with one another."

He shuddered.

Her eyes bulged. "Did you just *shudder?*"

"It was more of a shiver."

"A shiver and a shudder are very much the same."

"One can shiver if they're cold," he pointed out.

She paused. "Are you cold?"

"No."

If looks could kill, he'd have caught fire and burnt down the room, effectively putting an end to their family's feud before it officially began.

"Alexandra," the lady's sister called loudly, bringing their attention back over to the young woman still eyeing them oddly.

Alexandra gasped, and sweeping out from around him, she raced over to join her sister. "Cora! What are you doing here?" she demanded the moment she reached her side. She ducked her head out into the hall, and after she'd ensured they were alone, Alexandra pushed the door shut behind them.

"I . . . was looking for you," the younger girl replied, though as she spoke, her curious gaze remained locked on Dallin.

Alexandra took her sister by the hand. "We are done here," she said, and fixed another glare on Dallin. "We are done with this family."

Lady Cora drew her hand back and raced to put several steps between her and her sister. "But—"

"There are no 'buts,' Cora." Alexandra slid a brief glance back Dallin's way. "You must trust me on this," she murmured in gentler tones.

Lady Cora's eyes, however, flashed with a fury Dallin recognized all too well from her elder counterpart. "I will *not*, Alexandra."

The sisters fell silent, each glaring at the other.

And Dallin would have delighted in the young woman gainsaying her sister's wishes and cheered her on in her defiance if the outcome were something—anything—other than his cousin marrying into the Bradbury family.

Were Brone to wed the younger Bradbury sister, he'd either be distracted from his recent undertakings or, worse, be deterred by that family from sullying his hands in something so plebeian.

But the eldest sister proved stronger in this confrontation.

Lady Cora dropped her gaze to the floor.

Click.

As one, the three of them snapped their gazes to the doorway.

There was a long pause, and then a moment later, Brone entered.

Bloody splendid.

Brone's confused gaze went around the occupants of the room; it lingered briefly in confusion on Dallin before the big Scot again found Lady Cora.

Dallin turned a mocking look on the elder of the sisters. "You didn't lock the door. Given your earlier lecture, I'd have thought you'd the good sense to take your own advice. Alas . . . it required good sense."

Bright splotches of color exploded once more on the lady's fair cheeks. "Locking the door would have hindered me leaving with my sister," she said, between the most even, gleaming white teeth he'd ever seen.

"And yet, here you still are," Dallin drawled.

The fiery glimmer in her eyes darkened, and she took a furious step toward him, then seemed to catch herself.

Suddenly, aware of stares upon him, he glanced over. Both Brone and the younger Bradbury sister looked peculiarly at Dallin and Alexandra.

Alexandra followed his focus over to their audience, then took Lady Cora's hand in hers. "We are going, Cora," she said in low tones. "Lest we both find ourselves ruined."

"If a Bradbury marrying a McQuoid was a disaster, what would that make two Bradbury sisters being forced to wed them?" Dallin asked dryly.

Lady Alexandra glared at him. "As I'd never wed you were you the last lord in London, it makes it an impossibility." She returned her attention to the wide-eyed girl at her side. "We're leaving, Cora. Now."

This time, the slightly shorter, plumper young woman nodded and allowed herself to be pulled along by her shrew of a sister.

Only, it wasn't Lady Cora who forced her legs to stop before Brone, but rather Alexandra.

"Do you care about my sister, Mr. Smith?" she asked by way of greeting.

Even with the length of the room between them, Dallin caught the solemn darkening in his normally playful cousin's eyes. "I care about her." Brone's gaze slid over to Lady Cora's and locked with the young lady's.

Alexandra opened her mouth to speak when Brone continued, "And more, I love her more than any man has ever loved a woman."

Whatever words the eldest Bradbury sister intended to say hung silent on her parted lips. Her eyes darkened, and some emotion—disgust? horror?—sent her graceful features into a spasm.

The sight of it sent more of that furious annoyance rippling through Dallin. "One would have to be capable of that emotion to understand what you are speaking about," he called over to his cousin, all the while directing his focus on the statuesque beauty.

Another woman, anyone else, really, would have pretended to not know that indictment had been directed at her.

"Oh, I assure you," she said stiffly. "I love, and when I do so, it is deeply."

"Ah." Dallin inclined his head. "How could I forget . . . your future duke."

Her rosebud lips tightened.

This time, the lady didn't take Dallin's bait.

She returned all her attention to Brone. "If you do love my sister as you say, then I'd implore you to not again threaten her reputation and good name with any further clandestine meetings."

Not allowing Brone another word, she tugged her younger sister along, and the instant they sailed through the entryway, Lady Alexandra pulled the door shut behind them, but not before Lady Cora threw one last, desperate glance over her shoulder at Brone.

The moment they'd gone, Brone looked to Dallin. "What the hell was that about?"

"Do not give Alexandra Bradbury another thought. She has a temper and an ego," he explained, with a wave of his hand.

Details he'd failed to detect upon their first meeting. Nay, not the part about the lady's temper. The signs had been there. She'd been outraged at his arrival that night. Dallin, however, had been so blinded by her like fascination in the stars, he'd taken her affront as endearing. Well, that was a mistake he'd not make a second time.

Brone gave him an odd look. "How do you know that?"

Dallin's mind went blank for a moment, and then he found his voice. "In my attempts at finding you, I happened upon the eldest." He flattened his mouth. "She was quite forthcoming in her opinions about our family and insisted Lady Cora sever her connection with you."

"And you support me and Cora in our relationship."

Dallin blanched. "Egad, no. I merely sought to defend our family's honor."

"By insulting the lady?"

He frowned. That was how his cousin saw it? "By stating truths she herself freely expressed."

And just like they'd done when Dallin and Brone had been boys playing chess, his cousin found himself on the opposite end of winning, and his cheeks went ruddy. "I am twenty-four years old, Dallin. I'm hardly in need of looking after from you."

It was on the tip of Dallin's tongue to remind the younger man that, given the circumstances and his clandestine courtship of a woman undeserving of him, he was very much in need of looking after. However, just like Dallin and all the McQuoids, Brone also possessed the fiery temper they'd inherited from their Scottish line. As such, Dallin opted for a different approach.

"You are a young man who is too in love to see that which is in front of you."

Brone arched a brow. "Oh, and do tell me exactly what that is."

"That you only stand to find heartbreak by loving a woman from a family who finds you and your kin inferior." Dallin delivered that lecture gently, free of the previous anger roused by Alexandra Bradbury.

Dallin clasped a hand on his cousin's rigid shoulder. "Brone," he tried again. "You are *just* twenty-four, building a fortune. And you'll risk all the work you've already done, and your future efforts, by shifting your focus *now*."

Color splotched Brone's cheeks.

Dallin persisted. "I'd ask you to not lose sight of those dreams because of some momentary excitement you found with a beautiful woman."

Close as the McQuoids were, Dallin had always viewed Brone as more of a younger brother than a cousin. As such, he'd protect him from hurt and pain where he could. Even if that meant Dallin speaking uncomfortable truths to the other man.

"Promise me you'll put yourself first in this," Dallin implored. "Promise me you'll end this."

Brone met that plea with stony silence, then slid his gaze beyond a point over Dallin's shoulder. "You have my word," he said quietly.

Dallin eyed him a long moment. He'd capitulated . . . too easily. "You're certain?" he asked quietly. "Because—"

"Would you like me to sign a contract?" Brone drawled, this time with more of his usual humor. "Shake hands? You've my word, Dallin . . . I will put myself first."

The tension slipped from Dallin's taut frame.

He gave his cousin's shoulder another light squeeze.

Someday the other man would see Dallin had been right. For no good could come from a McQuoid falling for a Bradbury.

Chapter 8

Later that evening, in the dead of a darkened night, when hours were so late they were called morning, Alexandra lay glaring up at the mint-green brocade silk overhead.

Restless, she shifted and turned, attempting to relax so that she might get some sleep.

Alas, her efforts proved in vain.

Flipping onto her side, she punched the down mattress. All the while, the memory of that handsome face that had robbed her of rest this night stared back in her mind's eye.

Dallin McQuoid.

Alexandra seethed. To think she'd ever carried romantic imaginings about the man.

How dare he?

Turning onto her other side, she buried her fist a second time.

Insolent.

Alexandra punched the mattress again.

Rude.

She punched it once more.

Mocking.

And of all the affronts he'd leveled at her, accusing her of not knowing what love truly was because she was marrying for a title had struck the sharpest nerve.

And damn him for being right and wrong, all at the same time. Her love for her sisters and mother was what would ultimately force Alexandra into doing what she was doing—marrying the son and heir of a powerful duke.

Even so, hearing Dallin speak so condescendingly, passing judgment on her, when he knew nothing about her situation, hurt. Nay, he didn't know what it was to be impoverished. His family had obscene amounts of wealth and had made honorable matches for two of his sisters—matches that, from everything the papers had written and Alexandra had witnessed with her own eyes, were also *loving* unions.

Tears burnt Alexandra's eyes, and in a bid to keep those useless drops from falling, she blinked furiously. That fluttering of her lashes, however, only hastened the descent of those crystalline beads.

No, Dallin knew nothing at all.

She gave the mattress another *thwack*.

He knew nothing about her circumstances, and she'd sooner trim the tip of her own tongue than utter the truth to him about her family's finances.

That there was nothing.

Alexandra dealt her bedding another punch.

No security.

She let fly another blow.

No safety.

She buried another punch.

No *anything* . . . that was, unless to save her family, Alexandra made the match Dallin jeered her for making.

And when the frustration and fury remained, she continued pounding away until she was breathless and her shoulders heaved. Collapsing onto her belly, Alexandra buried her head in the mattress she'd just brutalized, dragged her pillow over her head, and proceeded to scream.

The down and feathers muted and swallowed those sounds of her desperation and resentment until at last, the fight went out of her.

Tossing her pillow down onto the floor, Alexandra angled her head and sucked in great, gasping breaths of air, letting it fill her lungs. She lay there, staring blankly at the drawn brocade curtains that concealed the windows, at the household directly on the other side of those panes.

Giving up on slumber, Alexandra climbed from the bed.

The instant her bare feet touched the hardwood floor, a chill coursed through her. Gathering her wrapper, she hurriedly pulled it on and belted it at the waist.

Only, it did little to bring any warmth.

Hugging her arms about herself, she rubbed them in an attempt to bring more heat to her body.

She stared at the heavy green silk curtains for a long moment, then slowly parted them.

A full moon hovered high overhead, so bright it illuminated the streets below. Only, it wasn't the streets that called her attention. Her gaze climbed up to the sea of stars dotting the night sky, and she instantly found the one constellation she'd been searching for.

"Legend has it that the hero Perseus saw Andromeda strapped to a rock and instantly fell in love . . . He would slay the sea monster and save her if he could have her in marriage. Though she was already betrothed, they agreed, only to then ultimately break their promise. Perseus, however, went on to interrupt the wedding and save Andromeda once more."

Unbidden, her gaze slid to that rooftop terrace across the way.

Alexandra's heart seized viciously.

The mocking gentleman this evening, so full of loathing for Alexandra, bore no resemblance to the charming, teasing one who'd shared the stars with her.

Those fanciful imaginings she'd carried, however, had been as fantastical as the Greek myth Dallin had regaled her with. For there was no great Perseus there to save her. There was no avenging hero to halt the marriage Alexandra was required to make.

Dallin could judge her all he wished, but he knew nothing of what it was to be an unmarried lady with two unwed sisters and a widowed mama, none of whom had the protection of a loving father or brother, and who had only an apathetic uncle to *watch after them*.

Nay, there was no one but Alexandra to look after her family, and that required she sacrifice not only her very happiness but also all of herself to a cold, unfeeling man she'd met but once.

A man who'd sent his father's solicitor to sign the formal betrothal papers.

Her teeth chattered. Only, this time that uncontrollable rattling had nothing to do with the chill of the night and everything to do with the future awaiting her.

For the thing of it was, she wanted her sister to have the loving relationship she swore she'd found with Brone Smith. Alexandra just . . . wanted all that for herself, too, which was silly. She well knew women of her station were expected to make advantageous matches, ones approved by their family that strengthened their security. But knowing that was a lady's lot did not mean Alexandra wanted or accepted that fate.

And for the first time that night, exhaustion gripped her, and that same mattress she'd so bullied now beckoned.

Shedding her wrapper, Alexandra climbed under the covers.

This time, the instant she closed her eyes, sleep enfolded her.

What felt like mere moments later, a hand on her shoulder brought her awake.

Inky darkness filled the room. The crack in the curtains had allowed the moon's glow through, illuminating the small clock beside her bed.

Nay, it didn't only feel like mere moments later; only several minutes had passed.

"Alexandra," her mother whispered. "It is a disaster."

Another one. "What is it?" she asked groggily. Surely there wasn't a catastrophe to supersede the passing of the marquess and the finances of their family.

"It is Cora." Her mother glanced about as if to confirm they were the only two present. "She is gone."

Alexandra stared at her mother. *"Gone?"*

"Shh." Her mother pressed a finger hard against her lips and stole another look around the room.

Alexandra's heart thudded against her ribs. "Where could she have gone?" she asked, even as she already knew. Just like Cora had secretly done this past year, her sister had gone off to meet Brone Smith.

Enormous tears swelled in the marchioness's eyes. "She left a note."

Alexandra stared dumbly at the paper. Why was there a note?

Wordlessly, her mother pressed the piece of paper into Alexandra's fingers, and the moment that note left her hands, the marchioness proceeded to pace.

When troubled, Alexandra's mother had always been a pacer. That frantic back-and-forth habit, however, had become a good deal worse following her husband's death.

Looking away from the dizzying sight, her fingers shaking uncontrollably, Alexandra, in a bid to steady them, tightened her grip upon the letter Cora had left. And then, flipping open the page, she began to read.

Dearest Mama and Alexandra,

It had been my greatest hope that you would each accept my love for Brone. After this evening, however, it became more than clear that you'd only stand in the way of a future between us.

Dread pitted in Alexandra's stomach and grew as she frantically scanned every scratched sentence in her younger sister's always sloppy writing hand.

The possibility of being parted from him has left me bereft, and although I know you both love me and want me to be happy, I do not trust you to either understand or accept that it is Brone who makes me deliriously so.

Oh, God. Alexandra's response that evening had driven Cora to this.

I know you will worry but ask that you please don't.

"I'm never more safe than when I'm with Brone." Alexandra mouthed those words as she read.

I'm going to be ill.

She finished the remainder of the letter. Alexandra's fingers shook all the harder, and to steady the digits, she tightened them reflexively, crushing the page.

Do not worry, her sister said? *Do not worry?*

Her flighty sister had run off with a young man, both headed for Gretna Green. And were it to be discovered, nay, *when* it was discovered, it would mean the end of Cora's reputation . . . and subsequently, Daphne's and Mama's and Alexandra's.

Whether right or wrong, or good or bad, that was the way of society. A person was seen first for the family they belonged to, and a sin upon one member meant a sin upon all.

This was bad.

Nay, this was worse than bad. This was—

"A disaster is what this is." Alexandra's mother furiously wiped at the tears staining her cheeks. Only, more swiftly fell to replace them. "An absolute nightmare."

And as Alexandra looked at her mother, she noted for the first time the tired set of her eyes and the haggardness of her features. The marquess's death had devastated the older woman. Alexandra had known as much. Until this instant, however, she had not realized just how much his passing had aged her mother.

Nay, mayhap it was simply that Alexandra had deliberately made herself not see it.

There'd be no match with Wingrave, and even as her soul wished to secretly rejoice at being spared that fate, the practical part of her mind that knew her family's security rested squarely on Alexandra went into an all-out panic at the implications.

A crazed buzzing filled her ears. She'd been wrong. There was something to rival those previous other two losses.

"Alexandra?" Her mother's frantic whisper came muffled in her mind. The marchioness gripped her by the shoulders and shook. "Alexandra?" she repeated.

Alexandra came whirring back to the horrifying present. "Daphne?" she croaked, her tongue heavy.

"Is still abed. She doesn't know."

And it needed to remain that way. Bright and chatty as the youngest Bradbury sister was, there could be no certainty Daphne wouldn't inadvertently blurt something out about Cora's elopement.

Swinging her legs over the side of the bed, Alexandra hopped up and marched over to her armoire. She flung the doors open and gathered the floral embroidered valise tucked in the back. Bag in hand, Alexandra returned to her bed and heaved the portmanteau upon the wrinkled sheets.

Her mother's eyes widened.

With determined steps, Alexandra swiftly reversed course, headed back to the closet, and proceeded to sift through the dresses there.

Bypassing cheerfully bright gown after cheerfully bright gown, she tugged free the closest thing to inconspicuous: a serviceable carriage gown made of fine India muslin with short, full sleeves.

Alexandra welcomed the purposefulness of her actions—a purpose kept her steady. It kept her from crumpling into a heap and joining her mother in a fit of tears that, once started, would never, ever stop.

She grabbed another trio of dresses and undergarments made for traveling and draped them over her arm.

Marching back to the bed, Alexandra heaved the garments onto the mattress.

She briefly eyed the growing pile.

For a woman, the only thing more valuable than a serviceable pocket sewn into a gown was quality footwear. Alas, society was of an altogether different opinion and insisted ladies jam their toes into silk slippers and elegant scraps that a puddle a lady failed to see would ruin.

Alexandra returned to the armoire and grabbed two pairs of sturdy boots: one black pair, one silver.

When she returned, Alexandra paused to evaluate the items she'd selected.

At her side, the marchioness took a like inventory. "You are running away, too," her mother whispered, and then promptly slapped a hand over her mouth.

Alexandra pursed her lips. "No, Mama. I'm not running away." Even though her feet twitched with the urge to do just that—flee and continue running until she could put everything behind her: her father's death, her family's finances, her impending betrothal.

But to do so would mean leaving behind her mother and sisters, and that she could never and would never do.

"I'm going to fetch Cora."

"Fetch her," the marchioness echoed.

Alexandra nodded and proceeded to fold her dresses as best as she was able and toss them into her valise.

"Three ladies running around the country will only attract notice and stories."

Yes, it would. Only, it wouldn't be three ladies.

"Which is why *I'm* going." Alone. "Davies will look after me to see I'm safe," she said, continuing to hastily stuff garments into her bag.

The old driver, who'd been with their family since the marquess and marchioness had wed, was one of the dozen servants they'd retained.

"We can rely on his discretion," Alexandra assured her mother. "Douglas"—Davies's identical twin brother and their second groom— "will see you and Daphne to Leeds. This way there will be none of society's eyes on you. We mustn't make a big production of following them, or Cora will be ruined. I'll be able to travel more quickly if I'm on my own."

From the corner of her eye, Alexandra caught the way the marchioness wrung her hands together. "This is dangerous, Alexandra. Any number of terrible fates may befall you."

Snapping her bag shut, Alexandra turned to her mother. "And what other options do we have?" she asked, her tone sharper than intended.

None. There were none. Again, the task of saving the Bradbury family rested with Alexandra.

Fresh crystalline drops formed in the marchioness's ravaged eyes, and the sight of her suffering wrenched at Alexandra.

"I could not bear it if anything were to happen to you or Cora. Losing your father broke my heart. Losing the both of you would destroy me."

How many other mothers would have their first concern be the advantageous match with a duke's son, which now, because of Cora's reckless actions, was at risk?

"Forgive me, Mama," she said softly, and wrapped her arms around her mother.

The marchioness immediately folded hers about Alexandra; it was an embrace so very much like the comforting ones she'd given Alexandra as a girl who'd suffered some small hurt. Only, time had left Alexandra taller, so that now their positions were reversed and her mother's head fit upon Alexandra's shoulder. "Oh, Alexandra, there is nothing to forgive," she said, smoothing her palm in soft, gentle circles upon Alexandra's back. "It is I who should be apologizing to you."

Alexandra drew back. "You've done nothing." Her mother was no more to blame for the marquess's financial mistakes than she was for Cora's ill-thought flight.

When a woman wed, she became her husband's property. Everything she owned, any money she had, and any knowledge she possessed of their family's finances rested solely with the man she joined herself to.

Not once in Alexandra's life had she regretted not having a brother. Her family had felt perfectly complete with the gaggle of girls, as the marquess had fondly referred to his wife and daughters. That was, she'd not regretted the absence of a male sibling . . . until now.

Alexandra, however, didn't have a brother or father or husband or even a loving sweetheart to rely on. She'd save her sister herself.

Chapter 9

The vast McQuoid family was known for gathering whenever the chance permitted: Always at the Christmastide season for an extended house party in the countryside (with the exception of when certain McQuoids went missing and the gentlemen assembled to recover said missing McQuoids, as had been the case with Dallin's younger sister). Usually in the heart of summer, when they took part in raucous games of lawn bowling and races in the lake. Invariably at the start of the launch of each London Season, when they all gathered for a boisterous dinner party that stretched into the early hours of the next morn.

Yes, above all else, of all the uncertainties in the world, one could always count on the McQuoid gatherings to be noisy and joyous.

That was, until now.

Every last member of the McQuoid family—including the younger siblings who'd raised the warning that had brought them together—had packed into every corner of the Earl of Abington's office.

And the McQuoids had achieved a familial first: dead silence.

That was, with the exception of Dallin's recently widowed aunt Leslie's quiet weeping.

At the head of the mahogany desk, Dallin's father sat, looking deuced uncomfortable; he cast the occasional glance back at the countess, who stood at his shoulder, resolute. And aside from the worry in her gaze, she revealed not even a hint of the concern etched across every last family member's face.

Aunt Leslie blew her nose loudly into the deeply wrinkled kerchief Dallin had proffered when she and her many children came streaming into the McQuoids' townhouse, as like a whirlwind as only someone with McQuoid blood could be.

"How could he do th-this?" She spoke through her weeping. "With my dear Francis recently passed, h-his brother off traveling, and a-absolutely n-no regard for the wrath he'll b-bring down on h-his sisters."

The countess rushed out from behind her husband's desk and promptly wrapped an arm around her sister's shoulder. "*Shh*, dearest. It will be all right," she said soothingly.

"A-all right?" Leslie looked up at the countess through swollen, red-rimmed eyes. "A-alll right? The Duke of Talbert d-declared our family a s-scourge after C-Cassia wed the gentleman his daughter was intended to marry." She cast an accusatory look at the pair in question, Cassia and Captain Nathaniel Ellsby. "The way he'll see it is another McQuoid is marrying into the family he is joining his son with."

"I, for one, do not see what is wrong with Brone marrying the younger Bradbury girl," Brone's sister Linnie intoned. "It is not as though he's run off with the marquess's betrothed this time."

The marquess. As in Lord Wingrave.

And his betrothed. As in . . .

Alexandra Bradbury.

Dallin's fingers tightened into reflexive fists. He didn't care that the renowned chit was poised to wed another. He did, however, care about the fact he'd secretly harbored romantic illusions about a woman who thought so ill of his family, and who was more concerned with marrying an eventual duke.

"It is that he"—and the Bradbury family—"believes we are inferior," Dallin said quietly, calling everyone's attention his way.

His aunt Leslie pointed her finger at Dallin. "Th-that is right. H-he's made no secret of his contempt for anyone and everyone associated with our family."

"He's even severed his relationship with Nathan's family," Cassia murmured.

Leslie looked about the room. "The two men were friends since they were lads and raised their families side by side, and he just"—she made a slashing motion—"cut the ties of that relationship. Wh-what does that mean for those of us without so much as the benefit of any connection?" His aunt's voice fell to a shuddery whisper. "The Duke of Talbert will see us d-destroyed."

"We could always give the captain back?" Quillon suggested, earning a collection of angry looks.

The boy squirmed. "What? It was just an idea, and it is not as though I *want* to give him back." Quillon glanced Nathaniel's way. "Nothing personal, of course, Nathaniel. I do enjoy our time engaging in pretend sea battles and far prefer you to my brothers."

Captain Nathaniel inclined his head. "No offense taken, and I'm honored."

It was Fleur who brought the room back to the matter at hand.

"Talbert's just one duke," she piped in. "*We* have two." She jabbed the index finger on each hand to where their brothers-in-law sat. "Aragon and him."

"Do you mean the *Marquess* of Winfield?" Quillon shot back.

Fleur tossed a hopeful look the serious-looking fellow's way. "Is your father—"

"I'm sorry to disappoint," Cassia's husband said, his features expressionless. "He is in the very best of health and will likely outlive us all."

Fleur's face fell as all the occupants grew solemn once more.

She perked up. "We still have Myrtle's duke, and that surely at the very least cancels out the other duke."

Their cousin Meghan shook her head. "No," she said matter-of-factly, as if she were the absolute authority on the matter. "Myrtle's husband doesn't like people and so has limited connections."

Dallin's mother slapped a hand across her eyes.

Myrtle bristled. "My husband likes people just fine." She turned to her stoic husband, who sat beside her on the leather button sofa. "Isn't that right, dear heart?"

The lone duke amongst them grunted. "I like *you* just fine. Love you, even."

Myrtle's eyes went soft, and she joined her fingers with her husband's, and for a brief moment, Dallin recalled that long-ago night when he'd joined his hands with Alexandra Bradbury's in a similar way and how annoyingly right it had felt.

Fleur called out to the Duke of Aragon, breaking Dallin's pathetic reminiscing. "What about us and your children, Val?" the girl asked, reminding Myrtle's husband of his twin babes.

"I like my *children* fine enough." The duke paused. "Most times."

Only the uncharacteristic twinkle in the serious fellow's eyes hinted at his teasing.

Quillon frowned. "Am I the only one who'll point out he did not confirm his like for the rest of us?"

"Which is *whyyyy*," Fleur said, bringing them back to the matter at hand, "he doesn't have any connections that will save our dearest cousins, Meghan, Linnie, Andromena, and Oleander. At least, not any connections that will match the Duke of Talbert's," she pointed out with a sageness better suited to a grown woman than a child.

Their aunt dissolved into another fit of tears. As the countess patted her sister's shoulder, she glared at Fleur.

"What?" Fleur mouthed. "It's true."

"And what of you, imp?" Arran drawled. He tugged one of the girl's ringlets. "You don't include yourself ruined as well?"

"Me? Ruined?" Fleur snorted. "I consider myself saved from having to marry and end up like those two." She jabbed her thumbs in the direction of her elder sisters. "All big-eyed and sighing and—"

"Why are they here?" Dallin asked the question that surely everyone present was thinking.

A bevy of icy glares belonging to his youngest siblings and cousins landed his way.

"I'll point out that if it weren't for the four of us, Dallin, none of *you* would have any idea that Brone had sneaked off to—"

The adults present gave a collective hushing that managed to drown out the rest of Fleur's damning words.

The countess took charge of a discussion that had rapidly deteriorated before it had even begun. "Thanks are, of course, in order for Fleur, Quillon, Andromena, and Oleander. At this time, I'd ask you to take your leave while we discuss the situation." She turned to her eldest nieces. "Meghan, Linnie, will you please see them to their rooms?"

Reluctantly, the children climbed to their feet.

Before they could take so much as a step, Dallin's mother spoke again. "There is, of course, still the matter of your utmost discretion I want assurances of."

The four children nodded in unison.

"And," the countess added, "a discussion tomorrow morning about the situation which led to your discovery."

The situation being that the four had sneaked off to the stables and saddled their mounts at the very moment Brone, with a cloaked lady at his side, had been having a carriage readied.

In unison, the children groaned.

Unfortunately for the eloping pair, Lady Cora's loose lips with the McQuoid children appeared likely to kill those plans. Or, in Brone's case, to save the man.

The moment Meghan and Linnie had ushered the youngest ones from the room, a blessed silence fell over the office. Of course, Cassia, the chattiest of Dallin's sisters, had never met a silence she didn't wish to fill.

"I for one find it romantic," she chimed into the grim quiet of the McQuoid parlor. "Star-crossed lovers of rival families. Why, it has all the makings of *Romeo and Juliet*."

Romeo and Juliet?

Dallin looked about his assembled family, searching for a like reaction to that parallel, and finding none, he made the obvious point. "You are aware *Romeo and Juliet* is no manner of romantic work."

His sisters gasped.

"It is one of the greatest love stories of all time," Cassia exclaimed.

"A love story . . . that ends with both Romeo and Juliet *dying*," Dallin muttered.

Even as his brother Arran snorted a laugh, every other McQuoid relative assembled, along with his sisters' husbands, turned in their seats to glare at him. At *Dallin?*

He was the one they'd take umbrage with, and not his blasted cousin, who'd absconded with their neighbor's middle daughter?

Dallin resisted the urge to tug at his cravat.

"Yes, well, in my days young ones didn't run off as this new generation does. It's a veritable epidemic, it is," the earl groused as he sifted around his cluttered desk. "Cassia, Myrtle. Now, Brone."

Myrtle shot a hand up. "I'd be remiss if I failed to point out I didn't run off, but rather was left behind by my entire family."

At the reminder of that oversight, the countess had the good grace to flush. The *earl*, on the other hand, continued muttering under his breath, while he fished about for . . .

"Aha!" Their father held his big gold magnifying glass aloft, and then pressing it against his eye, he proceeded to examine a large square sheet of vellum filled with a rhumb line.

"That had better be a map of Gretna Green, dearest," the countess said warningly.

"Hmm." Lost in his latest passion—ancient maps—it was a moment before Dallin's father registered his wife's displeasure. "Oh, uh . . ." With a visible sadness, the earl set down the eyepiece.

Ever one to take charge of their big family, Dallin's mother clapped her hands once. "Now, given the circumstances, there is but one thing to do."

Dallin spoke the same moment Cassia and Myrtle did. "Put a stop to the marriage."

"Help Brone," his sisters said.

The two young women instantly frowned at him.

Wait . . . his sisters actually supported the match? The world had turned upside down. That's all there was to it.

"Is that what you think we do, Dallin?" Myrtle asked quietly. "We stand in the way of true love?"

Having never experienced the emotion himself, he didn't know much about true love. He knew his sisters were deliriously happy with their far-too-grumpy-seeming husbands. Dallin was also mindful of the fact that, romantic as Cassia and Myrtle were, they'd be unable to disentangle emotion from logic.

He measured his response. "The whole of his life, Brone has made no secret of his hopes of expanding his family's trade ventures into the textile industry. He's only just begun seeing that dream realized."

His pragmatic reminder was met with an answering silence.

"Furthermore, Brone hardly knows the lady," he said gently. "And he certainly doesn't know her family." For if their cousin *did*, he'd have never done something so foolhardy as run off with one of their daughters.

"All this talk of trade . . . Someday you're going to fall in love, Dallin," Cassia murmured. "And at that moment, then you'll understand precisely why Brone did what he did."

The chances of that ran the spectrum from highly improbable to completely impossible. He'd already gotten too close to harboring romantic sentiments and had no interest in making a further fool of himself.

Myrtle looked accusatorily at the countess. "Surely you are not suggesting we prevent Brone from marrying the woman he loves?"

Color splotched their mother's cheeks. "Under other circumstances, I'd not . . ." She glanced over at their aunt Leslie. "But this is not most circumstances, Myrtle," she said with a quiet sadness. "Their marrying will make the McQuoids an even more powerful enemy of the duke. Your uncle has passed, and there are your cousins to consider."

Leslie looked to Dallin. "Were Francis here," she whispered, "I would, of course—"

"I will go," he interrupted her, saving her from asking a favor that was really no favor. They were family, and as loud, scandalous, and vexing as the McQuoids were, family looked after family. "I'll stop him." He'd stop him from making an irrevocable mistake that would not only have implications for the McQuoid and Smith girls' future but also for Brone's very happiness.

His aunt Leslie broke down crying, this time with tears of relief.

He stood. "I will head out immediately." There wasn't a moment to spare. Brone had a lead, but he was also traveling by carriage with a young lady and would not be moving as quickly as Dallin would on horseback.

His sisters' disapproving gazes followed him from the room.

It was fine. They were entitled to their disappointment.

Dallin, however, would no sooner wed Alexandra Bradbury than he would let Brone tie himself forevermore to a lady who'd only break his heart.

Chapter 10

When Alexandra had first boarded one of her family's carriages two days earlier and set out after her sister, only one thing had motivated her—stopping Cora from marrying a McQuoid.

Now, as the conveyance raced along the flooded, uneven roads at a breakneck speed, swaying left and then right, tilting precariously, Alexandra discovered a new, more pressing goal—staying alive.

Please, don't let me die.

In quick succession, several streaks of lightning flashed in the sky. The team of horses squealed.

Clenching her eyes tightly, Alexandra curled her fingers into the red-velvet squab and clung to it for dear life. Fear had left her palms slick with sweat, and she searched—and failed—to find a firmer purchase.

Her driver's shouts and curses blended with the horses' panicked whinnies.

Terror ratcheted up in her breast.

Davies didn't curse. She'd never heard a single harsh word from his mouth, and he'd never lost control of his always even, affable temper.

The carriage lurched violently to the left.

Alexandra lost her grip on the bench and went flying against the opposite wall. The moment she slammed into the side, pain radiated along her shoulder.

"Hell and the Devil." That curse slipped out with an ease that would have horrified Alexandra's mother as much as the words themselves.

As she wrapped her arm about her and rubbed the injury, a panicky giggle spilled from her lips.

Only a Bradbury would be moments from death and worry about not conducting herself appropriately in the midst of the accident that would claim her short life.

The carriage rolled through a large hole and emerged from it so quickly Alexandra's bottom left the seat.

She gritted her teeth.

Mayhap the Bradburys hadn't been as good as she'd always taken them for.

The carriage lurched, and she held on, tightening her already white-knuckled grip for all she was worth.

For surely, between Papa's passing and their financial woes, Cora's elopement, and Alexandra's eventual marriage to the Miserable Marquess, the Bradburys were very clearly being punished mightily for some past transgressions. That was the only thing accounting for the string of ill fortunes that'd followed them.

And anyone else connected to their family was paying the same price.

Alexandra made herself steal a glance out the window at the rapidly passing landscape; the inky night sky, together with the speed of her runaway carriage, made the world a blur.

She'd insisted they ride through the rain-clogged roads because she'd known her sister and Brone Smith would have likely been forced to stop. That desire to reach Cora had made Alexandra reckless.

"Whoaaa!" Davies shouted to the out-of-control team.

And then, miraculously, the carriage rocked back in a sudden stop that sent Alexandra slamming against the back of her squab.

She grunted as the force of that impact sucked the air from her lungs.

The old driver cried out, and then came silence.

But for the ringing of an eerie quiet in Alexandra's ears, she heard no sounds at all.

Alexandra sat motionless; the shock and terror of an almost collision held her immobile.

Then she heard it: a low, pain-filled groan, muffled through the carriage walls, snapped her from her dazed reverie.

Giving her head a firm shake, Alexandra grabbed for the handle, and leaning her head out, she squinted, attempting to make out her driver's form on the box—the empty box. "Davies?"

"F-fine, m-my lady." That assurance came from below.

"Davies!" Alexandra scrambled from the carriage; the sodden riding path shifted under her unsteady boots, and their soles sank into thick mud.

Hiking up her skirts to spare them from the elements, she trudged over to where the older servant sat in the middle of the mud, looking as bewildered as Alexandra felt.

Her heart lurched. "You are hurt," she said, and abandoning her attempts at saving her skirts, she dropped to her haunches beside Davies.

He gave his head a dazed shake. "Never seen the roads like this, I have. That last bolt of lightning came awful close, it did. Terrified the horses into galloping off."

Alexandra briefly closed her eyes. "You were thrown."

"It's not as bad as all that."

"Nay, it is worse," she said.

Davies made a sound of protest. "I was fit as a fiddle until we stopped." He pointed up to the box, and she followed that gesture. "Getting down was what did me in, my lady. Turned my ankle in the mud, and then came down hard on my hand."

The thick storm clouds overhead shifted, allowing the moonlight to peek through, shining nature's light upon the injured driver's swollen hand.

Alexandra briefly closed her eyes. "Oh, Davies. I'm so sorry." Sorry he'd been forced to set out at the breakneck speed she'd set for them.

Sorry her younger sister had put them in a position of doing so. And sorry he'd not had the deserved retirement a servant of his advanced years should because her father had bungled the Bradbury finances.

He bristled. "You're sorry? What for? I'm the one who got myself in this tangle."

A hysterical little giggle that hovered very close to tears spilled from her lips. "I assure you, Davies, you are certainly the last who is to blame."

Yes, despite the faithful driver's protestations, he bore no responsibility for any of this. They didn't deserve him.

To keep from dissolving into a full panic, Alexandra glanced around. Debating who was to blame, here on the side of the road, solved nothing. "We must find a place for—"

"We'd just reached Sand Hutton. There's an inn not far back. Passed it a short while ago, we did."

She'd no idea where Sand Hutton was, but she didn't need to hear anything more than "there's an inn not far back."

"Then we shall go there." She looked over her shoulder and peered into the distance, searching for a hint of anything near the empty, barren road—and found nothing.

Why had she insisted on leaving her maid behind?

Because you were worried about salvaging your family's reputation and didn't want to risk more people finding out.

Thrusting aside thoughts about a future she could not control, she turned her focus back to Davies.

Alexandra worried at her lower lip.

The pain lines wreathing his face had deepened.

"You should not move," she said, straightening. "I will go and fetch help." Even as she made that determination, the idea of going off alone in the dead of night set her stomach to churning.

Davies scowled. "You'll do no such thing. I'm more than capable of walking, my lady."

She eyed his injury dubiously.

"I'm accompanying you, my lady," he said, this time firmly, effectively putting an end to the debate.

Ignoring Davies's protestations, Alexandra collected her own valise and, mindful of the older servant's injuries, set a slow pace along the edge of the old coach route.

As they slogged along the muddied earth, a miserable cold seeped through the soles of her boots, chilling her through. The brisk night air penetrated the fabric of her cloak, and she gritted her teeth to keep from chattering.

With every slow step she took, she mentally composed a list of items that, if she survived this flight to Scotland, she'd never, ever take for granted again:

A blazing fire in a well-tended hearth.

Blankets.

Throws.

Warm feather mattresses.

Warm feather pillows.

Somewhere nearby, a twig snapped, and Alexandra froze.

A small red fox darted in front of her and Davies, and then scurried off, disappearing into the high grass.

Some of the tension left her shoulders.

Only, as she and Davies resumed their slow trek, Alexandra's discomfort from the cold was replaced by a heightened awareness of every rustle and foreign sound of the North Yorkshire countryside.

Gooseflesh dotted her arms, and Alexandra gritted her teeth to keep them from chattering.

Do not focus on those eerie noises. Focus on—

"Twoo. Twoo."

That ghostlike call pulled a gasp from her, and Alexandra lost her grip on her bag. It hit the ground with a *thwack*, sending muddy remnants spraying her skirts and startling a roundheaded bird from its perch atop a split tree trunk.

Davies doffed his cap and scrubbed the material over his sweat-dampened brow. "Just a tawny owl, it is, my lady," he said soothingly.

"Just an owl," she repeated, as much as a reminder for herself as to hear her own voice.

With every step taken on the sodden earth, however, the exertion of carrying her weighty bag chased away the cold and her fear of the unknown around them. Under her leather gloves, sweat slicked her palms, and her shoulders and muscles she'd not known she possessed in her back strained under her efforts.

Out of breath, she passed her valise into her other hand.

How had she failed to appreciate just how hard a task it was? How many times had she taken for granted her valises and trunks being carried and loaded whenever her family departed London for their country estates?

This time, she added servants to the list of people she'd never again take for granted.

That was, if there *were* servants after all this.

Tears built in her eyes, and she furiously blinked them back, refusing to let those useless drops fall. She didn't want to do this. She didn't want her sisters' safety and futures on her shoulders. She wanted to put it all in someone else's hands, if even for just a moment, so she could not be alone in her fear. She wanted to return to a time when she'd believed her life and future were stable and secure.

Alexandra stared blankly out at the smattering of stars.

But there was no going back, and there was no Perseus coming. There was just Alexandra to make this right—all of it.

As they made what felt like an interminable journey down the Great North Road, she stole worried glances at Davies. Every step taken put a further strain upon his wizened features.

They walked so far and so long she began to fear Davies had merely imagined a stop along the way, that there was, in fact, no inn, that there was no *anything* and she'd be left to die alongside Davies on this barren road.

Then at last, she saw it in the distance—the orange shine only candlelight and a fire's glow could leave upon a windowpane. Smoke made by a chimney billowed into the sky, big, lofty clouds of white.

Just like that, the desolation that had gripped her faded.

A giddy lightness suffused her chest and filled her with a renewed energy. "We have made it, Davies!" she announced happily. "We did it."

"Indeed we have, my lady," he said with the first grin since he'd suffered his fall.

"Come," she urged, adjusting her grip on her valise. "We've not much farther to go."

And as she and Davies headed for the inn, from the seeds of her earlier doubt grew a sense of triumph at her accomplishment.

Alexandra firmed her jaw. She didn't need someone else to save her or her family.

She would do it all herself.

——— ❧ ———

Two Hours Later

Standing in the narrow hall outside her modest rooms at the Fox and Hound Inn, Alexandra waited for an update on the injured driver. Or continued waiting. The old village surgeon who'd been summoned and now attended Davies had been with the servant for the better part of an hour.

On occasion, the men's voices came through the doorway, but just muffled enough that Alexandra couldn't clearly make out their exchange.

The squeal of rusty hinges filled the hall, and Alexandra jumped.

Her heart thumping in her breast, she looked toward a sallow-faced fellow with a balding pate and garments best suited to a dandy two decades prior. Unsteady on his feet, he dug around the inside of his jacket, muttering to himself all the while.

Alexandra burrowed deeper into her fur-lined cloak.

Clink.

"Bloooody hellll," the inebriated patron slurred, and falling to his knees, he proceeded to fish around for the key he'd dropped.

As if he felt her stare, the man suddenly stopped and looked up.

Heart hammering, Alexandra grabbed the door handle and raced inside her room.

Her fingers shook as she fumbled with the lock, and a wave of relief went through her at the satisfying *click.*

From the other side of the crude oak panel, there came the shuffle of unsteady footsteps. She held her breath as the stranger went ambling past her door, and then only the ring of silence and distant voices of patrons below and Davies and the surgeon next door remained.

Squeezing her eyes shut, Alexandra pressed her forehead against the door.

She wasn't the crying sort, but if ever there'd been a time for a lady to have herself a good weep, well, this situation more than certainly called for it.

She'd never been anywhere without the benefit of a companion or lady's maid or sister or parent, or anyone . . . and as such, she'd never known what it was to be alone in the world. Only to find herself unaccompanied at a packed inn filled with drunken patrons, and with only the benefit of an old—and now injured—servant to rely on.

Through her misery came the distinct guffaw of Davies's laughter.

Why, laughter went more with "Fit as a fiddle" and "Can you believe your good fortune" than . . . "You've suffered a debilitating injury that will keep you off the driver's box."

Laughter was surely a good sign. For the first time since her father's death, hope blossomed in her breast.

Fumbling with the lock, she let herself out into the empty hall just as the surgeon, with a bag in one hand and a cane in the other, slowly exited the room Alexandra had rented for Davies.

With a mane of wild white hair and a wrinkled face, he couldn't be many years older than the patient he'd just seen, and she felt another pang of guilt strike at yet another person she'd been forced to put out because of the Bradburys' circumstances.

"Dr. Sturgeon," she greeted the moment he closed the door behind him and they were alone in the corridor. "How is he?"

"He will be just fine. There are no breaks."

She briefly closed her eyes and sent a prayer above that the Bradburys hadn't inadvertently seen the old groom gravely injured.

And that beautiful hope that had been born before fanned brighter. The surgeon indicated Davies's injuries weren't so very bad, after all. Perhaps it'd been worse in the moment, but he'd still be fine to continue driving on to Scot—

"He cannot drive, Mrs. Alaister."

Dr. Sturgeon cleaned the lenses of his wire-rimmed spectacles on the front of his linen shirt.

With that pronouncement, Alexandra's earlier buoyancy popped like the flimsy soap bubbles her youngest sister had always enjoyed playing with.

The noisy clang of tankards and the ebullient laughter from patrons in the crowded taproom below stood in stark juxtaposition to that solemn declaration.

"The hand isn't strong enough to hold the reins," he explained, as if she'd voiced a protest of his assessment. "I'd expect within a week or so, he should be capable of using his wrist some."

"A week," she repeated dumbly. A week she did not have. Four days. That was the length of time it took to travel from London to Scotland,

and that was barring no unforeseen delays. And the accident which had sidelined Davies proved to be one unforeseen delay too many. As it was, Cora and Brone Smith already had a lead on Alexandra. She—

"Mrs. Alaister?" The surgeon's concern-filled question penetrated the rapidly rising panic aswirl in her head. "Mrs. *Alaister?*"

Mrs. Alaister? Why was this man calling her by that strange name?

Then she recalled the false identity she'd given to both the innkeeper and surgeon. *It's me. I'm Mrs. Alaister.* And likely that invented title would be the closest she'd ever find herself to actual marriage after all this.

"Yes, Dr. Sturgeon?"

"May I be of additional service?"

Additional . . .

Alexandra caught his slightly pointed look.

Of course. "No." Giving her head a shake, she removed several coins from a pocket sewn into the front of her cloak. "That will be all."

She laid coins in the doctor's hand, and as he pocketed those funds, Alexandra stared forlornly as they disappeared into his serviceable wool jacket.

How peculiar to have lived such a privileged life before that she'd never given a thought to money. Now, every singular aspect of her existence revolved around the total lack of it. Davies would need to remain behind. She'd leave funds so that he was cared for until a servant was able to return for him.

"Worry not," the merry surgeon said. "There are far worse fates than to be waylaid in the beautiful North Yorkshire countryside, Mrs. Alaister."

Worse fates. Among them: Destitution. Being assailed by drunken men at an inn far away from her family's home. A broken betrothal. And the subsequent ruin of not just one Bradbury sister but two, and because of the two, three.

Alexandra stared at the departing doctor and fought down the hysterical giggle that threatened.

She rather doubted it.

"Dr. Sturgeon," she called out the moment he reached the top of the stairway.

He glanced back.

"Do you mayhap know if there is someone who might drive my team?" she asked hopefully.

As if on cue, a swell of raucous laughter rolled like a wave through the establishment, cresting all the way to the narrow hall.

She followed the dubious look Dr. Sturgeon cast over his shoulder. Her heart sank. "I . . . didn't think so. Thank you again."

When he'd gone, she remained there, motionless. Afraid to move. Afraid to breathe. For surely, were she to do so, she'd splinter into a million shards, never to be put back together.

She remained trapped here without a single way to either get to her sister or return home. The weight of that realization knocked the earth out from under her.

Alexandra's legs shifted, and to keep herself from falling, she rested a shoulder against the stone wall. The cold of those ancient rocks, crudely assembled some centuries prior, penetrated all the way through her cloak and gown and chilled her.

There wasn't a single sober man throughout the entire inn who could help her.

Not a—

The stairs creaked, signaling too late the arrival of another drunken patron.

That self-indulgent moment where she'd allowed herself to wallow in her own self-pity forgotten, Alexandra made a move for her door handle.

This figure, taller and more broadly powerful than the foxed fellow who'd stumbled down this hall a short while ago, moved with steady steps.

Purpose-driven, he passed Alexandra and gave no outward indication that he so much as noted her presence.

There was something . . . strangely familiar about his assured stride.

Her heart thumped for the first time this day with something other than fear.

Edging her hood back the tiniest fraction, she peeked over at the stranger . . . who was, in fact, no stranger.

Dressed more finely than any of the other patrons she'd spied as she'd walked in, the gentleman possessed a singular handsomeness: his chestnut-brown hair, just a smidge longer than fashion dictated, and a day's growth of beard on his fine-featured face.

And this time, her heart fell for altogether different reasons.

Bloody hell.

There was one man who could help her.

Dallin McQuoid.

Chapter 11

As Dallin had suspected when he passed the nearly motionless, cloaked figure in the hall of the Fox and Hound, the woman had been watching him.

A short while later, as he sat in the corner of the bustling establishment with a tankard of ale between his chilled hands, it became apparent why.

Dallin narrowed his eyes.

Bloody impossible.

The lack of sleep merely had his mind's eye playing tricks on him. That was absolutely the only thing accounting for her being here.

And yet, the sight remained.

Lady Alexandra Bradbury.

Even seated as he'd been at the far back table in the Fox and Hound Inn, the room filled to bursting with patrons, Dallin spotted her the instant she walked down the narrow planks of the hewn log staircase.

Nay, mere mortals walked.

Almost celestial in her beauty, Lady Alexandra floated with fluid, balletic steps upon those stairs.

He'd hand it to the lady, she gave no outward reaction to the increasingly unruly patrons around her. Rather, she paused at the edge of the fray, and from under the hood of her cloak, she skimmed her gaze just over the tops of everyone's heads. The lady assessed the room around them like some queen, seeking a figure upon whom to bestow the honor of her stare.

And then, sure enough, she stilled, locking that imperious look on one—Dallin.

The lady contemplated him a long moment more, and then giving no outward reaction to the rowdy tableau around her, she adjusted her skirts, lifted her chin a notch, and sailed through the sea of drunken patrons.

Surely not to him.

He did a search around him for some other gentleman she could possibly be seeking out. Or the companion she joined.

Only . . .

The lady glided to a stop before his table.

"Viscount Crichton," she greeted, as if it were the most natural thing in the world for them to be meeting at a smoky, medieval tavern on the edge of North Yorkshire.

As if it were entirely commonplace for her, a young lady, to approach Dallin, at that.

Befuddled, he only managed to stare at her over the top of the metal flagon in his fingers.

Composed and collected enough for the both of them, the lady availed herself of the opposite seat.

He managed to find his tongue. "What are you doing?" What was she doing on the road at this ungodly hour? What was she doing wandering through this tavern? What was she doing sitting with him?

"It should be clear."

He heard the frown in her voice.

"It isn't."

"I'm sitting."

Had any other soul on the whole of God's green earth uttered that rejoinder, Dallin would have taken it for a jest. This proud, haughty woman, however, couldn't have picked a quip out of a wicker basket.

He sharpened his gaze on the lady. "Surely you aren't here alone?"

Alexandra scoffed. "Surely you don't believe I'd travel alone?"

He barely knew her, not at all, but enough to say with certainty: only one reason and one reason alone would send a woman of her station out at this hour on a desperate mission.

"Off to stop a wedding, are you?" he drawled.

"Hush," she whispered, stealing a quick glance about. Her hood slipped, revealing the rose-hued blush that filled her high cheeks.

"Do you think anyone here is attending to us?"

"I wouldn't be so foolish as to assume they're *not*," she countered, giving him a pointed look.

He sharpened his gaze on her. "Are you calling me foolish?"

"If you assume it's safe to openly discuss . . . what we're discussing amidst a crowded taproom, then *yes*."

As if to prove the impudent chit's point, the old innkeeper appeared. "May I fetch you a tray, Mrs. Alaister?"

"Mrs. Alaister?" Dallin mouthed.

She shot a foot out, catching Dallin square in the shins, and spoke with a smile in her voice as she did.

Dallin winced.

"Not at this time, Mr. Whipplewhite," Alexandra said. "I will take one in my room shortly after I finish speaking with *Mr.* Alaister's business partner."

The silver-haired, slender proprietor dropped a little bow.

"Are you truly so bad at this?" she whispered furiously the moment the other man had taken himself off.

"Bad at—"

"At being discreet. Furtive—"

"Deceptive?" he supplied, winging an eyebrow up. "I confess, you are undoubtedly my superior in that skill."

She didn't take the bait. Not that he expected a woman as self-possessed and uppish as Alexandra *would*.

A woman who could present herself as two different people: one an innocent young lady with a sudden interest in stargazing, and the other a lady so determined to be a duchess she'd traded in her status of Diamond before the season had started for the opportunity to marry a future duke.

In retrospect, she'd likely only feigned her interest in stargazing to avoid the humiliation of having been caught trespassing.

Alexandra continued to sit in silence, her palms resting on her lap.

"What brings you here, Mrs. Alaister?" he asked quietly.

"I thought I would say hello," she said softly. She turned her gloved palms up. "We are neighbors."

A memory he hated for being so vivid all this time later surfaced in his mind. "As such, you'd argue, given our neighborly association, I might be a good deal more welcoming?"

At those familiar words, the lady drew back so abruptly that the sudden recoil sent her hood slipping farther, revealing stricken eyes. However, she righted that fur-lined article so quickly Dallin may have only imagined that almost tragic glint in those exquisite azure irises.

And he hated himself for wanting to shove that ridiculously deep hood off her head so he could freely drink in the sight of those fathomless blue pools.

That reminder steeled him. It chased away all the wistful thoughts about that terrace meeting they'd shared. "How curious of all the surnames you could have chosen, you opted for a *Scottish* one."

Alexandra froze like a startled doe.

"I had no idea," she said, her voice weaker than he ever recalled.

He continued, finding more glee in this exchange than was healthy or good. "Allow me to enlighten you, lass. In Scottish, the name Alaister refers to a cruel demon of hell."

She gasped but promptly found her footing. "Do you know, in *English*, Alexandra means 'protector of mankind.' Or in this case, womankind."

Dropping his elbows on the table, he flared his nostrils and leaned in, shrinking the space between them. "And you think your sister needs saving from my cousin?"

"I know my sister needs saving from both herself and your cousin. Eloping to Gretna Green is dangerous not only to her reputation, but the journey in and of itself is perilous. All details your cousin should know."

—⊷⊶—

Alexandra's fingers twitched with the urge to snatch the tankard from Dallin's fingers and dump those frothy contents over the top of his smug, all-knowing head.

But she didn't do that.

Over the years, Alexandra had perfected every lesson passed down by her mother and the family's governesses.

A lady didn't ever lose control of her temper. Ladies, at all times, must be balanced and even and reveal no hint of any excessive emotion.

Those particular lessons had been instilled in Alexandra around the time she could talk.

Fortunately, it'd also been around the time she could count and when her silent habit of list-building formed to keep her emotions firmly in check.

This time, seated across from a coolly mocking Dallin McQuoid, she put that list-building to the test.

Obnoxious.

Condescending.

Rude.

Wretched.

The gall of this man. He'd pass judgment on *her* for attempting to save her sister. It was all she could do to tell him precisely what she thought of him, and yet . . . to do so would prove calamitous. For whether she liked it or not—and she decidedly didn't—Alexandra did need him. She needed his help getting to Cora, and for Cora, she could do or be anything.

Her temper safely in check, Alexandra attempted to start this exchange over. She glanced around the slovenly, low-ceilinged taproom.

"It is a lovely inn," she remarked as the fiddler at the front of the room brought his rollicking set to a close.

Cheers, and more shouts for another round, filled the establishment as the cross-eyed old fellow playing for the room adjusted his instrument and readied for his next song.

Dallin cast a dubious glance about, and she saw precisely what he saw: Stained tables. Uneven furniture. Rowdy patrons.

He made a show of adjusting his feet on the sticky, ale-covered floor, the little *pop* from the suction loud enough to be heard over the brief pause in song.

The gentleman wasn't going to make this easy, then.

Very well. Alexandra had become all too familiar with things being difficult. "I will be direct with you, Dallin," she said, laying use of his name as that familiarity put them on an equal footing.

"I believe we are past that point."

Do not let him get a rise out of you.

She spoke through lightly gritted teeth. "We are not dissimilar."

He snorted.

"In fact, we are very similar in the ways that matter most."

Dallin kicked back on the legs of his chair and nudged his chin her way. "This, I have to hear."

"We both care very much for our family."

He stilled.

Hmph. Well, take that. "We are loyal and loving of those deserving of our love and loyalty. You with your cousin and—"

"You with your sister."

She nodded. "Precisely." Alexandra locked her eyes with his. "And neither of us wish to see our loved ones make a decision they will come to regret."

A muscle ticked at the corner of his jaw. "Because your sister will regret marrying a McQuoid."

"Because my sister will come to regret and resent not having her family there for her wedding day, and she will eventually realize, after the magic of the moment wears off, that the clandestine nature of their meetings and secret relationship fueled whatever madness made her do this thing without a single care for her or her sisters' reputation."

He quirked a chestnut brow. "And that is what this is ultimately about."

"My lord?" she said carefully.

With an air of casualness, Dallin swirled the contents of his ale. "Your sister rushing off to marry a man your betrothed and his family do not approve of threatens the union you so desperately want."

Alexandra drew back but managed to find her voice.

"You know nothing of it," she said stiffly. And with the ways in which he'd judged her and found her so clearly wanting, she'd sooner wed the condescending lout than share her family's circumstances with Dallin McQuoid.

Dallin set down his tankard hard and stretched all the way across the table. "You see, Alexandra, my first and only thoughts are of my cousin's happiness and not my own. *That* is where we are different."

He stared boldly back, daring her to challenge him, and any other time, she was a woman who'd not allow such slights to stand uncorrected.

Her family was on the cusp of ruin.

Her sister had eloped with a man . . . a man Alexandra's betrothed's family now feuded with, at that.

She'd nearly been killed in a carriage accident.

The one servant she'd set out with had been hurt and declared unable to drive.

Given that rather lengthy catalog of problems facing Alexandra, one would expect the unkind opinions of Dallin McQuoid would have no effect on her.

Only, his insults left her chest aching in a most peculiar way.

Dallin thought so ill of her, and she really shouldn't care. But she *did*. And more, this mocking, icy version of the man she'd secretly harbored romantic thoughts of left her feeling a fool ten times over.

"You may profess to be somehow superior and more honorable in your intentions, my lord"—she spoke with the quiet calm she'd never been more grateful for having mastered in her lessons—"but if you are able to sit before me and pretend as though you and your family did not express some fear, even some small reservation, for the wrath they will incur were your cousin to wed my sister, then you are not only being disingenuous but you are also a liar."

The splash of red that spread over his chiseled cheeks spoke as loudly as his silence.

Alexandra swept to her feet and gathered her reticule.

As she stood over Dallin's seated form, she relished even the brief moment of being able to tower over the big, tall McQuoid.

"Furthermore, if Alaister means 'demon,' then that must make you boorish, nasty, rude *Mr.* Alaister."

"Wouldn't that then make us husband and wife?" he asked drolly.

She gasped. "Never. Never, ever, ever. Ever."

He paused. "Are there any more n—"

"Never!" she repeated.

"Ah, forgive me. That's right. Because I'm a McQuoid and you are a high-and-mighty Bradbury, destined to marry a future duke. I could always count on you for that reminder of your superiority."

Her cheeks went hot. "Because you're a foulmouthed . . . *shabbaroon*."

"*Shabbaroon?*" Amusement dripped from that echo.

"Yes, shabbaroon." Because she didn't know any other suitable—and what were surely far more satisfying—insults. Ladies weren't afforded those word choices, and never more had she regretted that oversight in a lady's education than right now.

She leaned down so close their noses nearly touched. "I'll have you know the surname is perfectly respectable and belongs to my family's butler."

He stared at her with unblinking eyes. "Does that make you the butler's daughter, then?"

She stilled, then gasped. "You, sir, are no gentleman."

He grinned. "If you are the butler's illegitimate daughter—"

Alexandra jabbed a finger at his face. "Do not even *think* of finishing that thought. Now, if you'll excuse me," she said with a toss of her head, "my mother and servants will be looking for me."

It was a lie he was none the wiser of, and she'd be damned if she admitted to the lout that she was, in fact, here alone and fear had prompted her to seek him out.

Bag in hand, Alexandra marched off, winding her way through the still-crowded taproom. All the while, she seethed. What had she been thinking, going to Dallin McQuoid for help? She'd been a fool to think she could request his aid, just like she'd been a fool on his rooftop terrace.

She'd been bloody mad. Or desperate. Or both.

Yes, both. That was precisely the manner of madness which had brought her to seek him out. For a moment, she'd let herself recall their far warmer meeting and believed that, with their shared goal, he might allow her to accompany him.

Foolish. Foolish. Fool—

A patron stepped into her path—or more aptly, stumbled into it—putting a swift end to her much-longed-for exit.

Christi Caldwell

Impatiently, Alexandra made to step around him, but with uneven steps, he matched her movements.

"Excuse me," she said, infusing a firmness into those two words.

Greasy haired, in crude wool garments, and stinking of spirits, he flashed an uneven, yellow-toothed smile. "You don't want to be rushing off."

"Actually, I do," she said between gritted teeth.

The tall, lanky stranger clapped a hand around her wrist.

In an instant, Alexandra's earlier annoyance rapidly gave way to fear as the depth of her vulnerability out here on the road, without a companion or able-bodied servant, hit her all over again.

"Release me, sir."

The drunken patron preened. "Like the sound of that, I do. All fancy."

Her heart galloping, Alexandra cast a desperate glance around the crowded room. They were surrounded by other patrons, and as loud as the place was, and as fixed on their spirits and good times as those patrons were, no one paid her or the man accosting her any attention.

"How about you partner me in the next set," he urged, tugging her toward the makeshift dance floor, where the fiddler fiddled away.

Alexandra dug her heels in. "I really must insist you release me."

Only, he paid her no heed; his focus on that spot near the hearth, he continued to drag her along.

Panic assailed her. "I said, release me." And still, when he gave no indication he'd so much as heard her, Alexandra brought her bag down over his ear.

He cried out. "What did you do that forrr?" he asked, rubbing at the spot where she'd clouted him. "All I wanted was a dance with a proper lady."

His eyes darkened, and Alexandra knew the precise moment the stranger went from determined to enraged.

134

Fear churned in her gut, and Alexandra tugged frantically at her wrist—to no avail.

"Unhand her. Now."

And where her own such requests had gone otherwise ignored by the brute holding her, this time, that steely command saw him rapidly releasing her.

Alexandra and her would-be dance partner whipped their gazes over to the handsome and formidable figure behind them.

And despite her earlier hurt and fury, Alexandra's heart jumped. *Dallin!*

Absently, she cradled her smarting wrist and took a reflexive step toward him, the unlikeliest of rescuers.

In the short span she'd known Dallin McQuoid, she'd seen him angry any number of instances: the moment he'd come upon her on his rooftop and believed her to be an intruder bent on burglarizing his unique household. And then all the times after that, where he'd been cold and jeering.

Never before, however, had she seen him like this.

Rage: it emanated from his powerful frame. He held himself with a stiffness that hinted at violence about to be unleashed, and the sight of that raw, primal power should have further roused terror inside Alexandra. Only, that fury was directed not at her, but rather another . . . because of her.

Dallin gave her a quick, cursory look, as if verifying she was unhurt. His gaze lingered on the wrist she still cradled with her opposite palm.

His lashes swept impossibly lower; pinpricks of rage burnt through those narrow slits. And she almost felt bad for the cowering fellow.

Almost.

Dallin returned his attention to the man, shorter by four inches.

"Didn't mean no harm," he stammered. "Wanted a dance with her, and she wanted it, too. Ask—*ahh.*"

Dallin shot out a hand, grabbing the patron by his wrist, and squeezed with a grip that pulled an agonized cry from the fellow's mouth.

Ignoring the man's blubbering apologies, Dallin jerked him close.

"Next time a woman tells you no, you'd do well to remember that she's said no," he said with an evenness belied by the fire in his gaze. He added more pressure and wrenched the man's arm behind his back.

The patron's face contorted with pain. "Will. *I will,*" he rasped.

Maintaining his merciless hold on him, Dallin angled the suddenly very sober-seeming stranger.

And despite her having earlier relished his misery, Alexandra's belly churned with the evidence of his real suffering.

"Make your apologies to the lady," Dallin ordered.

"Apologies. Apologies."

Dallin looked to Alexandra.

She nodded hurriedly, and he released the other man, who promptly scurried off, making a direct path for the front door.

After he'd gone, leaving Alexandra and Dallin alone in the middle of the crowded room, her heart continued to race.

"Are you all right?" he asked loud enough to make his voice heard over the confused noise of the taproom.

At that evidence of his caring, her heart shifted in a dangerous way.

"I am," she lied. The lie, however, stemmed not from her well-being after her run-in with that pawing stranger.

It was far easier to despise Dallin when he was churlish and disagreeable, just as it was far easier to despise him than remember him as someone different: someone Alexandra could have seen herself with.

Dallin did a glance about. "Come." And then resting a hand protectively on the small of her back, he proceeded to guide them through the crowded room.

As they headed for the private suites, she stole a glance at Dallin from the corner of her eye.

This gentleman? The one who'd swept across the taproom like an avenging warrior of old and defended and protected her proved dangerous in his own right.

This was a man who made her long for more, for things that could never be.

Chapter 12

As Dallin and Alexandra made the quiet walk through the lively tap-room to the private rooms above, not a word passed between them. He used the moment as an opportunity to rein in the primitive fury still knocking around his chest.

Nay, not just fury.

Fear. There'd been fear, too.

In his mind, he replayed the moment she'd left to go join her mother and servants, only to be waylaid by some drunkard. A man who'd dared put his hands on her.

That familiar anger tightened his gut.

All the while Dallin escorted the lady, his mind raced as the scene of her being accosted played over and over in his head.

They reached Alexandra's rooms, both of them still silent.

Alexandra avoided his eyes, and that sign of an uncertainty so uncharacteristic in this always bold, spirited woman hit him square in the chest.

"Thank you for your assistance earlier," she said softly. "My mother will be most appreciative of your rescue. I will be sure and let her know when she awakens."

Alexandra stood there, clearly waiting for Dallin to leave. Clearly not gathering he'd no intention of doing so without personally delivering her to someone else's care.

She puzzled her brow. "My lord?"

My lord. How strange to miss the sound of his Christian name on her lips.

"I would speak with the marchioness myself."

The lady instantly bristled. "So that you can tattle on me for getting myself into trouble with that patron?"

He frowned. "You weren't responsible for that man's effrontery. A lady should at the very least be able to pass without fear of being accosted."

Her features went soft, and her lips quivered, parting slightly. "Oh." The breathless exhalation slipped past that crimson, bow-shaped flesh.

And despite himself, despite the resentment that had sprung as fast as his previous enthrallment with the lady, his eyes of their own volition locked on her mouth.

Did he imagine the way her eyes fluttered? Or the slight way her body swayed toward his? The same way he'd once imagined she'd been as captivated by him as he was by her?

Dallin tensed. "I'd make my greetings for the sake of being neighborly and courteous."

A glimmer of befuddlement filled Alexandra's eyes, and she blinked slowly. As if belatedly registering his words, she gripped the door handle behind her and pressed her back against the crude oak panel.

"It would hardly be proper to call on her . . . *here.*"

And they were sticklers for propriety.

"Given the circumstances our two families find ourselves in, one would argue there's nothing conventional about any of this."

Alexandra dug in. "She is abed."

He narrowed his eyes. "Abed."

She nodded.

Dallin looked at her askance. "And you opted to leave and visit the taproom while she is so?"

The minx instantly became tight-lipped.

Dallin stared at Alexandra a long moment, and then the truth hit him square in the gut. Surely not. And yet he searched his mind and memory for some hint of a servant wearing the Bradbury livery . . . or a maid . . . or anyone who'd been with her in the taproom.

"Where is your maid?" he asked quietly.

The lady made a show of adjusting her skirts. "We are nothing to one another, my lord. At best, we are neighbors. At worst, we are now families at war with one another. As such, I do not have to answer to you and do not intend to."

How easily she spoke of both that feud and the lack of any true, meaningful connection between them. And yet . . . she lashed out like one determined to end their exchange without further probing on Dallin's part.

As if she felt his astute stare, the lady fumbled behind her for the door handle. "Now, thank you for your earlier . . . assistance, but I must bid you good evening."

Dallin's next quietly spoken words stopped her.

"There are no mother and servants. Are there?"

She bristled with her usual indignation. "*Of course* I have a mother and servants."

"Here with you," he gently clarified.

There was a discernible pause.

"I do."

Dallin gave her a look.

She hesitated a moment more, continuing to hold on to that admission.

"You really are a deuced liar, Alexandra."

"I have a driver," she insisted.

Dallin stared at her.

"And he may be injured," she said under her breath.

"*May* be injured?"

"Is injured." That admission came as if dragged from the proud beauty.

"And your mother?"

"She remained behind with Daphne."

Daphne?

"My youngest sister," she clarified.

It was just one more reminder of how little he knew of this woman and her family.

"They were to depart for the countryside to—" She instantly cut off from completing that thought on whatever it was the pair would do.

"Have you traveled with a footman?"

She shook her head.

"A maid?" he asked hopefully.

Again, she gave one of those very slight moves of her head, indicating the contrary.

Dallin scrubbed a hand down his face.

"I trust you *now* intend to lecture me on getting precisely what I deserve for daring to set out on my own."

"And why would I do that?"

"Because you find fault with everything I do."

He started. "I do not."

She slanted a challenging look his way.

Only, if he were being honest with himself, since the moment he'd discovered that he'd never have the opportunity to pursue whatever had been born on that rooftop terrace that cold winter's night because she belonged to another, he had been boorish and rude.

"I . . . forgive me," he said gruffly.

He'd been so caught up in annoyance with the lady that, when she approached him belowstairs, he'd been too clouded by his own pride to note the very obvious fact she'd been without the benefit of a chaperone.

"May we speak?"

"Isn't that what we are doing?"

Dallin motioned to her rooms.

Alexandra pressed her back against the door, rattling it in its frame. "That wouldn't be proper."

"Oh, I daresay we've moved past the point of proper long before this," he said drolly, with his first dose of real amusement since the Brookhaven ball.

Heavy footfalls echoed in the stairwell, and he and Alexandra glanced toward that approach.

She fumbled with the handle and hurried inside.

Dallin hovered there, waiting for permission to follow her.

"Well, do you intend to just wait for an invitation?"

"Actually, I do."

The lady muttered something under her breath, and then shooting a hand out, she gripped his sleeve and gave him a tug.

The moment he entered, she pushed the door shut behind them.

As the lady took off her cloak and moved to hang it inside a sturdy wooden armoire, Dallin glanced about the small but serviceable rooms.

His gaze settled on the single floral embroidered valise at the foot of the bed. That was all she'd come with.

He didn't know what he'd expected. Certainly not for her to be here—at least, not alone.

Given the exchange he'd overheard between Alexandra and her mother, and the frantic desire to keep the lady's match with the Duke of Talbert's son, it didn't surprise Dallin in the least that she'd come all this way to stop her sister's wedding to Brone.

He'd have expected, however, that she'd have traveled with trappings and a contingent of servants to see to both her protection and belongings.

Or mayhap the absence of those was a testament to her desperation.

He studied her as she hung her cloak, and God help him for noticing the way the silver material of her dress pulled about her when she lifted her arms. That fabric stretched, drawing his eyes to the graceful arch of her back and her saucily curved buttocks.

Assailed by a powerful wave of lust, Dallin averted his gaze. Only, his stare collided with her bed, and just like that, lubricious thoughts took root in his fertile mind and grew.

Thoughts of sliding that shimmery satin gown up about her waist until she was bared before him. Of filling his palms with the abundant flesh of her bottom and dragging her close against him.

Desire filled him, and to purge those lust-filled imaginings, he made himself stare at her valise. Anything but her or that mattress.

The lady had been correct. Entering her rooms had been a deuced bad idea, after all.

"Did you expect I'd travel with a cortege and trunks?"

Dallin whipped his gaze back over to where Alexandra, with her arms folded at her chest, leaned against the armoire and stared at him with more amusement than the situation merited.

With amusement that most certainly would not be there were she to have followed the salacious path his wicked thoughts had taken.

Dallin grunted. "I didn't say anything."

She quirked a wry smile. "You didn't need to." Letting her arms drop by her sides, Alexandra wandered over.

And God forgive him, he could not fail to note the seductive sway of her hips as she moved, as he imagined them moving in an altogether different way, in slow undulations as she arched—

She stopped with several paces between them.

"You wished to speak with me?" she prodded, a master of self-control and worse . . . indifference.

While he stood lusting after her, she remained wholly and completely oblivious to him. But then she was to wed the enigmatic Marquess of Wingrave, and Dallin had never been the sort to fascinate like those rogues and scoundrels.

Confusion brought a crease to Alexandra's regal brow. "My lord?"

"You cannot be out alone on these roads."

And certainly not alone with him.

The moment the words left him, the truth of them took hold. "It is far too dangerous for a lady to make this journey."

She narrowed her eyes. "Indeed?"

At that warning she managed to imbue into a single syllable, he'd be wise to, if not stop, proceed with caution. Alas, there were far greater dangers to him . . . and to the lady herself, were he to let his words go unfinished.

"Aside from facing the elements, there are brigands and highwaymen."

"I'm going, Dallin."

That quiet calm bespoke a woman who had no intention of taking the safer-for-her course.

He dragged a hand through his hair. "God, you are obstinate."

"You are rushing to rescue your cousin with the same intent as I: to stop him making the same mistake my sister is, and yet, I'm obstinate. While you are . . . what?" She didn't give him a chance to answer. She took a step closer, shrinking the space dividing them. "Am I to believe if it were *your* sister, you'd not do precisely what I'm doing?"

"It is different, Alexandra." And he certainly didn't mention that when his two sisters were in different but similar circumstances—one left behind at Christmas, the other rushed off to sea—he'd done precisely that. He'd set out in swift pursuit.

She lifted a beautifully arched eyebrow. "How so?"

"Do you really need me to say it?"

"Actually, I do."

"Because you're a woman," he said flatly. "And for that reason alone, it isn't at all the same." He took the last remaining step between them. "I'm not saying it's fair."

"It isn't."

"No, it isn't," he readily agreed. "I've three sisters, who at various points in their lives have chafed at their circumstances, and I understand why, but neither does it erase the fact that in addition to the world being unfair, it is also cruel and merciless." A visceral rage descended over his vision as a memory from moments ago slipped in. "And the danger you encountered with that drunken patron belowstairs, just moments ago, is proof of that."

Alexandra recoiled.

The moment the words left him, he wanted to call them back. Even as they were truthful ones. Even as they perfectly reinforced the very argument he made. Because to remind her of that near assault she'd encountered only wrought hurt. They may have become enemies of late, but he'd never intentionally bring her pain.

"Alexandra," he said quietly, reaching for her.

She jerked away from him. "If you think I somehow need you to point out to me the dangers I face for no other reason than because I'm a woman, I assure you, you don't. I know exactly what they are. I know my lot as a woman is much different than yours. And yet, you, a man with the benefit of a title, wealth, and power to your name, presume to lecture *me*?"

The incredulity she managed to pack into that uptilt of a question brought a dull flush to his neck. "I didn't intend it to be a lect—"

"And yet, whatever your intentions were, you did just that."

"Because I am worried about you."

———— ⟶◎◎⟵ ————

Because I am worried about you.

The solemnness of Dallin's admission bespoke the truth of his words.

Alexandra didn't want that pronouncement to matter. She didn't want her heart to quicken or for warmth to fill her breast.

And yet, after these many months of uncertainty, where she and her family found themselves at the mercy of distant relatives and Alexandra's betrothed, who couldn't be bothered, there was something so very wonderful about the thought of someone caring about her. Of truly caring about her. Not because she was a bother or a responsibility one didn't want, but for no other reason than they—or in this case, Dallin—worried about Alexandra as a person.

Her lower lip trembled, and she swiftly caught the quavering flesh between her teeth.

Dallin's astute gaze, however, missed nothing, and by his stricken expression, she knew the moment he detected that quiver.

"Forgive me," he said hoarsely. "I didn't mean . . . I would never wish to make you—"

"N-no," she interrupted, halting him before he could speak that last word.

Aside from the days following her father's death, Alexandra hadn't cried once over her circumstances. Nor could she or would she. For the moment she did, she'd weep a river of tears enough to drown in.

"It is f-fine." Alexandra drew in a deep, shaky breath.

She averted her head and composed herself.

Dallin allowed her that moment to do so. He didn't attempt to fill the silence or offer up any apologies. Instead, he remained silent, allowing Alexandra to feel her emotion, and she was so very grateful to him for that gesture.

When she'd gotten a full rein on her emotions, Alexandra turned back.

The fire crackling in the hearth cast shadows over his features, but even with that, tender concern radiated from his brown eyes, threatening to undo her once more.

Something shifted in his gaze, and in the very air around them, and as if in harmony, they took a step toward one another, and then instantly stopped.

"There is something I'd ask you, Dallin."

He worked his penetrating gaze over her face, and the piercing intensity and heat within his stare made her go weak in the knees.

"What is it, Alexandra?"

The low rumble of his voice proved as intoxicating as his stare.

Reaching out, Alexandra steadied herself on the old washstand with spindle legs as wobbly as her own.

Stop. You do not have the time to be a ninny about a gentleman who is now forbidden to you, nor the luxury of weakness.

"Might I perhaps accompany you?" she blurted.

He stared back puzzledly.

"To Gretna Green."

Dallin continued to just stare.

"To halt the wedding between my sister and your cousin," she clarified.

He remained frozen.

Alexandra frowned and waved a hand before his eyes. "Dallin—"

The sound of his name seemed to snap him out of that reverie. "I can see just fine. It is my ears that appear to be the problem, because it sounded as though you asked to—"

"Join you!" She beamed. "I'm pleased to report your hearing is just fine. You see—"

"No, I don't see."

And embarrassment at her circumstances, together with the forwardness of putting such a bold favor to him, sent words tumbling from her lips. "As my driver is indisposed, and as you pointed out, I'm here without the benefit of a chaperone or companion or servant, I'm what one might call"—she splayed her hands—"stranded."

"Stranded."

She nodded.

Once again, he went silent and continued to just look back dumbly.

147

"Stranded," she repeated for a third time when he still didn't speak. "As in helpless, without the means to escape. Placed in a location one cannot escape from. Detain—"

"I know what the word 'stranded' means."

"Oh."

He said nothing more.

Alexandra cleared her throat. "Are you certain? Because you've got a confused look to you."

"I assure you," he said dryly, "any confusion on my part has less to do with the word 'stranded' and *more* to do with, say, your proposing we travel together, alone." Understanding flashed in his eyes. "That's why you sought me out this evening in the taproom."

She nodded.

He dug his fingertips into his temples in that same way Alexandra had done after the headaches she'd begun having after her father's passing.

"You said so yourself, Dallin," she reminded him. "It is unsafe for a woman to travel alone, and yet if I remain behind here, then I'll be just that. The only logical course would be for me to follow you."

"That's the wise course, and not, say, have someone escort you back to London."

She scoffed. "Who will escort me? Some stranger belowstairs?"

"I will loan you the services of my footman and hire one of the village women to serve as a companion."

He may as well have added, *Anything, as long as I don't have to deal with you underfoot.*

Alexandra resisted the childlike urge to stamp her feet.

He'd all the answers. None of which included allowing her to make the remainder of the journey.

"I've no one else to rely upon, Dallin, so now, I am doing this with or without you," she said quietly.

His sharp, handsome features tensed.

"I'm not telling you this to garner pity." Pity was the last thing she wanted. Especially from this man.

"You're too proud for me to think you'd ever want pity from me or anyone. What about your betrothed?"

All the muscles in her belly clenched. Her betrothed.

"What of him?" she managed to make herself ask.

Dallin reached a palm out, and for a moment she thought he'd cup her cheek, and she wanted that. She craved the warmth and tenderness of his touch.

Only, he merely left it resting face up. "Why didn't you seek out his assistance? Accompany him."

Wingrave instead of Dallin.

"Is he not one you can turn to?" Dallin asked. "Not one whom you can rely upon?"

Considering she'd seen Lord Wingrave but once, she couldn't say she could pick him out of an uncrowded room, let alone rely upon him.

A distraught laugh built in her throat, and she swallowed several times to keep from choking on her hysteria.

Then Dallin placed his hand, in that gentle touch she'd craved, upon her shoulder. "Alexandra?" he asked with more of that worry that would be her undoing.

"It's not a love match, if that is what you are asking, Dallin."

But she couldn't fall apart. She didn't have the luxury of even allowing herself a moment of that weakness.

"I'd not do anything to risk my marriage to the marquess," she finally brought herself to say.

His fingers tensed on her arm, and she felt that clenching and sought to make sense of what it meant. If anything.

"Of course," he said stiffly.

Even as that curt reply gave her leave to say nothing further, Alexandra couldn't halt the remainder of that worrying. "If he were to discover . . . if his father, the duke, were to find out—"

"That your sister eloped with a relation of the McQuoid family."

She paused. "There is that, as well. Polite Society doesn't look kindly on families whose daughters dash off to Gretna Green."

He made a *tsk*ing sound. "Then just think what he'd do were he to find out his beloved betrothed was traveling alone with not only a McQuoid but also the future earl whose sister married the Duke of Talbert's intended."

Beloved betrothed.

Alexandra couldn't stop the wave of hurt from either the reminder of the cold union awaiting her or the resentment from this man for whom she'd once harbored romantic thoughts.

Dallin removed his hand from her person, and she grieved for that loss.

He turned as if to go, and her heart fell.

She really was all on her own. Even knowing his disdain for her, Alexandra found a calm, even a comfort, in Dallin McQuoid's presence, and the idea of him leaving her alone sent panic tumbling through her.

He stopped and wheeled back to face her.

Her heart thumped faster.

"Tell me, Alexandra."

She nodded.

"If Wingrave were to reject you because of actions that were beyond your control, actions belonging to another . . . would it be such a very bad thing?" he asked with a detached curiosity. "Might not you see it as you are saved from marrying a man who didn't want you enough?"

Were the marquess to break off their arrangement, it would be both a blessing and a curse.

Only, the blessing would be Alexandra's alone. The curse was one that her entire family would suffer the effects of.

"It would be disastrous," she finally brought herself to say.

A cynical grin curled his lips. "I see."

By the cold edge to his low baritone, she expected he thought he did. When in actuality, he saw *nothing*. He took her as a lady hungry for the future title of duchess, and a man she hardly knew, one so quick to form an ill opinion of her, was hardly a man she'd ever humble herself before by admitting the true nature of her circumstances.

She forced a frost into her voice. "Do you have any other questions for me, my lord?"

"I've nothing else to ask you. I will see you in an hour's time," he said, changing the topic as quickly as if they'd been discussing the heavy rains they'd encountered rather than the future which awaited Alexandra.

It was a moment before the realization hit her.

"You'll take me with you!" she exclaimed, clutching a hand to her chest.

"If you aren't ready—"

"I'll be ready."

"I'll leave my footman behind to see to you." Dallin tugged free his dusty riding gloves and stuffed them inside the front of his jacket. "I've learned in questioning the innkeeper that your sister and Brone passed through not long ago."

He'd gathered that pertinent information already. Alexandra, on the other hand, hadn't even thought to ask.

"I'm only staying long enough for the team to be changed out, and to switch mounts. I'll travel by horseback, and you may retain the use of my carriage." Dallin delivered those logistics as her brain, slowed from exhaustion and now an overwhelming relief, struggled to keep up.

"I do not intend to ride alongside your carriage. My goal remains to intercept my cousin."

"Of course," she said, so very grateful for his capitulation she'd have danced a jig had he asked it.

"Brone asked about coaching along the way. The innkeeper below advised them on their next stop."

My God, he'd thought of everything. He knew where they were, and where they'd stop. And never had she been more grateful to another person in the whole of her life.

"Dallin." Alexandra took a step toward him. "I cannot thank you enough—"

"I do not require your thanks. Just an assurance that you'll be ready in an hour's time."

With only that warning and not so much as a simple goodbye, Dallin took his leave, closing the door with a near-silent click.

The minute he'd gone, Alexandra crossed over and turned the lock.

There should be only relief. She was so very close to finding her sister, and Dallin would allow her to join him in Cora's rescue. So why, then, did the coldness of his tone and the antipathy for her hurt to the point of distraction?

It didn't matter what ill opinions he'd formed and carried about her.

Ultimately, when all this was said and done, she and Dallin would part ways and become strangers once more. Alexandra would go on to wed the Duke of Talbert's son, and Dallin would someday . . . live a life with another lady. A lady who'd be so very lucky to have a man such as him for a husband.

Closing her eyes, she rested her forehead against the cold oak panel.

Chapter 13

Less than an hour later, having changed his garments and broken his fast, Dallin exited his rooms at the Fox and Hound and headed down the narrow, now completely darkened corridor.

He must be mad.

Only madness accounted for the fact he had agreed to take the distingué Alexandra Bradbury along with him. A lady so desperate to save her match with a future duke that she'd risk her own reputation by traveling alone with Dallin.

An unnecessary reminder of the state they'd found themselves in, which only roused further thoughts. Improper ones. Of Alexandra and himself, alone in a quiet inn in some distant corner of the English countryside. A place where no one knew who he was or who she was, or that, ultimately, she belonged to another.

He slowly stopped in the middle of the hall.

For she *did* belong to another. A common goal had brought Dallin and Alexandra together, but when they succeeded in stopping a hasty wedding between their loved ones, they'd part ways. Alexandra would return to London and go from betrothed to bride and then wife of Lord Wingrave.

As her husband, Lord Wingrave would be the one to kiss that bow-shaped mouth as Dallin had once—and still—secretly longed to.

His hands curled into instinctive fists at his side; his fingers dug into the leather fabric of his riding gloves. But the thoughts continued to come.

The marquess would know what it was to uncover and explore every curve of her exquisitely graceful frame, tasting of her. Drinking of her.

An insidious poison spread like fire through Dallin's veins. Something akin to jealousy. Nay, not akin to it. This red-hot sentiment that fell like a curtain over his eyes and burnt his tongue could be mistaken for no other emotion.

Clenching and unclenching his jaw, Dallin forced himself to keep walking the remainder of the way to the lady's chambers.

Perhaps fate would hand him a boon and she'd have remained sleeping as any other lady likely would. It was an ungodly hour.

The moment he reached her room, he lifted a fist to quietly rap on the panel.

Suddenly, the door swung open. "Good morning."

He'd hand it to the lady.

At that, she stood there, bright-eyed, and with a valise at her feet and a reticule in her left hand. At some point, she'd changed into a new dress, the emerald-green material of which peeked out from the bottom of her cloak.

She'd not only been ready the moment he went to knock on her door but also waiting. How many women in the whole of England would have been set to go at this early hour? It spoke to the lady's resilience and determination and . . .

A determination to interrupt her sister's wedding so that hers could go off with the future duke without ado.

He found his voice. "You shouldn't open a door without an indication as to whom is on the other side."

She scrunched her nose in an endearingly affronted way. "I knew it was you."

"You couldn't know that."

"Given the fact we were meeting at four o'clock in the morning and your footfalls were the ones I heard in the corridor at exactly one minute past four o'clock, well, then I'd say it was a fairly safe assumption on my part that you were, in fact, the person knocking," she said dryly.

Dallin frowned. That logical reasoning did not erase the fact the lady could have unknowingly opened herself to danger. "One should never make assumptions."

She snapped her hood into place. "One also shouldn't lecture a lady on not being late, and then become so caught up in haranguing her on another point that he proceeds to make them both tardy. And yet"—she gave a wave of her hand—"here we are."

He opened his mouth to further debate her. "Come along," he said instead.

They reached for her bag at the same time. Their fingers brushed, the tips of their gloved digits kissing, and even through the leather barriers between them, there was an intimacy to that accidental touch.

Alexandra was the first to draw away. She wrested her fingers back and brought her palm close to her chest. She held it there against her heart almost protectively.

And the evidence of her distaste sent a dull flush up his neck.

Gathering her large, brocaded valise, he headed for the stairs.

Alexandra's footfalls echoed close behind.

They didn't speak another word until they reached the carriage. The McQuoids' loyal driver, Harris, sat atop the box, while Otis, one of the family's footmen, stood in wait, holding the reins of Dallin's mount. The pair had discreetly averted their gazes.

As a credit to both servants, neither man gave any indication there was anything at all untoward about Dallin escorting a cloaked and hooded woman into his carriage.

Clasping the handle, Dallin drew the door open, and after setting Alexandra's bag on the bench, he made to hand the lady up.

She hesitated.

Perhaps the lady had come to her senses. Maybe she'd finally realized that their continuing on together was not only the height of impropriety but also dangerous . . . for a host of other reasons.

"What is it?" Dallin asked quietly. "Are you nervous?" He didn't give her a chance to answer. "Because if you are, you're more than welcome to remain behind with my footman and your driver and—"

"No," she interrupted. "It isn't that . . ." Her voice trailed off.

He released a breath he'd not even realized he'd been holding.

He stared patiently. "Yes?"

"How long do you believe it is before we reach them?"

Alexandra surely asked out of concern for ending this journey before their actions, and their respective loved ones' actions, were discovered.

And yet, pathetic as Dallin was and had proven countless times to be where this woman was concerned, he could think of but one question: How much time did he have left with her?

Dallin scrubbed a hand over his face. "Riding at the rate I intend to set, I will need to change horses every thirty-five miles. Barring no unforeseen delays—"

"What might be an unforeseen delay?"

"I don't know, Alexandra. That's what makes them unforeseen."

Her eyes reflected back such hurt he immediately felt like he'd kicked a kitten.

With a murmur of thanks, Alexandra hefted herself inside the carriage.

That was what it had taken to get her moving. He should be only relieved and glad. He'd far more important matters to see to than remaining idle, locked in discussion with Alexandra Bradbury.

Except, as he pushed the lady's door closed and headed to collect the reins of his new mount, he was unable to tamp down bitterness that when their time with one another came to an end, she'd become the wife of the wicked Lord Wingrave.

————— ❧✦❧ —————

Alexandra stared out the carriage window at the passing hillsides. The farther the churning wheels took her from London, the wilder and more untamed the land around them became. The bumpier the roads. And the sky crisp and clear as it could only be in the English countryside.

Since the sun had pushed the night sky away, they'd stopped once to change out their mounts for another team. As Dallin had indicated, he'd not remained behind in wait for Alexandra's carriage.

However, when she had arrived at the coaching inn, there'd been an innkeeper waiting with a basket filled with bread, cheese, and apples. And . . . a note.

Unfolding the already well-read letter on her lap, she skimmed her gaze over the hastily written words.

I've received word they passed through earlier this morn. They remain with a lead of several hours; however, I've learned they are not switching out their team, which means they'll need to stop more frequently. At this pace, I expect we will come upon them sometime late tomorrow evening or early the next morn.

D

With the tip of her finger, she absently traced that single initial of his Christian name.

When they'd set out that morning, Dallin had been annoyed with Alexandra for pressing him for information. However, he'd not been so because she'd dared to ask questions he'd felt she had no place asking. Rather, he'd been impatient to begin their pursuit of Cora and Mr. Smith. Even with his restlessness, he'd still taken the time to answer her queries, and when he'd stopped later that morn, he'd taken time to pen a note for Alexandra containing the information he'd obtained about her sister and his cousin. In a world where ladies were viewed as inferior for no other reason than because they'd been born women, and where they eventually became the property of men, Dallin had kept Alexandra apprised as though she were an equal.

Her finger curled sharply, leaving a crescent mark upon the page.

When this trip came to an end and she and Dallin returned to London, parting ways forever, there would be a wedding waiting for Alexandra. She'd find herself with a bridegroom who couldn't be bothered to meet her, and who only married her to appease his father and see to his responsibilities as a ducal heir.

Alexandra's chest grew tight, making it impossible to draw in a breath.

She'd wager her very name and reputation—which made her marriageable to the marquess—that such a man would never dare take questions or explain himself.

The air slipped from her lips on a soft, breathy exhale.

Then there was Dallin. Dallin, who even when clearly annoyed with her hadn't deemed her undeserving of knowing her fate. And she knew beyond all doubt and any certainty the woman he one day wed would be one whom he cherished and viewed as a partner in life. And . . .

Alexandra went still as a thought she'd not previously considered slipped in.

If she managed to delay Cora's wedding until after her own, then eventually, Cora would be joined with the McQuoid family, which would also mean Alexandra, too, would be joined to Dallin's family. As a result, she would not be able to separate completely from him. She'd be forced to witness his courtship of another woman and eventual marriage . . . an eventual marriage that would be nothing like the cold union Alexandra was certain to find herself forced into.

She focused on breathing. Only, her chest hurt and her lungs hurt and her heart . . . *Oh, God.* Her heart did, too. It was as though a vise had been wrapped around the organ, squeezing the blood from it so it could manage nothing more than a sickening, slow thud against the wall of her chest.

There couldn't be a crueler, more miserable fate than one day being tied to one man while imagining what might have been with another.

"Whoaaa!"

Suddenly, the carriage lurched, knocking Alexandra momentarily free of those torturous thoughts.

She let out a scream and reflexively curled her hands around the bench, gripping hard to keep her seat.

This time, her heart thudded at a sick pace against her chest.

Not again. Not another near-death moment in a bloody carriage.

When this journey was done, she wasn't getting in another damned conveyance. She didn't care if it was a blasted phaeton, curricle, carriage, or mail coach. She didn't care if she had to walk until the soles of her slippers wore out. She was—

The carriage came to a graceful glide. That anticlimactic halt confused her panicked mind.

Alexandra frowned.

They'd stopped.

Alexandra drew back the curtain and peered outside. "Why have we stopped, Harris?" she called.

A deep voice that belonged to neither Harris nor Otis the footman boomed back a response. "Stand and deliver."

Her heart dipped. So *that* was why they'd stopped.

And here she'd thought there couldn't be a crueler, more miserable fate, only to have actual fate make an absolute liar of her.

There came a muted exchange of rapidly fired words between Dallin's servants and the masked man with two pistols, each pointed at Harris and Otis.

Alexandra's heart lurched.

The driver nodded to the footman, who tossed his box pistols at the brigand's feet.

Of course her mother would be proven correct when she'd raised the outlandish possibility of highwaymen waylaying Alexandra. Mother knew best and Mother knew all.

Dragging the curtain closed but for a crack, she took in the scene.

Motioning his pistol toward that slight gap she'd left in the fabric, the highwayman said something that instantly compelled both servants to dismount and lie down on the ground upon their bellies.

Alexandra glanced about for something with which to defend herself.

Back when she was a girl, she'd discovered that her stern governess— who'd proven strict in the books she'd allowed Alexandra to read—hadn't been quite as fastidious with her own literary interests. When she'd come upon the young woman napping, Alexandra had plucked the small leather volume from her lap and read . . . discovering her stern governess had an interest in the wicked.

While the governess had slept, none the wiser, Alexandra had availed herself to that copy of a gothic novel. It'd featured a grand love between a lady traveler who'd been stopped by a dashing highwayman. Alexandra had devoured that tale, and for some time had even longed for such a romantic meeting of her own.

She must have been out of her head. How dare the world feed women stories of danger and package them as ones of romance. There was nothing romantic about any of this.

There came a stretch of silence so long, hope kindled in her chest. Mayhap he'd leave her be. Mayhap—

That surprisingly cultured voice again called out and swiftly put an end to Alexandra's wishful thinking. "Come and join us, good sir."

Nausea churned in her belly, and desperately, Alexandra looked about once more for a weapon. She eyed the opposite door. Perhaps if she climbed out and . . .

And what? Made a run for it? Leaving Dallin's servants behind to face the highwayman's wrath? No, Alexandra was many things. Cowardly, however, was not amongst them.

Only, as she reached for the handle with unsteady fingers, she secretly wished she were a touch more craven.

"Very good, now your hands up in front of you," the highwayman ordered. "Or I'll—"

The moment she pushed the panel open, the masked brigand went silent.

With his midnight-black hair drawn back into a neat queue and classically handsome features revealed under his black domino, he may as well have been one of those dashing characters pulled from her books.

Only, there wasn't anything romantic about him or this moment.

He looked her up and down. "You're a woman," he said flatly.

Alexandra quirked an eyebrow. "Indeed. Is this the first time you've seen one?"

He flashed a rogue's grin that would have been perfect in that old gothic book she'd read. "Not at all." His smile vanished. Around that black domino, the man's eyes went hard. "Step down and instruct whoever else is riding with you to do the same."

Alexandra caught either side of the McQuoid carriage and awkwardly lowered herself to the ground. "There is no one else."

"Do you expect me to believe a young lady is traveling without the benefit of a companion or chaperone?"

Alexandra lowered her shoulders in a little shrug. "It's not my place to care what you believe or don't."

"Actually, it is."

Alexandra headed in the direction of Harris and Otis.

"Uh-uh. I'm afraid not, my lady. Other side of the road." He kept his gun on her, and the sight of that big, double-barrel pistol compelled her to follow those orders.

The highwayman came and did a quick search of the carriage for additional occupants. After confirming Alexandra was in fact alone, he headed back down the road, and for a second, she was gripped by a desperate hope that he'd continue on walking. That mayhap he was a sort who didn't rob from ladies and only—

He stopped at a distance where he'd Dallin's servants in his line of vision, and her hope died an all-too-quick death.

"Your money or your life," he yelled over.

"Which is it? My money or my life or stand and deliver?"

"They mean the same."

She blinked slowly. "Oh." She paused. "You're certain?"

"Quite."

He sounded mildly amused, which she took heart in. Mildly amused hardly hinted at one about to end her life here on the side of this old Roman road.

"I rather think they are different. You see, 'Your money or your life' implies if I do not surrender my personal effects, my life is forfeit. The other is more of a statement, if you will. You're telling me to stand and deliver anything of value I may have."

The highwayman's eyes revealed a befuddlement.

Good. Befuddled was far better than angry or lethal.

Determined to use confusion to find her way out of this, she took advantage of his silence. "Let us say I do not deliver anything of value, then there's no indication as to the outcome."

He narrowed his eyes on her. "Then the former applies."

Oh, hell. "You're certain."

"Very."

And here she'd thought there was something romantic about these fellows.

As if to illustrate his very point, the highwayman waved that heavy-looking pistol at her breast. His large hand, however, handled it with an ease and steady fingers.

"My lady," Dallin's driver pleaded from where he lay. "Give him what he seeks."

Prior to her father's death, she'd have not only handed over her sack and bracelet but also offered the ruthless man with his flinty gaze the promise of more funds from her family. But that had been before. Before she'd known the truth. Before she'd known what it was to be nearly penniless with creditors bearing down on her family.

The moment he divested her of the precious funds she did have, she'd have nothing for the remainder of the journey, and either way, they were monies that mattered to her.

"I'm waiting." The brigand shook the head of his double-barrel gun at Alexandra. "And you can begin by handing over your bracelet."

"My bracelet," she dumbly echoed.

She reflexively covered the gold, topaz, and chrysoberyl bracelet, that gift a token of her late father's love, given to Alexandra's mother and then passed on to Alexandra as a symbol of hope at her future happiness.

Wordlessly, she shook her head.

"My lady," the footman urged.

"I . . . really cannot."

The thief narrowed his eyes. "You cannot."

There was a warning there.

Alexandra shook her head. She couldn't be parted with that cherished bracelet. Not with the memories attached to it. Not with what it meant to Alexandra's still grieving mother. "I'm afraid not."

The highwayman leveled his gun at a point just over her shoulder and fired.

Alexandra's entire body recoiled in fear and shock.

That loud report ricocheted around the countryside, startling birds from their perches in nearby trees. The acrid smell of smoke filled the air around her, nearly blinding Alexandra.

"Now," the bandit said, repositioning the pistol at her breast. "Bracelet and reticule, and be quick."

Chapter 14

That morning, as Dallin had climbed astride his mount outside the Fox and Hound, he'd been resolved to keep his distance from Alexandra Bradbury.

Yes, he'd agreed to take the lady along to intercept the proceedings between her sister and Brone, but neither did that mean they needed to be in close quarters.

She'd ride by carriage and have the protection of a footman and Dallin's driver. Dallin would travel by horse, and enough of a way ahead of her that he needn't even *see* the conveyance, let alone the lady herself. They'd stop as needed, and when they did, they would be in rooms next to one another. Why, that sleeping arrangement was really no different from when lords and ladies gathered for summer house parties and inhabited the guest chambers next door.

And after all was said and done, they'd part ways and never again have any dealings with one another. She'd go her way, happily marrying the Marquess of Wingrave. Dallin would go his way, at last traveling as he wished, and now, after his rescue of Brone, he would have his family's blessing to do so.

So why did that prospect not stir the same longing it once did? Why wasn't he filled with elation at the prospect of at last enjoying some freedoms he'd been denied as the heir?

You know why, that silent voice in his head taunted. *You secretly waited for the lady to make her debut and thought to have those dances you promised, the ones her eyes lit up at the prospect of.* He'd imagined reconnecting and doing so with a talk about the stars.

In short, he'd been a deuced fool, harboring fanciful thoughts about a woman so bloody beautiful and clever she'd made a match with a future duke without even needing to make a formal debut.

But damn it, he wasn't the romantic in his family. That miserable trait belonged to his sisters Myrtle and Cassia, and his cousins Meghan and Linnie and Brone . . . *not* Dallin.

Only, with Alexandra he had been, and he'd never not be humiliated for having imagined more with her.

Dallin's mount, Pegasus, let out a high-pitched whinny.

Dallin instantly relaxed hands he'd not even realized he'd tensed.

"Forgive me," he said, and holding the reins in one palm, he stroked the tense horse along the neck. "I'll put it from my mind," he promised. "She is far behind us, and I promise to keep it that way in my though—"

Boom.

Dallin's entire body tensed at that thunderous report. Pegasus reared, pawing fearfully at the air around them, and Dallin struggled a moment to regain control of the gelding.

His heart pounding rapidly, Dallin wheeled the creature in the direction of that sharp, unmistakable explosion. He did a quick scan of the horizon. That shot had traveled from the south—around the vicinity of where Alexandra's carriage would be.

Terror slickened his palms with moisture.

You are being melodramatic. First romantic, now given to hysterics. What was next? Singing damned ditties and snipping a lady's lock of hair in the middle of a crowded ballroom, like his brother-in-law?

Nay, Dallin was a man of reason and logic, and with that logic, he well knew the echo of a pistol wasn't at all uncommon in the countryside. Gentlemen hunted, as did local farmers. There were any number of rational explanations accounting for the pop of a gun.

Even telling himself as much did nothing to lessen the knot in his chest. But then there was nothing rational about fear.

"Hyah!" Keeping his back long and his elbows close to his knees, Dallin stood in the stirrups and turned Pegasus loose into an all-out gallop.

Alexandra is fine. She's no doubt sitting in her carriage, stewing over the fact that I've a lead on her. He told himself that over and over.

The likelihood of encountering peril on the roads wasn't what it had been decades earlier. Why, as long as Dallin had lived, neither he nor his family had encountered anything more than a wheel that had become stuck in the mud or snow.

Furthermore, he wasn't one for the tales he'd hung, fascinated, on to from his aunt Leslie, who'd regaled the McQuoid children with stories of the highwaymen she'd encountered as a young lady. The roads were far safer now than they'd been.

Still, Dallin applied a gentle inward pressure, urging Pegasus to a faster gallop.

And then as he crested a rise, Dallin spied her some one hundred yards away.

Only, it wasn't Alexandra and the servants Dallin had left her with. But rather, a darkly clad fellow.

Oh, hell.

Dallin's chest tightened with that earlier emotion that had sent him doubling back to check on Alexandra: fear.

Reflexively overlapping his reins, Dallin sat up, steadying Pegasus under him.

As he neared the group, the dread in Dallin's belly spread and threatened to poison him with panic. The servants he'd counted on to protect her had been divested of their weapons and lay face down on the ground, ten paces apart from one another.

Alexandra stood with the tall, wiry stranger's double-barrel pistol pointed at her chest.

Dallin's pulse pounded loudly in his ears, momentarily deafening as it muted the sounds around him.

Dismounting in one fluid movement, his feet hit the ground hard, and the moment they did, he started in a near sprint.

Only Alexandra Bradbury could have a gun pointed her way and exude not fear but a thunderous fury. The sight of her, calm and cool and braced for battle like some Spartan warrioress, managed to steady him.

In an instant, the brigand shifted the barrel of his pistol from Alexandra to Dallin.

Relief assailed Dallin and he reached behind to collect the gun tucked into his waistband.

"Halt," the masked thief cautioned.

The hell he would. As long as the highwayman's weapon was pointed Dallin's way, Alexandra was safe.

The dark-haired stranger's brow flared over the black mask covering his face. "If you know what is good for you, you'll set down your weapon," the man said.

In an instant, he retrained his gun at Alexandra's breast.

Dallin stopped midstride; that abrupt stop sent gravel and rocks kicking up around him. "Don't," he said sharply.

A small laugh shook the highwayman's frame. But then as quick as the man's hard lips had quirked up, they flattened into a lethal line. "I'll not ask again." As if to punctuate that warning, he cocked his gun.

With a glare, Dallin tossed his pistol into the overgrown grass beside him.

"Let us commence with introductions." The highwayman doffed a gold-trimmed tricorn hat befitting the not-so-distant time ago when these blasted scourges had infested the roads. "Robin of the Rookeries, and I take it you are both *esteemed* members of the peerage." Disdain dripped from his unexpectedly crisp tones.

"And you are an esteemed member of *what?*" Alexandra planted her hands on her hips. "Some band of merry thieves?"

God, what was she thinking, baiting the man?

"Enough," Dallin gritted out.

Disimpassioned, the thief passed a look back and forth from Dallin to Alexandra, before ultimately settling on Dallin. "I trust by your reaction you are acquainted with one another," he deduced.

Bloody hell.

"No."

"What business is it of yours?" Alexandra flung back at the same time.

Bloody, bloody, bloody hell.

He gritted his teeth.

The thief smirked. "Oh, it is just . . . *useful* information. It is clear the gentleman cares deeply for you."

Once again Alexandra and Dallin spoke in unison.

"He doesn't."

"I don't."

Alexandra nodded and pointed at the highwayman. "See?"

"I see he at least cares enough that you don't inadvertently see yourself hurt because of your disagreeable nature?"

"My disagreeable nature?" she echoed. "This from a brigand intent on divesting me of my property. Tell me, *good sir*," she began jeeringly.

Dallin closed his eyes and sent a prayer skyward.

"What is the proper response I should have to being robbed? *Hmm?* Should I be polite and respectful and—"

"You should close your mouth, my lady, and turn over your possessions," Robin cautioned.

Alexandra seethed. "You bastard."

"You wound me." In a false affront, the highwayman touched his spare hand to his chest. "Actually, my parentage was never in question," the brigand said. "And I've earned a reputation for being an honorable sort."

"That I find hard to believe," Alexandra muttered.

Dallin shot a silencing glance her way.

Alas, the fiery minx would have had to be looking at him to note that soundless warning.

Again, the highwayman laughed. "That is, honorable amongst the company *I* keep. But my origins are neither here nor there."

Dallin balled his hands.

Did the chit not realize the peril she was in?

"Alexandra," he gritted out.

Instead of taking heed, she took a furious step toward the danger. "Never tell me. You fashion yourself as a Robin Hood, stealing from the rich to give to the poor."

The stranger's eyes hardened. "How condescending you are. A cherished, pampered lady, I trust, who's known nothing except a life of luxury and who's not had to worry a single day about her security, should balk at being made to turn over one of her certainly many trinkets."

Alexandra set her jaw at an intractable angle.

His mouth dry with fear, Dallin took a frantic step toward her.

"Not another move, my lord," the brigand directed, never once taking his focus from Alexandra.

Dallin's patience snapped. "You released one round, and only have one shot more. As such, if you do intend to fire your pistol, I'd advise you use it on me, because if you so much as harm a hair on her head and leave me living, I promise, I'll end you."

That managed to pull the highwayman's attention briefly from Alexandra and over to Dallin. The tall, wiry stranger considered them a long moment, and something indescribable passed in the other man's veiled gaze.

"That is . . . quite the noble sacrifice from someone who claims to neither know the lady nor care about her," the thief remarked.

Dallin tensed. Once more he'd said too much.

He passed a cold, dismissive stare over the raffish fellow. "Any decent gentleman would defend an innocent lady, regardless of the status of their acquaintance. As the case may have it, we are from rival families, who really quite disdain one another. Isn't that right, my lady?"

At her silence, Dallin looked to Alexandra.

She found her voice—a little bit *too* much. "That is correct. Given our family's histories, we are even less than nothing to one another."

Even less than nothing? Her words were simple, matter-of-fact, and helpful, given their current circumstances. Why, then, did that statement still set his teeth on edge?

Alas, the minx wasn't done.

"Why, given the antipathy between us"—Alexandra continued to prattle her never-ending list of proof that where she and Dallin were concerned, absolutely no feelings existed; at least, none that were warm—"it's a wonder His Lordship didn't turn around the moment he spied me with you. He really quite despises me."

Dallin frowned. Now, that was really enough. "Of course I wouldn't ride off," he snapped. "Do you think me so dishonorable?" And furthermore . . . "I don't—" *Despise you.*

"We travel in completely different social circles," she said, cutting Dallin off and handing that explanation to a very bemused-looking *Robin Hood.* "Why, I'd be hard-pressed to name more than one event we've simultaneously attended."

One—there'd been just the one—and not the one he and she had spoken of, where he'd have danced two sets with her. Instead, that single gathering had been rife with tension and anger and resentment. And after overhearing Alexandra's discussion with her mother, Dallin now knew why.

She gave him a pointed look, a look that said them pretending they were nothing more than aloof almost-strangers was the wisest course.

"In fact," Alexandra continued, "after His Lordship and I part ways, we'll have absolutely no further contact with one another, and that is how it's been and will always be. And also how we prefer it." She said that last part quietly. She looked to Dallin. "Isn't that true, my lord?"

When they parted ways, they'd go their own ways, in every way. Just as she'd said, they'd move amongst different members of the *ton* and attend different events, she with her husband, the future duke, and Dallin . . . wondering about Alexandra and her happiness and—

An increasingly familiar pressure weighted his chest.

A question filled her eyes, and she cocked her head. "Dallin?" she mouthed.

That noiseless deliverance of his name on her lips brought him to.

Dallin gave his head a hard, clearing shake. "The lady is accurate," he said coolly.

He felt Alexandra's eyes upon him but couldn't bring himself to look at her lest she see the truth reflected back in his—the one that said when she was gone, he'd miss her more than he could ever admit aloud, even to himself.

"I thank you for that rather lengthy history of your families' enmity. However, at this time, I'm all out of patience." Dismissing Alexandra, Robin turned his focus back to Dallin. "Why don't you demonstrate what I expect of the lady by divesting yourself of your timepiece."

Dallin hesitated a moment before withdrawing the perpetual gold timepiece.

Engraved with Urania, the muse of astronomy, the pocket watch had been a gift from his brother Arran upon returning from his first journey. Dallin eyed it a moment longer, and then regretfully tossed it over to the thief.

The other man caught it in one fluid motion, then stuffed that cherished piece inside his jacket. "As you've proven the logical one of your pair," he said, "I'd advise you to instruct the lady to follow suit and give me the bracelet *now*."

Alexandra growled, "I am not a child to be spoken about and over."

"Alexandra," Dallin said tightly. "I'd ask that you give the bracelet over now so that we can all be on our way."

She gasped and clutched that coveted piece close and looked at him as if he'd kicked a beloved pup. "I won't."

At his wit's end, Dallin opened his mouth to give her another warning that would, once and for all, put an end to this. The words died before they even formed on his lips.

He ran his gaze over her face.

The fury and fire of before had been replaced with a quiet panic and desperation. "I can't," she silently mouthed.

She'd fight that valiantly, that hard to retain those jewels? They mattered so very much to her? How could she not see that *she* mattered far more?

"Alexandra," he said, this time infusing a softness into those four syllables. "It is just a trinket, and it does not matter more than your life."

He gave her a long look.

A battle played out in her expressive eyes: frustration, devastation, and at last . . . regret, a regret that could only stem from her capitulation. Her lower lip trembled, and then clamping it between her teeth to steady that quiver, she snatched the bauble from her wrist.

Still, she retained her hold upon that bangle of gold, topaz, and chrysoberyl.

The highwayman held out his spare hand. "Give it here, love," he ordered, giving his palm a shake.

Alexandra's fingers folded around the glittering piece so hard her knuckles went white.

"Give it to him," Dallin said, again with more of that tender insistence.

Alexandra bit her lower lip, and then as if startled, she flexed her fingers.

The jewels fell with a noisy little jingle into the thief's gloved hand.

"If it is any consolation," the highwayman said as he pocketed Alexandra's bracelet, "the funds fetched from this will be put to very good use."

"I'd have to trust the words of a thief to believe that," she said bitterly.

Dallin slid her a warning look, one that went unheeded.

Robin gave his gun another wave. "The purse next."

Alexandra hesitated once more, but this time turned over the green velvet, beaded reticule without objection.

The minute he'd secured both, Robin proceeded to back away. "I will say the last couple to pass this way proved a good deal more agreeable in handing over their valuables, but then that couple was on their way to Gretna Green and eager to be along."

Dallin tensed.

Alexandra gasped, and then surged toward the thief. "When did you see them?"

Understanding flashed in the highwayman's eyes. "*Ahh*, off to disrupt a wedding, are you? I wish you good luck with that, as the couple appeared very much in love . . . which is why I left them to most of their coins." He grinned. "No one would ever accuse me of not being a romantic."

"When?" Alexandra pleaded.

"Alas, I'll not be one to aid in your meddling." He touched his brow. "Now, I, along with all the good people of the Rookeries, thank you for your generosity this day."

Not taking his gaze from the quartet, Robin backed away, heading for Dallin's mount.

"Worry not. I'm not so foolish as to rob a man of his horse," he said, and still pointing his gun at Alexandra, he managed to loosen

174

Dallin's saddle with his opposite hand. "They don't take as kindly to horse thieves." The highwayman smiled, and then tipping his cap, he whistled once.

A black horse trotted over.

And with nary a glance back, the stranger climbed astride the big mount and was gone.

The moment he'd left, Dallin raced the remaining way to Alexandra.

"Are you all right?" he asked frantically, running his hands over her arms to verify for himself that she'd been unharmed.

"Yes. Fine," she said, her gaze and voice equally dazed.

Fine. She was fine. He briefly closed his eyes and let that wave of relief assail him.

The moment that realization took root, so, too, did the reminder of the danger she'd put herself in.

"Are you *mad*, Alexandra? What were you *thinking*?" he asked, his fingers sinking reflexively into her soft, warm skin.

"I was thinking about keeping my bracelet," she said so matter-of-factly his brows went shooting up.

Dallin instantly drew his hands back. It was all he could do to keep from shaking her.

"My God, woman, do you not have a brain in your bloody head?" And the same terror that had filled him the moment he'd heard that gunshot in the distance came rushing back with that same powerful force. "You could have been killed. And for what?" he demanded, not allowing her a chance to speak. "For a damned fancy bauble that you didn't want to be parted from."

"You know nothing of it," she said through gritted teeth.

"No, I don't. Because I'd never be so reckless with my damned life." And yet she had been, and had nearly lost hers for it. The acrid bite of fear singed his mouth.

"It is *my* life," she said, her voice as steady as the lady herself, in ways Dallin suspected he'd never be again. "My life," she repeated, thumping a fist against that place where the highwayman had fixed the barrel of his gun. "As such, I'd choose what I do with it."

Her last words came muffled as he stared at that place where her heart beat.

How very close she'd come to dying this day. And how casual she was about that near-death experience. Frozen, Dallin's gaze remained fixed and unseeing on her chest. In his mind's eye, the scene from before played out differently: this time with the highwayman's ball striking her chest, ripping apart her skin, and leaving her forever silent as her very life's blood seeped from that hole onto the ground around them.

His breath grew ragged and muffled in his own ears. That horrific imagining snapped the last thread he'd managed to retain of his patience. "It is your life," he thundered, "but whether I like it or not, you have made it so that I'm responsible for you."

The lady drew back slightly, and if he were a better gentleman, that involuntary reflex would have silenced him. Dallin, however, was too far gone. How could she be so indifferent to the danger she'd faced? Determined to get through to her, he took the last step between them and lowered his head so their noses nearly touched. "You think nothing of sacrificing yourself." A truth that would never not haunt him. "And for what?" he spat. "A bloody bracelet and"—he flicked a hand—"a handful of coins. Your cupidity, combined with the indifference you have for your own life, put at risk the lives of others. Men who *do*, in fact, value the air they breathe more than the baubles on their wrists." He glanced pointedly over to where his servants remained.

To their credit, both men had set to work, collecting Dallin's mount, who'd wandered off, and adjusting his loosened saddle. All the while, they kept their gazes averted from the scene Dallin had made.

Alexandra followed his stare over to the two men, who made a show of looking busy so as to not be obvious in the fact that they were privy to such a very personal exchange.

"I . . ." Distress filled her eyes. "Forgive me," she said softly. "You are . . . right on that score."

Silence filled the air around them, and had Alexandra yelled back or cursed or fought Dallin, it would have been easier to bear than this damning solemn acceptance.

She glanced down at her feet.

At the sight of her dejectedness, the fight at last left him.

A dull flush slapped at his cheeks.

God, when had he ever behaved so around a woman? Never. Not even the million and one times his troublesome sisters had gotten on the very last of his nerves.

What was it about Alexandra that robbed him of reason and turned him into someone he neither liked nor recognized?

A fitting thunder rumbled in the distance.

"My lord?"

He started and glanced over at his driver.

The servant removed his cap and held it against his chest. "Storm is rolling in. We'd be wise to continue on."

"Yes," Dallin said. "As it is, we've lost enough time on the day."

Alexandra flinched.

Silently cursing, Dallin swiped the hat he'd not realized he'd lost up from the ground and jammed it atop his head. He'd not intended to hurt her with that statement. His thoughts were still all chaotic over how very close she'd come to dying this day.

"Here," he said gruffly. "Let me help you inside."

She didn't protest as he handed her up. Beyond that offer, neither Alexandra nor Dallin spoke a word to one another.

Moments later, they were on their way.

Chapter 15

Thunder shook the countryside, and rain angrily pelted the carriage Alexandra rode within.

Blankly, she slipped the velvet curtain open and peered out at the raging storm that had slowed her and Dallin's journey. The thick grey storm clouds which had chased away the day's earlier sun ushered in an ominous, dark sky.

It was as though the sky wept the tears Alexandra couldn't bring herself to cry.

She'd lost her mother's bracelet.

She followed a raindrop's windy path down.

It was a fitting, and no doubt telling, loss.

Alexandra's misery should stem from only that great loss.

So why could she only think about how much Dallin McQuoid, Viscount Crichton, detested her? And that he'd rather ride in a downpour, getting soaked through, than share a carriage with her?

But then, what else would you expect from a man who so clearly despises you?

Through the sheets of rain slanting down at the window, Alexandra searched for and found Dallin.

Despite the deluge and the certain misery of being soaked through, Dallin sat tall and proud in his seat. He rode beside the carriage, but just far enough ahead of the conveyance that his back remained to her. Never once did he pause to so much as glance back.

His charged words from earlier that morn whispered around her mind, as crisp as when he'd spoken them two hours prior.

"It is your life . . . but whether I like it or not, you have made it so that I'm responsible for you. Your cupidity, combined with the indifference you have for your own life, put at risk the lives of others. Men who do, *in fact, value the air they breathe . . ."*

Alexandra caught her lower lip hard between her teeth. The aching hurt of his loathing remained.

Alexandra would have been so hurt by any person thinking so little of her. It had nothing to do with the fact that it was this particular man. She told herself that. Mayhap if she told herself enough, she'd even come to believe it.

For even as he despised her, he'd still returned for her. Surely that must mean somewhere deep inside, he liked her some small bit?

"You are pathetic, Alexandra Alison Bradbury," she muttered into the quiet, hoping that in hearing that spoken aloud, she'd snap out of this blasted state of dejection.

As he'd stated to the highwayman, the only reason he'd intervened was because Alexandra was a lady and he was a gentleman, and he'd have attempted to rescue any woman who found herself accosted by a brigand.

Because that was the manner of man *Dallin* was. He was honorable and clever and fiercely protective, and didn't couch his words but rather spoke to Alexandra as though she were an equal. In short, he was everything she would have dreamed of in a partner for herself.

He, on the other hand? He'd rather risk contracting a fever from the cold rains than share a carriage with her.

Just like that, Alexandra's melancholy lifted, as with a frown she sat up.

The stubborn lummox. She'd given him too much credit in her earlier cataloging of his attributes. After all, one who'd subject himself to those elements, all for the sake of avoiding a person he despised, was a thickheaded dolt.

Fiddling with the latch, she tossed the window open. Wind gusted inside, and the ice-cold air sucked the breath from her lungs. Drops of freezing rain pelted her face, briefly blinding Alexandra, and she blinked furiously to see.

Cupping her hands around her mouth, Alexandra shouted into the storm. "You're going to catch your death."

The howl of the wind, however, and the thundering of the horses' hooves, swallowed her cries.

Raising her voice to make herself heard, she tried again. "I said, you're going to catch your death."

To no avail. Dallin remained wholly oblivious to her shouts.

Drawing the window shut, Alexandra sat back in a huff. She drummed her fingertips together, and then stopped.

Alexandra tossed the window open a second time, and then forming a circle with her thumb and index finger, she licked her lips, and placing the tip of her tongue against that circle, she closed her mouth, and blew.

That piercing shriek managed to penetrate even the storm raging outside.

Dallin cast a glance back.

Alexandra motioned him over.

His eyebrows came together in what would have been an endearing line of confusion if she weren't so cross with him.

Frowning, Dallin adjusted his gait so that he and his mount rode directly alongside Alexandra's window. Water ran in rivulets down the hard, chiseled planes of his face. His long chestnut lashes were slick with rain, and the sight of him, raw and unfettered in the storm, did wild things to her heart's normal rhythm.

"Are you mad?" he shouted, instantly quashing that moment of daydreaming. "Shut the blasted window."

Alexandra kept her features expressionless. "Oh, yes. You're the one riding in a violent thunderstorm, getting soaked through, but do tell me how I, with the window open, am the one of our pair who is mad."

He may have growled. Given the latest round of thunder, it was really hard to sort out one rumble from another.

"What is it you want, my lady?"

My lady.

Funny how two words, a simple form of address directed her way since birth, should both hurt and grate when it came from this man.

"You are going to catch a chill," she said, forcing aside those ineffectual sentiments.

"Yes, and given that, slowing our pace to discuss as much seems fruitless to me preventing such a state."

"You should ride in the carriage."

He puzzled his brow. "And have you ride what?"

Alexandra prayed he attributed the sudden rush of color to her cheeks to cold, rather than humiliation. "I'm too clever to risk fever by riding in such elements." She gave a little toss of her head for good measure.

Understanding filled his eyes. "You mean . . . *together.*"

Being removed from the rest of the world, out here on their own without society's eyes prying into their every move, she'd thought he'd at least share a carriage if for no other reason than to avoid the risk of catching a fever. And yet, it appeared the idea of sharing a carriage with her repulsed him.

He found his voice. "I can't do that. You are a lady and I—"

"You are a gentleman. Yes, I'm aware." Alexandra scoffed. "Rest assured," she said, resentment teeming inside, "I've had every last rule of propriety ingrained into me since I was a babe in the nursery. I'm also well aware those same rules forbid me, a lady, from riding alone with a gentleman." That was, in anything that wasn't a curricle.

It was as if in speaking her frustrations aloud, she'd shaken those invisible chains constraining her and every woman, so that they grated like metal striking metal. "There is a great hypocrisy to all of it, you know. You, my betrothed, all men are free to take mistresses and lovers. There are no questions or criticisms. It is accepted as simply as Sunday sermons. Whereas I? I cannot even be in a carriage with a man during a rainstorm without destroying my name and reputation." Her voice grew in volume. "If any of the details about my sister's elopement and my attempt at rescuing her emerges, I'm ruined. As such, it doesn't really matter either way if we share a carriage."

Embarrassed by her display of emotion, she braced for some barbed response, and when it came, she'd slam the window and leave him to his misery in that cold rainstorm.

Only, his eyes grew gentle, and it was a gentleness she recalled from long ago, that tender warmth which she'd not seen since, and God help her, this proved somehow worse, more agonizing.

"And yet, I would know. Just as I know it wouldn't be proper for me to join you, Alexandra," he finally said in that same beneficent way, and she balled her hands on her lap.

After all she'd said, after all the frustration she'd given voice to, that was all he'd say.

She forced a smile. "But then, nothing about any of this is?"

He grinned in return. "This is true."

It was the first smile they'd shared in so very long, and her heart ached with the feeling of rightness to it . . . to them when they were this way.

Something more powerful and potent than the tempest ravaging the countryside passed between Dallin and her.

Their smiles faded.

"My lord." The driver's booming shout slashed across whatever it had been.

Dallin trotted on ahead to meet Harris, and with fingers that shook, Alexandra brought the window back up into place.

It was just a smile. Nothing more than an upward tip of his lips and yours.

Reminding herself of that, however, didn't do anything to settle her racing heart.

Dallin doubled back, and she hurried to lower the window.

"There is an inn a short distance ahead. We will be sheltering there for the evening."

She nodded, grateful for that information.

And as she drew the window up yet again, she stared out past the drops of rain racing in a zigzagging path down the glass, and at Dallin.

This time, she didn't make any attempt to hide her study of him.

Even with his annoyance at having been forced to take Alexandra on with him to Gretna Green, since their fight, along every step of the way thereafter, he'd still taken the time to share their plans of travel and discuss their course of action.

Were she in this situation with her betrothed, Lord Wingrave, Alexandra could say with absolute certainty he'd not be so enlightened. Why, they were about to enter into marriage, and he didn't believe in having any relationship with her beforehand, or even at all. Such a man would never see Alexandra as a partner in life's struggles or triumphs.

Her eyes burnt, and she brushed back the remnants of the rain.

———— ❧❧ ————

At last, they arrived.

As servants from inside the King's Arms came to help with their team and belongings, Alexandra and Dallin raced down the cobblestones, slipping and sliding as they went, to the front of the inn.

How long had it been since she'd raced through the rain or jumped in puddles or done anything that wasn't purely ladylike? The feeling of freedom at being far and away from the rest of Polite Society and her mother and the world set on constraining ladies left her giddy.

Despite the scandal bearing down on her family and the threat to her future marriage and her family's security, a laugh spilled unexpectedly from her lips.

Alexandra stopped, and with the rain falling down upon her, she tipped her face up and let those waters slap her cheeks.

How very good it felt.

Dallin paused and glanced back to where Alexandra remained, soaking in the storm. "Alexandra?"

She tossed her arms wide. "It is wondrous, is it not?" she shouted, directing those words to the nearly black sky overhead.

Another laugh escaped her as, with her eyes closed, she allowed the downpour to wash away the misery that had become a permanent part of her existence since her father's passing. She let herself recall when life had been simpler and the expectations about how women behaved—or didn't behave—were not fully set in her still-forming mind.

She wanted to go back. She wanted to return to that long-ago time and steal more of those moments which were eventually forbidden women.

Feeling eyes upon her, she straightened her head.

Dallin stared at her in the most peculiar way.

"What?" Alexandra's hand went to her drenched hair. "I'm a fright," she called.

His stare remained riveted on her face. "No. Not that."

Not that, which implied he did stare at her. But for what reason?

A streak of lightning snaked across the sky, followed almost instantaneously by a sharp crack.

"Come." Dallin bounded over, and catching Alexandra's arm in a protective way that only brought more of that radiant warmth, he escorted her the remainder of the way.

Entering through the arched oak doors, Dallin motioned for Alexandra to precede him. When they stepped inside, silence greeted them in the empty taproom. Water dripped from their persons, leaving a puddle at the previously dry entryway.

A generous fire crackled in the hearth, emitting a welcome warmth throughout the cozy inn, and shivering inside her soaked garments, Alexandra rubbed her hands together in a bid to absorb some of the room's heat.

They stepped deeper inside the establishment.

But for that fire and the muffled song from a fiddle being played from somewhere within the inn, one would have otherwise believed the place empty.

Suddenly, there came a collection of whispers. Alexandra and Dallin looked toward that smattering of sound. The pine door, previously cracked, was suddenly shut.

There came a flurry of footfalls and more whispers.

The cheerful off-key whine of the music came to an abrupt stop.

An instant later, the door opened a fraction, and a ruddy-cheeked, smiling fellow dipped his head outside. If possible, that already boundless grin grew bigger.

"My lord. My lady," he called in rumbling, jovial tones.

An enormous fellow with a smile as wide as his huge barrel chest, and with a fiddle in his right hand, hastened over.

The instant he reached them, he dropped a bow that sent his shaggy sandy-brown hair tumbling over his kindly brow. "How wonderful it is for you to visit our merry establishment on this lovely spring day," he welcomed.

Lovely spring day?

As if to highlight the ridiculousness of that overstatement, the storm still raging outside released another violent rumble of thunder.

"I am Gus, the owner of this fine establishment." He puffed out his chest, proud as a peacock displaying its shimmering blue-green feathers. "Not every day I have noble lords and ladies to visit," he said. "Once, I'd a pair travel through. Found themselves snowed in at Christmas during that stormy winter a year back, they did."

There was something infectious about his geniality, and despite the cold and the misery of wanting a man who so very clearly despised her, and the miserable marriage awaiting Alexandra upon her return, she found herself smiling.

"Came through, they did, with their dog as big as a wolf," Gus went on with his telling of that momentous day of his. "They called him Horace, but I privately nicknamed him Horse on account of his size."

Dallin emitted a strangled sound, and she glanced over and frowned.

He'd gone all red in the cheeks.

There was hardly a reason to be rude.

"It is a *most* fine inn," Alexandra praised, and the innkeeper grew impossibly taller under that flattery. "And it is a wonder that, from that visit, more lords and ladies did not come to discover for their own the greatness of your establishment."

The older fellow preened once more under that praise and proceeded to prattle on about some great wonders of his place.

She felt Dallin's gaze on her and glanced over. He'd managed to get himself under control. However, he stared at her with an odd expression.

He was annoyed by her? Him, when he'd been the one reacting so rudely to Gus's telling?

What was it he took offense with now?

"The villagers tend to gather here, but the storm has scared everyone off. They like my music, they do. Mayhap you've heard of some of my work?" the garrulous fellow asked, pulling their full attention back his way.

"Mr. Gus?" she asked hesitantly.

"Just Gus." He flashed another one of those giant grins. "We don't stand on ceremony here in Yorkshire. My works," he clarified. "'The Rakes of Madeley'?"

"'The Rakes of . . . Mallow'?"

A twinkle in his eye, he pointed the bow Alexandra's way. "*Madeley.* Rewrote it, I did, adding some different chords and runs." Raising the instrument to his shoulder, he proceeded to play the quick ditty. *"Laughing, dancing, singing, cleaning, Ever working, always thinking, Live the Rakes of Madeley."*

Alexandra laughed and clapped happily. "Bravo! You've turned the rakes into honorable gentlemen."

The big man beamed. "Indeed, I did. Everyone in Yorkshire is still talking—"

"And I see why—"

"Gus," Dallin interrupted Alexandra and the innkeeper. "Might you have rooms available?"

At that rudeness, Alexandra shot him a glare.

Of course he'd have to be looking at *her* to note as much.

"Why, I've got any number of them, I do," Gus said. "On account of the rain."

"May we have two of them?" Dallin said.

The innkeeper tapped the back of his fiddle against his forehead. "Of course. Your wife standing there, soaked from the storm."

Dallin's wife.

Alexandra's heart did an all-too-wild pitter-patter at even the thought of it, and she braced for Dallin to refute that incorrect supposition, to instead offer up a different falsified relationship between them.

Only, he didn't.

"If you'd be so good as to follow me," Gus said, and led the way.

As he led them abovestairs, his instrument now tucked under his arm, he proceeded to hum an off-key rendering of "The Rakes of Mallow," pausing only to share an occasional piece of information with them.

Dallin could have just as easily corrected the innkeeper and claimed they were brother and sister. But he hadn't.

Why hadn't he?

You're looking for there to be a greater meaning than there is, a voice in her head silently chided.

Even knowing that, however, did nothing to stop dangerously insidious thoughts from taking root, and like a stubborn plant that could not be chopped down, those imaginings grew and grew: of Alexandra and Dallin, joined not as rival members of enemy families, but as husband and wife. Of the two of them, laughing and teasing one another. Of them on that rooftop terrace, studying the stars overhead.

And a hungering so great and equally perilous in nature gripped Alexandra—a hungering to have a real marriage, not just with any man, but with the one beside her.

Bitterness singed her veins and left a sour taste in her mouth. She was a fool, yearning for things that could never be. Even had Lord Wingrave not stood between them, Dallin's antipathy did.

Only, he hadn't always been that way. He'd once exuded only warmth and kindness and—

Big Gus brought them to a stop before a single door. "These are the fine rooms stayed in by my last noble guests." He frowned his first frown. "Though they only used the one—"

At her side, Dallin growled, and she cast him another sharp glance.

"Therefore, I'm not sure which of you to—"

"Her Ladyship may have the honors," Dallin demurred.

Alexandra entered the room, taking in the pine bedframe at the center back wall. A clean white coverlet had been draped over the mattress. A cheerful, welcoming fire filled the hearth.

A Sure Duke

"If you would be so good as to have a warm bath readied for Her Ladyship?" Dallin asked Gus.

"Of course. My daughters will be along shortly to see to it."

At Dallin's consideration, a fresh wave of pain seized her breast, and Alexandra wandered deeper inside, stopping at the fireplace. She gripped the hard stone mantel, welcoming the sharp sting of pain as the ancient rocks dug through her gloves and into her palm.

"I'll see to it first thing," Gus was saying.

Must Dallin be so thoughtful? Mean and surly were preferable, as the tender side of Dallin only made the idea of their eventual, forever parting unfathomable and left her cut up and ragged inside.

Misery weighted her eyes shut, and even the cheerful fire emanating from the grate did little to chase away the chill left at the thought of losing him.

Losing him?

You never even had him.

But she'd wanted to. She'd wanted to have those two waltzes he'd vowed to dance with her. She'd wanted him to come to her with an answer to the question that the two of them had vowed whoever found out first would share with the other. She wanted—

A big, warm hand fell on her shoulder.

She gasped, her entire body jerking at that unexpected interruption.

Dallin caught her firmly by the arm, and he held on to her to keep her from tumbling forward into the fire.

Her heart jumped, and as she stared at the high flames she'd come so very close to falling into, fear escorted her back to the present.

Dazed, she gave her head a hard shake.

Unable to meet Dallin's concerned gaze when he gently guided her to face him, she looked miserably to the door Gus had closed on his way out.

"He went to see to your bath," Dallin said, misunderstanding the reason for her averted eyes.

And she gave thanks to retaining some level of pride.

"Are you all right, Alexandra?" Dallin asked in hushed tones, infused with such a gentle concern that tears filled her eyes, and this time, Alexandra didn't even fight the idea those drops were anything other than what they were.

No, I'm not all right, she silently screamed. *I'm miserable and falling apart inside at the future awaiting me. And angry and resentful that my father has left me to sort out the mess he made of our finances and future.*

And she was agonized. Agonized at everything that could not and never would be with the tender man next to her.

Nothing, absolutely nothing, could make her happy again. Not truly.

"Alexandra?" Dallin repeated, giving her arm a light little squeeze.

"Fine," she said, her voice thick. "I am just"—*heartbroken, resentful*—"tired."

And she was. Tired of the responsibilities which had fallen to her. Weary to the bone of the Bradburys' financial secrets that, upon her father's death, had been bequeathed to her.

Dallin stroked both his big hands along her arms with more of that warm gentleness, and it threatened to break her at last.

He moved his gaze over her face. "What is it, Alexandra?"

"It's been a lot, is all," she managed to say, her voice thick as she uttered the truest words she'd spoken to him since the night her father died.

"Are you regretting undertaking this journey?" he asked without any condemnation in that question. "Because if you are—"

"No!" she exclaimed, lest he get the thought into his head of leaving her behind with his servants and ending the last of the time they had together. "No," she repeated, this time more modulated in her reply. "As I said . . . it's just been . . . a lot."

"I know it has," he murmured.

You don't know. He assumed she spoke of their flight to Gretna Green. He didn't know any of the truths surrounding her response or her family's circumstances.

"Is there anything else you need, Alexandra?" he asked quietly, still rubbing her arms in that soothing way as, all of a sudden in this moment, Alexandra became aware of him in a different way.

So much. I need so much.

He slowed that gentle back-and-forth glide of his hands but remained holding her, his broad arms framing her.

And she became aware that she'd spoken her previous admission aloud, and she should be horrified. She should be mortified, and a host of any other sentiments.

Only, she remained incapable of feeling anything other than the touch of his palms on her.

Dallin abruptly drew his fingers back, recoiling those long, powerful digits, like he'd been the one to burn himself in that fire.

Alexandra reached for them, taking them in hers, linking their fingers, and they wrapped about each other as naturally as two different branches of ivy that had twined themselves as one.

She simply stared at their joined hands.

How natural this was. How natural it felt. It was as if their palms had been made for one another.

"Alexandra," he whispered, a thread of pleading contained within her name.

To release him, no doubt.

Alexandra, however, let herself imagine a different reason for the desperation layered within his entreaty.

She imagined a world where he wanted her as she wanted him. Dallin may be forever beyond her reach, and content to remain so, but in this, she imagined he shared a like yearning for her, and it was an all-too-powerful illusion.

For she'd one day soon marry and be forced to give every part of herself to another, but she'd at least have Dallin's kiss to take with her when she went.

Freeing herself of those invisible chains, Alexandra leaned up and touched her lips to his.

Dallin stilled, and then with a groan that rumbled from somewhere deep inside his chest, he folded his arms around Alexandra and kissed her in return.

He devoured her mouth. He kissed her like a man who not only wanted to but also had secretly dreamed of doing so for so long he was half-mad from the want of it.

And she allowed herself to have that fantasy, and in this instant, her body didn't care whether she lied to herself. It cared only for the feel of being in Dallin's arms.

Never breaking contact with her mouth, Dallin glided his hands over her body. He stroked the curves of her hips with a possessive touch that threatened to undo her.

Alexandra moaned, and Dallin slipped his tongue inside, swallowing that hungry little sound, and then filled his palms with her buttocks, keeping her upright and pressing her close to the hard ridge in his trousers.

When she'd first met Dallin, she'd wondered what his kiss might be like. She'd imagined them embracing. None of those contemplations could have prepared her for the raw, primal heat of this actual moment.

Alexandra climbed her arms up around his neck, and she twined her fingers in the silken strands of his slightly-too-long chestnut hair. Angling his head, she kissed him deeply in return.

He tasted of the peppermints she'd so favored as a girl, and Alexandra would never see or taste one of those sweet treats without thinking of this man and this moment.

And Dallin kissed her with the same ferocious intensity, of a man who sought to devour her, as if he sought to sear this encounter in his mind so that he, too, might commit their embrace to his forever remembrances.

They tangled their tongues in the forbidden waltz they'd been denied, stealing this more wicked dance as their own.

He thrust, she parried.

She thrust, he parried.

Then Dallin sucked lightly on the tip of her tongue, teasing that flesh, tormenting Alexandra.

A restlessness filled her, settling someplace between her legs, and she shifted and undulated in a bid to escape it. Nay, not escape it, to have it assuaged.

She dimly registered the backs of her knees colliding with something.

The bed.

Alexandra gripped Dallin by his jacket and tugged him closer.

They collapsed on the bed in a tangle of limbs. He pushed up her damp skirts and ran his left hand over the expanse of her leg.

Alexandra whimpered, and in a futile attempt at getting closer, she bucked against him.

Dallin growled, that low, primitive reverberation filling her mouth. He gripped her hips hard and pushed himself against her.

She moaned and kissed him more desperately.

She wanted this moment to go on forever. She wanted to live in it and be devoured by Dallin and his embrace.

RapRapRap.

That light knocking at the door filled the room.

Dallin wrenched away.

Horror filled his eyes, and the tangible hint of his repugnance chased away every last vestige of warmth left by his touch.

He jumped away from her . . . and the bed.

"Just a moment," he called in a completely steady voice that revealed no hint of his earlier passion.

Whereas Alexandra? Alexandra would wager her very soul that she'd never, ever be the same again.

Forcing herself up onto unsteady elbows, Alexandra made herself stand.

She patted her damp hair with quivering fingers.

Standing at the entryway, Dallin glanced back.

She instantly dropped her arm to her side, lest he see the effect he and his embrace had wrought on her senses.

He passed a sweeping gaze over Alexandra, lingering an impenetrable stare upon her mouth.

Was he recalling the kiss they'd shared? Did he also wish, like Alexandra, that there'd been no interruption, so that they could have drunk more of one another?

Only, his unblinking brown eyes remained opaque.

Dallin, however, must have found she'd composed herself more than the riotous emotions inside her felt, for he looked away and opened the door.

"Here we are!" Gus boomed in his jovial voice, and bowing deep at the waist, he picked up one end of the empty wood bath he'd arrived with. "Matilda has come to help, on account of her being my biggest girl."

Alexandra and Dallin looked to the daughter in question. Possessed of broad shoulders and thick hips, the young woman couldn't have been much older than Alexandra.

Matilda dropped a curtsy, and at her father's directives, she reached for the opposite end of the tub.

Dallin sprang forward.

"Please," he said, rushing out into the hall. "Allow me."

God help her. During that rooftop exchange with Dallin McQuoid a year ago, she'd fallen a little bit in love with him. In this moment, she'd lost every last remaining untouched corner of her heart to him for that kindness no other gentleman would have shown the young woman.

No, most lords and ladies took everything as their due and saw servants not as people first, but as figures who existed to see to the needs of their employers.

As Dallin and Gus proceeded to carry the small tub into Alexandra's room, Gus's pretty, wide-hipped daughter watched Dallin with moonstruck eyes.

Oh, how I can commiserate, Matilda.

She was unable to look away from Dallin—this man who was like the sun to her, and just as dangerous to stare upon—and yet in her eagerness to get even closer to him, she remained as hopeless and greedy as Icarus.

For Dallin wasn't the rogue or scoundrel most ladies thrilled at the prospect of reforming. He was something that posed a far greater peril to a woman's heart—he was a gallant, honorable man who actually saw the people around him and offered them every kindness.

Dallin remained while a stream of girls and young women, all bearing a striking resemblance to the jovial innkeeper, carried in bucket after bucket of steaming water.

"I am here to help you, my lady," a tiny voice piped in, managing to at last sever Alexandra's focus on Dallin and recall her attention to the girl speaking before her.

"I'll return to assist you with your bath, miss, after I see to this." Little hands hefted the object in question, an empty wood bucket, up. "My sisters said they should see to you because they're older and I'm just ten, but I told them I was as capable as anyone ten or twenty years my elder, and my da agreed. Said *I'd* be the one to have the honor of helping."

Alexandra dropped to a knee beside the smallish girl, diminutive and quietly spoken, where the rest of her kin were big and gushing.

"What is your name?" Alexandra asked softly.

"Rebecca."

Near in age to Alexandra's sister Daphne, Gus's youngest daughter also revealed hints of Daphne's same take-charge spirit.

"Rebecca," she murmured. God, how she missed her sisters. They were the other half of her soul, and for them she'd do anything. Nay, for them, Alexandra *was* doing everything. At that unnecessary reminder, an excruciatingly sharp pain ripped through her.

"My lady?" Little Rebecca's concerned voice slashed across those self-pitying thoughts.

Alexandra forced a smile. "Well, then, Rebecca, I believe you'll be the finest person to ever help me, and I'm most grateful to you for your assistance."

The girl puffed her small chest out with pride.

Feeling eyes upon her, Alexandra glanced up.

Dallin remained at the entryway with Gus talking away at his side. Dallin's attention, however, remained fixed on Alexandra.

"Well, then, we should be along, so I may show you to your rooms." Gus's booming voice jolted Alexandra.

Only when Rebecca had sprinted out the door did Dallin quit the room, with Gus at his heels, leaving Alexandra alone. And standing in the middle of the room, her skirts dripping a puddle about her, Alexandra had never felt more alone than she did at this very moment.

Chapter 16

Nearly an hour later, having toweled off and changed into a pair of dry garments, Dallin sat in the taproom beside the warm fire and contemplated the contents of his tankard.

He'd kissed her.

Nay, she'd kissed him, but he'd happily and eagerly returned that embrace.

He took another long swig of ale. It didn't help. The memory of the taste and feel of her in his arms remained far more potent than even the strongest spirits he'd ever consumed.

He wanted to despise her.

Loathing the lady would make it far easier to let her go when this was all done. If she were haughty and exuded her own self-importance, he could hate her.

But after this day, he wasn't certain that he ever could. Oh, he'd made a valiant effort to convince himself he despised her and her kin.

Given the rigor of their travels and the elements they'd encountered along the way, the lady should have been foul-tempered. Dallin knew it because he'd raced through the same elements of the storm outside, and he'd been deuced miserable in his soaked garments.

One would have never known, looking at Alexandra. Why, the ease with which she'd stood there, talking with the garrulous Gus, and the gentle way she'd spoken to Gus's youngest daughter, she and Dallin may as well have waltzed in during the middle of a soft summer's day.

Nay, she'd stood there, smiling and laughing, and without revealing any indication of the station divide between them, she'd patiently chatted with the innkeeper and his daughter.

With each exchange, she threw doubt into every opinion he'd developed of her after hearing her that night of Lord and Lady Brookhaven's ball.

She'd been prepared to lose her life over a piece of jewelry, but she showed a genuine concern about him being out in the storm, putting his well-being first.

Such a woman didn't fit with the supercilious lady he'd taken her for.

And Dallin preferred a world in which she was the self-important Diamond who looked down on his family and coveted that all-powerful title of marchioness and future duchess. Because it would be easy to forget such a woman.

Now that he'd held her in his arms, Dallin knew the lies he'd been telling himself. He'd never, ever forget her.

Nay, instead, Alexandra Bradbury would live on; thoughts of their embrace would be forever seared into Dallin's deepest memories.

Only, the time would soon come when the lady joined herself to another man, another man who'd have the right to kiss that mouth whenever he wished, and who would look upon her bare body, stroking it, learning it . . . Cruel and unrelenting jealousy threatened to take Dallin apart.

In a bid to eradicate the festering thoughts of another man knowing Alexandra in all the ways Dallin longed to, he took another drink—a long one.

It didn't help.

She lived in his mind.

She was everywhere.

She is here.

Dallin looked across the room.

She'd traded her wet garments for a pale-yellow dress, and in that shimmering silk, she was the sun amidst the storm.

Warily, from under hooded eyes, he followed her approach. All the while, he found himself an unwilling witness to the memory of their embrace. It played over and over in his mind, and he lived it all again, recalling the sweet, fragrant hint of apple on her breath. The feel of her delicate tongue wildly exploring his own equally eager flesh.

Dallin's breathing grew more ragged.

The moment Alexandra reached his table, he stood. "What are you doing here?"

She arched a single elegant brow. "Where *should* I be?"

"In your rooms, taking a tray."

"Why aren't you in your rooms, taking a tray?"

Touché.

And then with Dallin still standing there, Alexandra availed herself of the opposite chair.

Dallin flexed his jaw, and then reclaimed his seat.

The stubborn woman opposite him paid him no heed. Rather, she passed her opaque gaze around the quiet taproom, moving her focus over the empty round tables and the mismatched chairs of varying types of wood neatly tucked underneath.

Alexandra shifted her attention, and Dallin followed her stare to the pressed metal wall plate hanging over the hearth.

The piece had begun to tarnish around the outer rim and within the raised scene depicted upon the plate.

"I trust such an establishment does not meet the very high standards of the uppish Bradbury family," he said testily, as much to get a rise out of her as to remind himself of who she and her family in fact were.

As if she'd forgotten his presence, Alexandra blinked slowly.

"On the contrary," she said softly, looking back at Dallin. "There is a coziness to the place."

He snorted.

Alexandra's mouth dissolved into a frown as she dropped her elbows on the table. "With you turning your nose up at our accommodations, perhaps the Bradburys aren't the uppish ones, Lord Crichton."

"I wasn't—"

"Weren't you? And furthermore," she said before he could speak, "I'm not the one cutting off the proprietor whenever he speaks."

They glared at one another.

"Here we are."

They both looked up to find the always smiling Gus with his fiddle and bow in hand and two serving girls, who both bore a striking resemblance to the big innkeeper.

The older man gave no outward indication he'd sensed any fraught tension, but then, with his perpetual smile, Dallin rather doubted him capable of picking out any unpleasantness were he handed the sentiment in a bag.

One of the young, sandy-haired girls set down two tankards of ale between Dallin and Alexandra, and the bashful young woman beside her ducked out from behind Gus long enough to place glasses of water down before both, then rushed to the door leading back to the kitchens.

"Two of my daughters, they are."

"They are lovely," Alexandra kindly remarked.

Gus beamed. "The others are preparing your meals. Good girls, all of them. Look after me, they do."

Some emotion Dallin couldn't place filled Alexandra's eyes.

"May I play you a song?" Gus asked, abruptly changing the topic. He brought the fiddle up into place.

"I'd very much like to hear the rest of your 'Rakes of Madeley,'" Alexandra said.

The old proprietor needed no further prompting. He immediately launched into the merry tune, dancing off as he did; he moved from empty table to empty table as though there were other guests present whom he regaled with his happy song.

Picking up his tankard of ale, Dallin studied Alexandra from under hooded lashes.

Her eyes fairly sparkled as she followed the fiddler as he went. Her lips moved soundlessly as she silently mouthed the new lyrics Gus had shared earlier. All the while, she tapped her feet in an endearingly enthusiastic way under the table.

Being close to her in this way, witnessing her in this light, harkened back to their first meeting and proved perilous to Dallin.

He tightened his hold upon the pewter glass.

For any other man, having had Alexandra Bradbury in his arms would have been enough.

Don't think of her with Gus and Rebecca. Don't think of her happily taking in the mediocre playing with a delight better reserved for the finest symphony. Think of her as she was, disparaging your family, and then this night, so bent on keeping jewelry she nearly got herself killed.

"You shouldn't be down here, Alexandra."

"Where *should* I be, Dallin? *Hmm?*" She didn't even take her eyes from the fiddler. "You have all the answers, so tell me."

"Back in London," he said flatly.

"While you see to my sister?" She scoffed. "I think not."

"Because I'm a bumbling McQuoid incapable of interrupting the proceedings and escorting her safely back?" he asked coolly.

The fact she thought him incompetent rankled more than it should.

"It has nothing to do with your family," she said, exasperated. "I'm determined to escort Cora back because she is *my* sister. Why can't you understand that?"

"Oh, please spare me." He clipped out each syllable. "Do not *pretend* as though you and your flaunted Bradbury kin do not look down on the McQuoids."

As if he'd struck her, she recoiled.

She swiftly found her voice. "At every turn, you make barbs and assumptions about me and my family. How little you truly think of me," she spat, disgust and hurt wreathing her every word.

He'd not allow himself to feel bad. "This from a woman who's been very clear in how she feels about my family."

Color exploded in her cheeks. "I have never—"

"Haven't you?"

"I most certainly haven't—"

Dallin brought his tankard down with more force than he intended. *"You know how that family is viewed."* He repeated verbatim every last hurtful word she and her mother had uttered that day. *"We do not mingle with the McQuoids. Not then, and not now. Especially not now, with you girls having made your debut. Cora must not be seen with him, ever."*

Alexandra paled.

She didn't, however, attempt to refute her earlier claims. But then, how could she?

"I didn't . . ." Her fragmented response emerged no more than a desolate whisper that stood in stark juxtaposition to Gus's merry playing.

"You didn't?" he shot back. "You didn't say, *I will make it right, Mother? I'll speak to her the moment the set ends and make it clear she's not to partner with a McQuoid?*"

Alexandra's eyes slid shut, those pale, golden lashes briefly concealing her stunned gaze. "You shouldn't have heard that," she said, her voice threadbare.

There could be no feigning the hurt wreathing her flawless Grecian features, and that he was the one responsible for it sent an unwanted guilt spiraling through him.

Guilt he'd not feel.

"You expected I should happen to stumble upon an exchange involving a dear, beloved cousin and his future and just walk away because it's impolite to eavesdrop?" he returned in a hushed whisper.

"Nay," he went on, letting free all the anger and resentment that had gripped him since he'd discovered her betrothal to Lord Wingrave. "We are good enough to kiss," he hissed, "but not seemly enough for you and yours to have any respectable connection with."

She recoiled. "It isn't that."

He flexed his jaw. "I'm sure whatever reasons exist in your lovely head are good enough for you, but honestly, Alexandra," he said coolly, welcoming the rage, "I don't care what they are."

"Here we are!"

That cheerful greeting hung in the charged air a long moment as Dallin and Alexandra remained with their gazes locked.

Dallin looked away first.

The serving girls from before, wearing their father's same big smile, had returned with two plates.

"Thank you," Dallin said as they set the wooden dishes down before them.

— ⟨⟩ —

Oh, God.

No wonder he believed her a capricious miss concerned above all else with snagging that elite title of duchess. He'd heard Alexandra's exchange with her mother and formed the exact opinion anyone else who'd happened to overhear it would have.

Not only that. He'd also memorized, word for word, every single awful sentence uttered . . .

Which could only mean . . . he'd been hurt that night at Lord and Lady Brookhaven's ball.

Nay, more accurately, she had hurt *Dallin*. Inadvertently, and he'd misconstrued what he heard, and yet that didn't change the pain she'd caused him. He'd no idea the reason for her words that night.

He took her for a title-grasping miss who'd kissed him out of curiosity but otherwise found him unworthy, when there could never be anything further from the truth. Dallin and the dream of them together had been one she'd fleetingly carried for a whisper of time.

And after she'd learned her true fate, the dream of Dallin had remained—only this time, the idea of them together was nothing more than a fantastical imagining of what would never be. It was why she'd taken that kiss from him, to keep that part of him forever.

Only, he'd seen it as something ugly and vile.

She yearned to crawl under the table or dissolve and disappear into the floor. The moment Gus had gone, Alexandra made herself speak.

"You think so poorly of me. At every turn, you question my honor. If I had remained safely tucked away in London while my sister is alone on the road with a man she hardly knows, you'd have undoubtedly found fault with me for putting myself first."

Dallin frowned. "I'd not. I'd say you were wise for realizing the peril awaiting a lady alone on the road and instead entrusting the task to another."

It was on the tip of her tongue to keep from pointing out that there wasn't a male relative or gentleman in her life to be trusted with the task of fetching Cora. Only, she knew the lie there. Even having known Dallin a short while, Alexandra trusted that if she herself had asked it, he'd have seen to Cora's safe return.

"I love my sister, Dallin," she finally said. "I love both of my sisters, and I'd do anything to protect them, even if it means putting their"— *happiness*—"futures before my own.

"As to what you shared," she continued, "you heard a conversation that was taken out of context and fit whatever narrative you already had existing in your mind about me."

Uncertainty filled his eyes. That hesitation lasted but a moment.

"You were both very plainspoken that evening. As such, it would be hardly possible to envision a somehow different *meaning* to your words."

Actually, there was, and yet to say as much, to tell him the truth about her and her family's circumstances, would only strip Alexandra of the last vestige of her pride before him.

As he grabbed his fork and knife and proceeded to carve up the boiled fowl on his plate, Alexandra picked up her own fork and, staring wretchedly at her dish, pushed one of the boiled potatoes around the perimeter.

Dallin hated her.

Which was really for the best. Once Alexandra married, she and Dallin could never be anything to one another. Nor, for that matter, did society permit her, as an unwed lady, to have any relationship with Dallin *now*.

Let him despise her. Let him think the absolute worst of her. Then she'd be left with the memory of a man who'd disdained her and not the teasing, smiling, gentle man he'd proven to be so many times.

Miserable, Alexandra speared a small boiled potato, popped it in her mouth—and instantly regretted doing so. The salted vegetable sat heavy on her tongue, and she made herself chew. She swallowed, attempting to choke the remnants down.

Giving up on the chore of eating, Alexandra grabbed her tankard and took a long, deep swallow.

She stared into her glass the way Dallin had done. Now, as one who sought to avoid his gaze, she gathered the real reason for Dallin's earlier interest in his drink—he had wished to evade Alexandra's notice.

She took another, longer drink.

And then as she sat there on the spindled oak chair, the most peculiar thing happened: a welcome warmth wound its way through her, dulling her humiliation, hurt, and shame.

"Alexandra." Dallin's quiet murmur brought her head slowly up.

God, she'd never not see him in her mind the way he sat before her: his cheeks chiseled from stone now ruggedly covered in even more stubble than when they'd first set out. His square jaw firm but not too heavy, bearing a slight and endearing cleft.

"I don't want to fight with you, Alexandra. I'd . . . propose something."

How desperate he was to be rid of her. She hated how very much that rankled.

She set her jaw at a resolute angle. "I'll not be deterred, Dallin. I'm going to collect my sister."

"That isn't what I was going to suggest . . . Rather, a truce. At least for the remainder of the journey. I expect we're close to reaching them."

Hours? A day? More, if there were further delays? Alexandra's heart wrenched. It wasn't enough.

"We needn't be friends, but neither must we be combatants," Dallin finished.

She stared sightlessly at him.

A year ago, she'd innocently dreamed of so much more, only to have Dallin propose something that wasn't even friendship. And how pathetic did it make her that she'd grasp at that offering?

"Alexandra?"

She stretched her palm across the table. "I would like that," she murmured.

Dallin looked at her hand a moment, then placed his bare fingers in hers.

A voltaic charge surged to the point where their palms touched; it radiated a thrilling heat that robbed Alexandra of her breath.

How right it felt to be joined so with him. It recalled Alexandra back to another night, when the future had been wide open and there'd been the promise of waltzes with him, and discussions about and under the stars.

With a like speed, Alexandra and Dallin drew their fingers back.

At the loss, Alexandra curled and clenched her hand, and when that failed to steady her, she grasped her tankard and made a show of drinking. The stout, pale spirits infused Alexandra with a welcome warmth, and relishing the restorative quality of the brew, she took another long swallow.

"Do you know," she said, resting her elbows on the table, framing her nearly untouched meal, "I've never had ale."

Her voice emerged languid to her own ears.

"Or port," she added, taking another sip and another. "Or claret." She hiccuped. "Or whiskey."

Nothing. She'd tasted nothing beyond watered-down lemonade and water.

"Because"—she drew her shoulders back and spoke in a near perfect rendition of her mother—"ladies do not drink spirits."

"A stern governess?" Dallin asked of her impersonation.

Alexandra lifted a finger. "A stern *mama*."

Holding her tankard in one hand, with her other, Alexandra dragged her chair closer. "I quite like ale, and it begs the question, Dallin," she said, hefting her glass toward him.

"What is that, Alexandra?"

"What other wonders are ladies being prohibited?"

His lips twitched in a crooked, charming grin that would never not muddle her senses. "I'd hardly call ale a great wonder."

"Oh, not to you, perhaps. But that is only because, as a man, you are afforded luxuries that women are denied until splendors become commonplace and you take them for granted. But I never would. No lady would." Alexandra closed her eyes and tipped her much lighter tankard back.

When that pale, bitter drink failed to touch her tongue, Alexandra frowned. Lowering her glass, she peered into the contents. "Thasodd," she said, those two words rolling together. "I've all done."

To demonstrate that sad point, Alexandra tipped her glass over.

A lone drop tumbled atop a salty potato. She stared wistfully at the small vegetable. "Lucky potato." Alexandra dissolved into a giggle.

Dallin's lips twitched in another one of those disarming smiles. He hesitated a moment, took a long drink, and then handed the remainder of his ale over to Alexandra.

"Why, thank you, good sir." She accepted that offering and raised it to her mouth . . . and frowned.

"A problem?"

Alexandra stared accusatorily at him. "You drank most of yours."

"It was my ale," he pointed out.

"Thas true."

A shadow fell over the table.

One of Gus's daughters had returned with a pewter pitcher. "More ale?"

"No."

"Yes," Alexandra said at the same time as Dallin's declination. "Don't mind him," she said to the pretty, plump girl filling her glass. "He's starchy."

Dallin bristled. "I'm not starchy."

Alexandra cupped a hand around her mouth and whispered to the serving girl, "Starchy."

The moment the girl had gone, Alexandra said, "We should toast."

"And what should we toast?"

She tapped her fingertips against her chin. "Thinking. Thinking."

"To better weather?" he suggested.

She pulled a face. "Dull."

"To no further incidents in our travels?"

"Better," she said.

"But not the focus of our toast."

"Not." While she thought, Alexandra took a drink from her foamy ale. "Wass it?"

"You've something here," Dallin murmured, his gaze locked on her lips.

Then, reaching across the table, he brushed that froth away.

His touch lingered there.

Alexandra sighed. *I like when you touch me.*

Dallin went absolutely motionless.

Uh-oh. "Did I say that out loud?" she whispered.

"You . . . did."

"Oh." She expected she should feel a greater sense of embarrassment, and yet the spirits helped with dulling that sentiment.

Alexandra straightened. "I've it! Our toast," she said excitedly.

"I'm ready."

"No yourrr not." She pointed to his newly filled glass.

Dutifully, he picked it up.

Alexandra cleared her throat. "To ale," she hailed.

"To ale!"

That merry chorus came from Gus and his daughters amidst the innkeeper's playing.

Alexandra laughed, and toasting the quartet tapping their feet in time to the latest jubilant set, she took another big drink.

Dallin frowned.

"I donnt like when you frown." She pouted.

"I'm sorry."

"But you're still frowning."

Dallin cleared his throat. "Perhaps you might refrain from any further spirits."

Gasping, Alexandra drew her ale protectively close to her chest. Liquid sloshed over the side and splattered the lacy fichu bodice of her gown.

"I thought we were almost-friends," she shot back. "Almost-friends don't deny their almost-friends things they enjoy."

"*Friends*," Dallin clarified, "do not let their friends overindulge to the point where they'll regret it mightily in the morning."

Alexandra waggled her brows. "Well, it is a good thing we're only almost-friends."

His hard, thin lips twitched again.

Alexandra shot a finger out. "You want to smile because you know ah-m right."

"That we're almost-friends?"

"That you shouldn't spoil my fun. Everyone is always trying to keep a lady from having fun." She spoke in between sips. "From what we weaaar, to the miserable pastimes they train us in since the nursery, fun is stripped." She made a slashing motion with her other hand that somehow sent ale sloshing over the side of the glass.

Alexandra frowned at the spirits staining the table. "That isssa shame," she lamented.

"You were saying?"

"I spilled my drink."

Dallin smiled. "I see that. What were you saying before that?"

Alexandra searched her sluggish mind. "I . . ."

Gus launched into a new song, this one a merry jig that brought his daughters to clapping their hands in time to the older man's playing.

Then she recalled. "Fun! It is denied us from the cradle, and we're left with nothing but. Sewing. Stitching. Singing."

"You have a problem with music?" he asked curiously.

"I dislike the songs ladies are expected to sing. And I was nahhh finished."

"My apologies," he said, inclining his head.

"Socializing," she added to her list. "Three *S*s. Henceforth, they should be called the three *S*s."

"I believe that was four," he murmured.

"Was it?"

Dallin nodded.

"Dallin!" she exclaimed, setting her nearly empty tankard down. Reaching across the table, she grabbed for his hand and tugged.

"What is it, Alexandra?"

"We will make a newww four. Oh, please. Do it with me."

Shoving back her chair, Alexandra hopped up, and gathering her skirts, she danced nearer the women gathered, stomping their feet.

Laughing, she shot a hand up. "Stomping!"

Gus drew nearer, his bow flying at a dizzying rate as he plucked those strains of the gay tune.

Holding Dallin's gaze, Alexandra made a quick turn. "Swirling!"

Alexandra looped each of her arms through those of Gus's nearest daughters.

"I want to dance, too," Rebecca called into the happy din of the song.

Gasping with laughter, Alexandra made to trade partners, but then Dallin was there.

He sketched a deep, sweeping bow. "My lady," he said solemnly to the little girl. "Would you do me the honor of partnering me in this set?"

Rebecca's big, guileless eyes grew, and she quickly placed her hand in Dallin's, allowing him to lead her through the improvised steps of the dance.

Her chest rising and falling from a breathlessness that had nothing to do with either her exertions or merriment, Alexandra slowed her steps. While Gus's elder two daughters danced off, Alexandra stared on at Dallin.

And through the merry haze left by liquor, the world shifted into greater clarity and focus as her gaze tunneled in on the unlikely pair.

Rebecca laughed and followed Dallin's lead.

The girl gazed up at him with adoring eyes, and bewitched herself, Alexandra rather knew the feeling.

She'd never known a gentleman could be this way, free and abandoned. Capable of not only seeing servants but also treating them as equals.

Her father had been doting, but neither had he been a man who'd have waltzed an innkeeper's small daughter about an empty taproom.

Over the top of the girl's head, Dallin caught Alexandra's eyes.

They shared a smile, and the whole world stopped, and Alexandra preferred it so. She wanted to remain trapped, frozen in this moment with him.

Gus's exuberant song came to a swift conclusion. Dropping to a knee, Dallin said something to the girl.

How effortlessly he spoke to the small girl. Would another man treat a child so? She'd never known such a man and wagered that, after Dallin, she never would. She had a glimpse of the father he'd be someday—one who played pirates with his daughters and had pretend sword fights. He'd be one who put his child atop his shoulders and . . . Envy snaked through Alexandra for the woman who'd one day have such a husband in Dallin.

She briefly closed her eyes, attempting to squeeze out the agony wrought by that realization. When she opened them, she found Dallin's stare upon her.

Alexandra forced a smile that she suddenly did not feel.

His gaze still on Alexandra, Dallin said something else to young Rebecca.

The girl gave a happy nod and rushed off.

Coming to his feet just as Gus launched into a slower, somber ballad, Dallin headed Alexandra's way. She followed his approach, appreciating the grace with which he moved.

When he reached Alexandra, he held a hand toward her. "I believe I owe you two sets, my lady."

Oh, God.

How was it possible for a heart to both break and swell?

A lump formed in her throat, making it impossible to speak. Words, however, weren't necessary.

Wordlessly, she placed her hand in Dallin's and let him lead her through their slowed-down version of a waltz that Gus now played.

How good it felt, being in his arms. How right it was to join her hand with his.

Then Dallin began to quietly sing.

Closing her eyes, she turned herself over to the seductive pull of his low, mellifluous baritone, slightly but endearingly off-key as he sang.

"We'll hear one, two, three, four, five, six
From the bells of Aberdovey."

And as Dallin whirled her into another slow, sweeping circle of the waltz, she let herself imagine they were somewhere else, in a different version of this moment she now had with him.

"Hear one, two, three, four, five, six
Hear one, two, three, four, five, and six"

In that fantasy they'd indulged on that winter's night long ago, he'd approach and sign his name to two waltzes.

"From the bells of Aberdovey.
Glad's a lad his lass to wed"

And she'd wait in breathless anticipation for each dance.

"When she sighed, 'I love you!'
When but today on air I tread"

They would have spoken of the stars, and she'd confess she looked but couldn't discover the answer to the question they'd pondered.

"For Gwen of Aberdovey.
While the heart beats in my breast"

She'd have asked what places he would soon travel to.

"Cariad, I will love thee."

Dallin would confess that he couldn't and wouldn't go because he did not wish to be parted from her.

"When we are married, you and I
At home in Aberdovey.
If to me as true thou art
As I am true to thee, sweetheart"

Not even the earlier spirits she'd indulged in could stop the cold that suddenly filled her.

For those dreams she allowed herself in this instant were just that—dreams.

This dance, in this empty inn, would be all she ever truly had of, and with, Dallin McQuoid. At least when she married the cold, heartless Marquess of Wingrave, Alexandra would have this memory with this man.

It would be enough.

It had to be.

Chapter 17

What are you doing? What are you thinking? Dancing with her like this?

With her eyes closed, Alexandra swayed to the rhythm of Gus's playing, and Dallin openly studied her graceful features, soft from the spirits she'd drunk and from the song they now danced to.

Only, if Dallin were being honest with himself, he knew the truth: he hadn't been thinking. When he'd asked her to dance, he'd been so swept up in the moment . . . with her . . . in them together . . . that he'd let himself forget the hurtful words she'd once uttered about his family and the fact she'd soon be married to another man.

He wanted to brush off the passion with which she'd spoken of her sister. He wanted to believe only that courage and devotion were just further proof of Alexandra's avaricious nature. He told himself her worry about losing the future title of duchess drove her.

Only, he'd be hard-pressed to name a single genteel young lady who'd have undertaken the journey Alexandra found herself on.

There is no one like her. There never would be.

Time and time again, she proved wholly different from that icy image, and very much like the woman he'd fallen more than a little in love with under the stars a year ago.

His hand at her trim waist tightened reflexively, and his fingers curled into her hips in a way some other man would grip her as they waltzed. As he would when he made love to her.

A visceral rage and jealousy snaked through his being, and Dallin jerked.

Alexandra tottered and stumbled over his feet.

Dallin quickly steadied them. He opened his mouth to put an end to this madness.

"This isss nice," she said dreamily.

"Yes," he murmured. Only, it was far more than nice. The feel of her in his arms and the sound of their laughter joined as one would be a memory he'd keep with him when he was an old man with a too-big paunch and a monocle at his eye.

And in that world they'd one day live, she'd grow old with grace, and in the arms of another.

Where prior that reality had riddled him with anger and resentment, now a malignant ache swallowed whole that place around his heart, and the very organ itself. Her impending marriage may have been easier to accept had she proven icy and self-important, so determined to stop her sister so she could herself ensure her future title of duchess.

But Alexandra wasn't those things.

She was a devoted, loving sibling, who'd brave any danger to rescue her younger sister. She'd bravely square off with a thief who wronged her. She'd treat an eccentric innkeeper and the man's daughters with kindness, speaking to them and dancing with them as if they were equals.

It was only because she was in her cups. He told himself as much. He repeated it in his head several times. Mayhap then he could actually believe it.

However, lying to himself didn't make any of those harsh thoughts of Alexandra's character true.

And it didn't erase the fact that he knew Alexandra in ways he'd never known any other woman, but Lord Wingrave would learn far more of her.

The notorious scoundrel would know the hue of her nipples and the sounds she made while making love.

Dallin's stomach muscles seized like he'd been feasting on poison. And mayhap he had for the agony wrought at the thought of her with another.

Do not think of her with Wingrave. Do not think of her walking the aisle of some distinguished church and approaching some other man and giving herself over to him.

Those silent reminders proved futile. Those insidious thoughts remained and ravaged Dallin.

Stop.

One day soon, the marquess would have a claim to Alexandra in all the ways Dallin wished to. But unlike the other man, Dallin had this precise moment with Alexandra, and not even her eventual marriage to Wingrave could take that away.

Embracing that truth, Dallin surrendered to his and Alexandra's waltz. As he twirled them about the room, Dallin committed to each additional moment spent.

They continued their waltz until Dallin registered that at some point the music had stopped and he and Alexandra moved only in the rhythm of one another's bodies.

He glanced to the old innkeeper. With his usual big smile, Gus held his fiddle aloft.

It was over—the dance. This moment. *Them.*

Alexandra brushed a fingertip over Dallin's mouth.

Her radiant smile vanished. "You're sad." Tears filled her eyes. "I hate it when you're sad."

"Only because the set has ended," he lied.

"I'm sad, too," she whispered.

That admission hit him square in the heart and gave him pause. "Why are you sad?" Because he'd fetch that star they'd once stood under the night sky studying to make her smile once more.

"Ohhh, los a reasons. But now I'm sad because I wannna be your friend," she slurred as she clung to him. "Nah your almost-friend."

"We are friends."

"You don't like me."

He grunted. "That isn't true."

"You *like* me, then?" She batted her exquisitely long lashes.

"Alexandra," he said pleadingly, doing a sweep of the empty tavern. "Come." He needed to escape her and this moment and the thoughts of what would never be.

"You're annoyed with me," Alexandra said as he tugged her along. "Wasmy dancing?"

He grunted again. "You dance just fine." She possessed the grace of all three of the Kharites.

"But you are annoyed with—"

"I'm not annoyed with you." He was only annoyed with himself for this unbreakable captivation with a woman he could never have.

"I *always* annoy you."

"Alexandra, you do *not* annoy me," he said gruffly.

Her eyes went all soft. "Oh. Do you knowww, Dallin. I do believe my list of Ss is complete," she declared, and then promptly fell against his side.

Dallin caught Alexandra to him, and then wrapping an arm around her waist to steady her, he proceeded to guide her abovestairs, trying not to think of the feel of her body against his. Or of the hint of lavender that clung to her skin.

"Your list is short," he said in a desperate bid to distract himself from thoughts he oughtn't be having, particularly given the state Alexandra found herself in.

She ground her feet to an unsteady halt, stopping Dallin at her side. "Howw dare you insult my list. Mah list is very tall."

"There were only two Ss upon it," he pointed out.

Four adorable lines creased her brow. "Was there?"

Dallin nodded.

"I'm sure there was more."

"There wasn't."

"Oh, dear," she said, and they resumed their walk. "We musss correct that. Muss thing. Muss thing."

Despite himself, Dallin smiled.

They reached the top of the landing.

Her eyes lit. "I've it."

"Well?"

Alexandra drew her shoulders back and, like a courier making a declaration on behalf of the king, said, "Singing."

"I thought 'singing' was one of the bad *S*s."

"That was before *theeese* songs, silly. Henceforth, singing shall be on the good list, as long as it is the *good* song."

"So it is written, so it is done."

"It isn written."

"So it is spoken, so it is done?"

She smiled. "Better."

Alexandra swayed.

Silently cursing, Dallin caught her.

She climbed her arms about his neck and kept herself upright against him so that the only things separating every last soft curve of her body from his were the thin layers of garments they wore.

His body betrayed him as a gentleman, and he hardened.

Groaning, Dallin angled himself away and resumed the agonizingly slow march to her rooms.

Alexandra blinked big, guileless eyes. "What isit?"

Oh, nothing. Just me ensuring my entry into hell someday. "You're still short an *S*."

At last, they reached Alexandra's door, and he reached for the handle . . . and redemption.

Alexandra slid herself between Dallin and the oak panel. "Uh-uh." With her hands clasped behind her, she rested her back against the door. "You canna leave until we finish our list."

"Isn't it *your* list?" he reminded, his ragged voice pleading, even to his own ears.

"Ours now."

Ours.

Funny, that. Dallin had never previously considered how a single word could so powerfully join two people.

"Sleeping," he volunteered. "Sleeping is your fourth *S*." He reached for the handle.

She shifted, blocking his attempts a second time. "Sleeping isn fun."

"Skipping?" he suggested.

Alexandra caught her lower lip in her teeth and troubled that flesh, and in an instant, Dallin recalled the taste of that plump, crimson skin. The feel of Alexandra in his arms.

"I'm afraid that isn fun *enough*."

Of course it isn't. The Lord was determined to test him this night.

"Sailing?" he managed to croak out.

"Ahm sure that is enjoyable, but I've never been. But you will, and then I'll be all alone."

Her mouth trembled.

"No, you won't," he couldn't keep from reminding both Alexandra and himself. "You'll have—"

Anger tightened her flushed features, and she slapped a finger against his lips. "Hush. Don speak of him and ruin the fun we're having."

"But, Alexandra," he said quietly, even as he knew in her inebriated state she'd not be reasoned with. "You will marry—"

"Don say his name, Dallin," she pleaded. "Please."

Dallin heard something in her voice, and he moved his gaze over her strained features. "Why?" he asked quietly.

"It'll ruin this." A study of contemplativeness, Alexandra tapped her chin, and then stopped. A radiant smile wreathed her lips. "I've it."

"Yes?" he prodded, desperate for this night to end, even as he wanted his time with her to go on forever.

"Smooch."

Oh, hell.

Dallin pressed his eyes closed.

"Dallin?" Alexandra tugged at his lapels. "Do you know tha word?"

He did. Lord help him, he did.

Giggling, Alexandra stretched up and made to touch her mouth to his.

Dallin turned his head, and her kiss landed noisily on his cheek.

Fumbling with the handle, Alexandra brought them stumbling backward into her room. With a laugh, she kicked a leg around Dallin and shoved the panel shut with the sole of her boot.

"Alexandra, you need to rest," he begged.

She pouted. "But sleeping isn one of the fun *S*s," she reminded him. "Smooching is."

And this time, she stretched up, cupped his face in her hands, and kissed him. The feel of her lush lips soft under his teased him. Tested him. Taunted him with everything that would never be. Her curves were supple and soft against him. She was a veritable Eve dangling that succulent fruit destined to bring about his fall, and Dallin was only too happy, devouring that forbidden offering.

In further proof he was being tested, Alexandra whispered against his mouth, "I love kissing you, Dalllin."

I love it, too. I love it so much.

Dallin groaned. His hands came up reflexively and he caught her hips, pressing his fingers into that flesh; his body, which hungered to explore all of her, waged a battle with his honor as a gentleman.

Think of something, anything other than how bloody good she feels and how much you want to divest her of her gown and show her all the wonderful ways it could be between us.

She belongs to another. She belongs to Lord Wingrave. She can never be yours.

That stone-cold reminder proved sobering, vanquishing Dallin's ardor.

"Dallin?" Alexandra whispered against his mouth.

"We can't, Alexandra," he said quietly.

"Of course we can. We are. Or were. Won't you kiss me, *please*? I really quite love it."

"I can't, Alexandra," he said quietly. Not like this. Not in any way, really. "You've been drinking. It wouldn't be right." It wouldn't be right for a whole host of reasons.

Confusion replaced desire in her red-rimmed eyes. "But I want it."

Oh, God.

Dallin squeezed his eyes tightly shut and prayed to the Lord overhead for strength.

Alexandra tugged his sleeve. "I want you to kiss me."

"Alexandra, I cannot."

"Then I can kiss you."

As if to illustrate that very point, she leaned up and into him.

With a strength that came from he knew not where, Dallin managed to turn his head to avoid that which he hungered for.

"Wingrave." That other man's name emerged strangled and harsh from his own lips.

Alexandra wrinkled her nose. "I don't want to kiss him."

Dallin's heart lifted. She didn't want Wingrave. As soon as the organ took flight, an invisible needle punctured it, dashing that embarrassingly jubilant thought and sensation.

She may not want the man's kiss, but she wanted his eventual title and connections. More than she wanted anything else. And in marrying

Wingrave, she'd give that other gentleman the right to both kiss her . . . and more.

Alexandra smoothed her palms over the front of his jacket, and Dallin's muscles jumped under her light caress. "I can kiss you," she suggested again, and leaned up and into him.

"No, Alexandra," he said more sharply than he intended.

A fresh wave of hurt wreathed her features, hitting him like a blow to the belly. The last thing he wanted was to bring her pain. He lo—

He blanched, his mind recoiling from the remainder of that unfinished thought in his head that he'd let stay unfinished because it wasn't true. Because he couldn't let himself even contemplate that it might be or was. Or—

"Wass it?" she whispered.

"It is late," he said, this time more gently. "I'll see one of Gus's daughters returns to help you."

"But I want—"

Then like a coward, before she could protest, he bolted and continued running.

He returned a short while later. Rebecca opened the door, but before she disappeared inside, Dallin caught one more glimpse of Alexandra standing there, her fingers pressed against her mouth.

He pressed his eyes closed to blot out the sight. His efforts proved in vain.

Alexandra said that the mention of Wingrave, the man who, upon her return, she'd marry, would ruin "this."

What was "this," exactly? An all-too-brief and memorable moment between almost-friends, as she'd called them? Only, he knew the truth. This escapade, from their journey to this intimate moment at an empty inn, would remain with him forever.

The irony was not lost on him. He'd spent his life longing to know the excitement that came in exploring the world, only to discover that thrill wasn't a place, but rather a person.

Chapter 18

Over the years, Alexandra had been so very certain her mother and the world on the whole enacted rules of propriety with the express and sole purpose of controlling women. She'd secretly suspected all the strictures were nothing more than arbitrary directives meant to strip ladies of their autonomy, and she'd never not believe there was truth in that postulation.

But several hours later, with an incessant throbbing in her head, she acknowledged there were at the very least justifiable reasons for women to avoid spirits.

Or mayhap it wasn't really that at all. With the way men drank spirits and the women didn't, mayhap it was really just that ladies had sorted out long ago that libations were bad news and had the sense to avoid them.

Alexandra rolled onto her side, and her stomach pitched. Nausea roiled in her belly, and she . . .

She was dying.

Wait, that thumping wasn't in her head.

It was . . . the door.

Alexandra groaned, and her skull split apart another fraction.

Then it all came rushing back to her—first the volatile tension between Dallin and her . . . followed by the unfettered joy in dancing around the empty tavern. He with a small, adoring girl, and then with Alexandra.

The kiss.

She stilled. Her heart thumped in time to that incessant beating in her head as she tried to pull together memories shrouded in darkness from too much drink.

The kiss. Their lips had met, and she'd tasted of him as he'd drunk of her.

Only . . .

"I want you to kiss me . . ."

"Alexandra, I cannot."

"Then I can kiss you."

And she *had*.

Those murky memories shifted into clearer, crisper focus: of Alexandra curling her fingers into the loose lapels of his jacket. Of her dragging him closer. Of her leaning up and pressing her mouth to his. His groan of disgust before he'd pulled away.

Alexandra squeezed her eyes shut more tightly and welcomed the briefly distracting pain that clenching of her face wrought. Anything to distract her from the humiliation of having kissed Dallin—against his will, at that—and his subsequent rejection.

Oh, God. She wanted to die, and the misery of shame and humiliation was so acute she thought she just might. And that might be preferable to facing him today.

Alexandra groaned, that low rumble wreaking further havoc on her skull.

She'd thrown herself at a man. Not just any man—*Dallin*.

How could she have behaved so wantonly?

And worse? She'd behaved so while engaged to another gentleman. Granted, that same *gentleman* had been abundantly clear about his absolute indifference toward Alexandra. The papers endlessly reported on the string of mistresses he kept at any given time. And in no uncertain terms had he given the illusion they'd have anything more than a formal arrangement, one that would not impugn on his lifestyle.

Were it not for the double standard that came all too easily for society, by that logic, Alexandra should be free to conduct herself as she would, regardless of when she married the marquess.

That, however, didn't mean she'd proven herself dishonorable . . . and where she could muster the strength to say to hell with it, she did care very much what Dallin thought of her.

Alexandra groaned.

Never again would she overindulge. Never, ever, ever.

Alas, the proverbial damage to her pride had already been done.

Do you truly care more about doing the right thing by society's standards? Or about breaking free of those chains that bound her, so she might have whatever she could with Dallin?

Dallin, who'd also rejected her.

She groaned again.

Tap Tap Tap Tap.

She whipped her gaze over to the door, and promptly pressed a hand against her head to steady the spinning world around her.

Oh, hell. She'd overslept.

"Alexandra?"

"Coming," she called back, and then instantly regretted speaking in anything more than a whisper.

Tamping down a groan of misery, Alexandra clamped her hands on either side of her face. Swinging her legs over the side of the bed, she surged to her feet. Ignoring the way her stomach dipped precariously at that sudden movement, she raced across the room.

Resting a palm on the side of the door, she caught the handle in her other palm and opened the panel a fraction.

"Good morning," she blurted, her voice raspy and lower than usual.

Though "Miserable Morning" far better suited her condition.

Dallin frowned. "Are you all right?" he asked gently.

Only, this time that downward tilt of his lips wasn't of disapproval or disdain . . . but rather, worry, and the evidence of his concern left her warm in ways she didn't want it to.

Because Angry-Dallin-Who-Despised-Her would be far easier to let go than Gentle-Tender Dallin.

"Alexandra," he repeated. The concern in his voice threatened to undo her.

"Fine," she said quickly, too quickly, and immediately regretted that haste. She groaned. "I'm sorry for having overslept. We'll be late—"

"We're not, and the weather will have slowed them down as well," he hurried to assure her.

Unable to meet his eyes lest she see the disgust that certainly twined with the pity in those brown irises, Alexandra directed her next words to the slight knob of his Adam's apple. "That is reassuring." She cleared her throat. "I'll be along shortly."

She made to close the door.

"You didn't oversleep."

His words stopped her.

"I didn't." She puzzled her brow, and even that slight tightening of her facial muscles wrought havoc on her head.

"I suspected you would be feeling a bit under the weather."

Under the weather?

"It's sailor speak," he explained. "A clever phrase handed me by my brother, the sea captain. When the crew fell ill during the storm, they'd retreat belowdecks to recover—hence 'under the weather.' Clever in its simplicity, is it not?"

Alexandra managed nothing more than a blank stare for him.

"May I come in?"

She stilled. He'd asked to enter her rooms. Her hesitation came not in the wickedness of allowing a gentleman to step inside the place where she slept, but because this was the place where she'd kissed—

"Alexandra?" The slight uptilt in his soothing baritone transformed her name into a question.

Wordlessly, she drew the panel wider and stepped aside, allowing him to enter.

A glass in hand, Dallin hurried inside the room.

Alexandra closed the panel behind them. Her heart thumped madly at the thrill of being alone with him. Tongue-tied in a way she'd never been around him, Alexandra struggled to find words.

They both found them, at the same time.

"You're certain I—"

"I brought—"

Alexandra and Dallin both ceased speaking.

He motioned for her to go first.

"You're certain I did not oversleep?" she asked, glancing over at the dark sky outside.

"You didn't," he assured her. "I suspected after last evening, you might have need of a dram. This is an old Scot's cure, sure to ease your splitting skull and churning stomach."

He held out a small glass filled with murky water.

She eyed it dubiously. "Are you certain you're not attempting to poison me?"

"I was going to save the poisoning for the next leg of our journey." A teasing glimmer danced in his eyes.

Alexandra hesitated, then accepted the drink. Her fingertips kissed his, in an accidental meeting that harkened back to the shadowy memories that remained of their embrace.

Her hands shook, sending several droplets tumbling over the edge. In a bid to steady her palms, Alexandra tightened her grip upon the glass.

Eyeing the thick, dubious contents, Alexandra experimentally sniffed at Dallin's offering.

"It doesn't smell horrendous," he said. "It just looks so."

"The not-poison drink."

"It's a heated mix of corn flour and buttermilk, topped with salt and pepper."

She gagged.

Dallin laughed. "I assure you, it isn't half as awful as it sounds."

Alexandra scowled. "I'm so happy one of us finds humor in this."

And yet, as horrendous as it looked and sounded, he claimed it healed headaches and eradicated nausea induced by overindulging, and she was so desperate for relief that she'd have downed a jug of the stuff if it meant feeling even half-human again.

Alexandra took a sip and promptly gagged again.

Dallin laughed, but when she shot another glare his way, he had the good grace to cover his merriment with a cough that he buried in his fist.

"If I may make a recommendation."

"Another one? Is it half as good as this one?" she said drolly.

"It works better if you guzzle it."

"Guzzle it," she echoed.

"Like glug, glug, gl—"

"I know what it means to *guzzle* something. What I *don't* know is how you expect me to down this." Alexandra hefted her glass up.

"As I said, the best course is to close your eyes and do it quickly."

As advised, she closed and then promptly opened them. "You'd best not be making light of me, Dallin McQuoid."

"I'd never," he murmured in suitably solemn tones, and he marked an X at his heart.

Alexandra pressed her eyes shut.

"That is"—her eyes went flying open—"I'd never do it when you're in this state," he said playfully.

And this side of him, a man who was so easy to speak to, renewed her impossible dreams for a future with him.

"Glug, glug, glug," Dallin repeated.

"All right, all right," she muttered.

Alexandra looked at the drink Dallin was determined to poison her with, and then closing her eyes, she downed the nauseating mixture.

"Keep drinking," he said, encouraging her along.

As she finished, Alexandra glared at him over the top of her tankard. When she'd drunk the last drop, she dusted the back of her hand across her mouth. "H-"—*hiccup*—"happy?"

"Immensely so."

"Of course you are," she said archly, and set the empty glass down.

"How do you feel?"

"I . . ." Alexandra stopped. Actually, interestingly, strangely, she felt leaps and bounds better than she had upon waking up.

Dallin smiled a smug smile. "I thought so."

"Oh, hush," she chided, giving him a playful swat on the shoulder. Only, the moment her bare fingertips touched his sleeve, she froze; her fingers remained on Dallin in a possessive hold.

"Alexandra?" he asked, his voice strained.

Because just as he abhors you, he is repulsed by your touch.

Alexandra made herself release him. "I wish to apologize for my behavior last evening," she began, directing that apology down to the floor she desperately wished would open up and kindly swallow her whole. "My behavior last night was—"

"You needn't apologize," he said on a rush, even as he cast a glance over at the stairs with the speedy look of a man desperate to be out of her company.

That further evidence of his rejection hurt her to her core.

"Alexandra, we must be on our way. What happened last night? You needn't feel badly for. It was merely the spirits and nothing more."

"Yes," she said woodenly. "It was only the drink."

Surely, he heard the lie in her mortifyingly weak concurrence. If he did—which he surely did—he was, of course, too much a gentleman to say.

"I'll allow you to . . . see to your morning ablutions." And with that, he quit the rooms.

A short while later, after Alexandra had changed and seen to her hair, she opened the door to her rooms and found Dallin waiting, as he'd promised. Without a word, he gathered up her now packed valise, and without so much as glancing back to see if she followed, he started for the stairs.

She'd be grateful to put this place behind them. Then she could forget about the utter fool she'd made of herself and their entire time here.

They reached the bottom of the stairs.

Gus and his daughters stood in wait alongside the front door, each member of that big family smiling.

And as Dallin handed over a hefty purse and expressed their thanks, Alexandra's gaze drifted over the still quiet inn. With the exception of a lone patron at a table near the hearth, the room remained empty but for the crackle of the cozy fire.

She closed her eyes and saw them as they'd been last evening.

"When we are married, you and I
At home in Aberdovey."

She heard the sound of Dallin's voice as he'd sung.

"If to me as true thou art
As I am true to thee, sweetheart
We'll hear one, two, three, four, five, six
From the bells of Aberdovey.
Alexandra . . ."

In her mind, the only alteration of those lyrics came in the addition of his low, husky voice speaking her name, making the joyful folk song specific to her . . . and them.

Alexandra . . .

"Alexandra?"

Alexandra came whirring back to the present. She blinked wildly. Dallin stared concernedly back.

He'd actually been speaking her name. She, however, had been so lost in the memory of last night she'd failed to hear him.

Alexandra cleared her throat and looked to Gus and his daughters. "I cannot thank each of you enough for the finest night." Stepping forward, she took the older man's big hands in her own smaller ones. "Your inn is a most special place, and I will . . ." Emotion wadded in her throat, and she gave his hands a light squeeze. "I will treasure the time spent here," she said thickly.

The big fellow managed to grow several inches more under that praise. "An honor it's been, serving you. An absolute honor."

Making their goodbyes, Alexandra and Dallin quit the inn, leaving behind only the whisper of the memory of them as they'd been last night.

Chapter 19

The sun shone again, reclaiming its rightful place in the sky.

Unlike the previous three days of travel, which had been rife with rainstorms, highwaymen, and unsafe roads, there wasn't a single incident to slow Dallin and Alexandra's pursuit. Dallin rode alongside the carriage bearing Alexandra, and this time, unlike yesterday, there was no reason for him to join her in that conveyance.

From the moment day broke, they continued at a quick, steady clip until the sun traded its place in the sky with an enormous full moon that illuminated the old Roman road, lighting the way.

Yes, unlike every previous travel day, everything had gone perfectly.

And as they arrived at the last inn before their final destination the next morning, Dallin couldn't be more miserable for it.

Dismounting outside The George, Dallin studied the medieval inn. With its courtyard constructed about the original stone gateways, the establishment may as well have transported its patrons back centuries ago.

I don't want to go back hundreds of years. Just days would do.

Dallin stared sightlessly at the bustling courtyard.

Just days, so that Alexandra and I are at the beginning of our journey and not nearing the end of it and our time together, and her marriage to Wingrave.

"My lord? *My lord?*"

Dumbly, Dallin looked over to Otis. The young servant stared concernedly at him.

"May I?" the footman asked hesitantly, and stretched a hand out.

Dallin followed Otis's gaze over to the tired horse, whose reins he still held.

Handing Pegasus's reins to Otis, Dallin looked past the footman to where Alexandra stood. Her expressive eyes glinted with a question and concern.

A dutiful Otis had already handed Alexandra down.

So Dallin wasn't even to be granted that fleeting moment of taking her palm in his to help her from the carriage.

You are a pathetic, foolish man.

Silently berating himself, however, didn't help. It didn't erase the regret or yearning for things to be different from how they were.

Dallin picked up her valise, filling that empty hand with something of hers. Wordlessly, he stretched out an elbow, and as if it were the most natural thing in the world to link their arms, Alexandra was instantly at his side.

She paused only long enough to bring her hood higher into place, then laid her fingertips upon his sleeve.

Dallin and Alexandra started down the paved stone path that led them to the last place they'd stop before they arrived at their destination tomorrow morn.

From the moment they'd met, words had always come easily between them. In this moment, making the trek at her side under those ancient arches and through the courtyard, Dallin discovered silence came with a like ease.

Neither Dallin nor Alexandra felt compelled to fill a void. When together, they were just as comfortable with the quiet.

This was what he'd wanted in a wife. Someone whom it felt so very good and easy to be with. Only, he'd not given prior thought to whom or what he wished for when it came to marrying. He'd been so focused on the idea of traveling like his younger brother did. Only to discover too late it wasn't a place he longed to explore, but rather a woman—a certain woman, *this* woman, who remained forever beyond his reach.

His chest muscles seized painfully.

The moment they reached the front, Dallin drew the carved wooden door open. A deafening swell of sounds rolled outside—voices raised and music played into one great big chaotic din.

As Alexandra entered, Dallin followed behind her and took in the crowded taproom.

Unlike their previous night spent at Gus's quiet, empty inn, The George offered only noise, and once a person surrendered their spot at the entryway of the establishment, it spared hardly a space with which to move.

A tall, slender innkeeper with a scowl etched in his sharp, pointy features appeared. He gave their garments a swift up-and-down look.

"What do ye need, my lord?" the aloof fellow asked by way of greeting in a deep, booming voice that managed to rise above the noise.

Cold and brusque, even the proprietor revealed himself to be the opposite of the last innkeeper.

"I was wondering if you can tell me whether a couple has passed through. A husband and wife. The lady is several inches over five feet. Has blonde hair and—"

"Big brown eyes," Alexandra jumped in.

"And the gentleman," Dallin added, "is near my height and of similar coloring."

The innkeeper gave them an annoyed look. "Got a lot of guests here who look like that."

Dallin fished a coin out and gave it over. "Perhaps this might help you remember a bit more clearly."

The innkeeper pocketed that money. "A fancy couple like you? Dressed fine?"

Dallin and Alexandra nodded.

"They would be," Alexandra added quickly.

"Were they traveling with anyone? Servants? Family?"

"They would have been alone," Dallin answered.

"Ain't got any lords and ladies without servants and family." The greasy-haired proprietor promptly killed the very real hope that they'd managed to reach their loved ones. "Can I do anything for you, my lord?"

Dallin should only be frantic and frustrated at learning the journey to reach Brone continued. Yet there was also a lightness inside him at the idea of his having more time with the woman beside him.

Feeling Alexandra's questioning gaze on him, he gave his head a clearing shake. "Two rooms, if you would, please," he requested.

"'fraid I can't. Inn's full, it is." The proprietor gestured needlessly to the crowded space around them. "Only able to offer one."

The older fellow took a step closer, leaned in, and cupped a hand around his mouth. "For the right amount, I might be able to displace another patron," he said with a waggle of his brows.

"That will not be necessary."

Dallin and the innkeeper looked over at Alexandra.

"My husband and I will make do with just the one," she said coolly.

The fellow grunted, then jerked his chin. "This way," he said with none of the warmth or hospitality all the previous innkeepers had shown them.

The hell they would, he silently mused as he and Alexandra followed the proprietor abovestairs. Dallin couldn't spend a night alone with her, in a room, with just one bed.

Only, wicked thoughts supplanted those gentlemanly intentions as his mind conjured images of that lone room with its one bed . . . and Dallin and Alexandra twined together—

Lust bolted through him.

Hell. I'm going to hell.

Alas, the road to hell is paved with good resolutions.

The innkeeper stopped at the first door, immediately adjacent to the cold stone stairwell. "Only got this one," he said. "On account of it being nearer the noise."

As if to illustrate that very point, a rowdy swell of laughter rolled like a wave through the establishment and climbed the stairs, flooding the hall.

Their latest host wagged his brows and, cupping a hand around thin lips, leaned in. "For the right price, I can move another patron out of their finer rooms and put them h—"

Alexandra cut him off. "That will also be unnecessary. We'd not displace another patron for our own comforts," she said, tugging off her gloves, and like the queen she was, Alexandra swept past the avaricious proprietor, effectively ending all further attempts at bilking them of their coin.

As she did a turn about the small, surprisingly clean and cozy room, Dallin's gaze was inexplicably drawn to her.

"If you'd be so good as to have a meal brought up and a bath."

"It'll cost ye—"

"That will be fine," Dallin interrupted. "And if you'd be so good as to send a serving girl to help Her Ladyship."

"It'll cost y—"

"That will be fine."

"More than usual. On account of how busy it be," the old man added.

Silently cursing, Dallin reached inside his jacket and drew out a heavy sack of coins. "I trust this will be sufficient to see Her Ladyship well cared for this evening," he said coolly.

The proprietor shot greedy fingers out, and with his long neck, small head, and beady eyes rabidly devouring the contents within, he had the fitting look of a weasel to him.

"This will do," the man said, stuffing the purse inside his jacket.

More amiable now that the offering had been made, he dropped a deep, extravagant bow and then backed out of the room, closing the door behind him—leaving Dallin and Alexandra alone.

They stood there alone.

And he'd been wrong. Not all silence between them was comfortable and easy. This moment stood testament to that truth. For being alone here, in this bedroom, with that surprisingly clean and well-made bed, conjured more of those desirous thoughts of him and her *in* that bed. Their mouths meeting as they'd recently done in a kiss that was seared in his mind, destined to ruin him for every other woman after her.

They found their voices at the same time. "Thank—"

"The room . . ."

Dallin gestured for her to continue.

"I merely wished to say thank you for your generosity," she murmured.

He grunted. "It is nothing."

Alexandra took a step toward him. "Not to *me*." She took another step and another, and Dallin found himself reflexively retreating.

His back collided with the door panel, barring him from any further escape.

Alexandra stopped just a pace apart from him. "I know you did not wish to bring me along," she said softly, and then rested her palms along the front of his dusty jacket.

He swallowed hard.

Or tried to.

Alexandra stroked her fingers in an entrancing way over his chest. The Devil taunted him, tormented him.

Then there were small mercies, after all. She ceased that intoxicating, distracted touch.

Very, very small mercies, as she left her palms there, resting against him.

"I will be forever grateful to you for all you've done for me these past days, Dallin."

Forever grateful.

She spoke of forever; her forever, however, belonged to another man. And there wasn't a more sobering thought than that one.

"Lock the door when I leave," he said tightly. "I'll wait outside until your bath is prepared."

Those proved the wrong words to speak. A mental image slipped in: of Alexandra, completely naked and dipping a toe into those hot waters. Of Alexandra with a red flush from the heat of that bath spreading over her bare skin.

"You don't have to leave."

He choked.

"Not yet," Alexandra clarified, a pretty blush filling her cheeks. "You can stay—"

"I cannot stay here, Alexandra," he said sharply. "This isn't the first night where we happened to stumble upon one another. Or last evening, where we stayed at an empty inn. We are in an establishment filled to the brim with guests, and the possibility of us being discovered grows exponentially, and I'll not risk being seen with you."

Confusion filled her gorgeous blue-green eyes. Nay, confusion and hurt. "I see."

No, she didn't.

Discovery would mean the end of her betrothal with Wingrave. And even as he yearned for the dissolution of that arrangement, Dallin wouldn't be the one who wrought the end of a union she was so very desperate for.

He gave his head a nod and turned to go.

With his fingertips a mere moment away from pressing the handle, Alexandra stayed him with her next words.

"I don't want to be alone, Dallin," she whispered.

Oh, God.

For he'd have an easier time gnawing off a limb than denying her anything she asked for in that heartbreakingly small way.

He closed his eyes and prayed. He prayed for patience. He prayed for resolve. He prayed for his honor.

"Alexandra," he said, his voice hoarse. "No harm will befall you. I will sleep outside your door to ensure as much."

"I'm not afraid."

Then, why? Why could she possibly want him to stay with her, in this way?

He knew what he wanted the answer to be. Just as he knew it was madness, wishing for the answer he sought. She wasn't for him.

She touched a hand to his shoulder.

Dallin briefly closed his eyes, then turned, faced her, and dislodged her touch. The feel of her fingers on him, however, lingered still.

"Alexandra, it isn't a good idea."

"I can sleep on the floor," she said on a rush. "No one will know."

"*I'll* know." He'd know she was right there, in nothing but a nightshift, with no walls between them and but one bed in the room.

Alexandra stared down at her hands. "I don't want to be alone," she confessed.

Dallin's sharing a journey—and now a room—with this woman put Brone and his sisters, and Dallin's youngest sister, at risk of earning the Duke of Talbert's wrath. The duke, with his hatred of the McQuoids, would see Brone's business ventures quashed and do his best to ensure most unmarried lords wouldn't so much as think of marrying the McQuoid women.

So why can I not deny Alexandra's request? Why, in this instant, when I should only be thinking of the future and my family, can I not put them first and force this woman from my mind?

Because I am lost . . . and fear I'll never find my way back to reason . . .

Dallin cursed roundly. "Fine," he clipped out in harsh tones.

Her face instantly brightened, and based on the beatific smile that wreathed her features, one would never know he'd spoken to her so coldly.

"Thank—"

"And you are not sleeping on the floor," he interrupted, putting an end to that ridiculous thought.

She went silent and just stared up at him with the biggest, bluest eyes he'd ever seen. Those eyes he couldn't resist. Though in fairness, in truth, he could deny this woman nothing.

"I will sleep on the floor. Over there." He pointed to the farthest corner. As far as he could get from her.

"Of course," she said quickly.

"This time, given the size of the crowd, you'll need to take a tray in your rooms. I'll remain downstairs while you eat and return after you sleep."

Her gaze grew stricken. As if she were devastated at the idea of him leaving her. Why?

He slid his gaze over her face. She did a like search of his own.

The air around them shifted, growing thick and heavy, pulsing with a palpable energy that hinted of want and desire.

Or mayhap that is what I want to see . . . because I want her so desperately. She, on the other hand . . .

Alexandra's lashes fluttered, and she tipped her face up.

He dipped his head a fraction, and then closing his eyes, he was lost—

KnockKnockKnock.

That efficient rapping sounded on the door, breaking the momentary madness.

He and Alexandra drew back abruptly.

"Good night," Dallin said quickly, and hurrying out into the hall, he stood in wait while a pair of burly servants hefted the bathtub inside.

Dallin remained while pail after steaming pail of water was carried in and dumped into the wooden bath, and only when one smaller girl remained behind to help Alexandra and the door had closed and the lock had turned did Dallin leave.

He made his escape below, finding one of two still empty tables. Helping himself to a seat, he stared sightlessly out at the crowded room.

She wanted him to sleep in the same room with her. She wanted him close. Why? For what reason, when her affections belonged to another?

That memory of her, when she'd been cup-shot and drink had left her careless and free with her words, slipped in.

I don't want to kiss him . . .

Dallin frowned.

Why would she say as much about Wingrave?

Because it's further proof that what she wants above all else is the title of duchess. Because Wingrave wasn't there, and Dallin was, and any man would have done in that instant.

It could have been any number of things. None of which meant Alexandra cared in any real way about Dallin.

Grimacing, he shook his head hard.

"My lord?"

Lost as he'd been in his own thoughts, he looked up.

A pretty serving girl with a big bosom and inviting smile instantly appeared. "Care for a drink, my lord?" She leaned forward, putting her bounteous breasts on full display. "And . . . mayhap something more?" She purred that invitation.

Any man would have salivated at the mere sight of that generous flesh spilling over the bodice of the low-cut dress; the woman's neckline plunged deep enough to reveal the tips of her nipples. Any other time before, he would have welcomed the sight . . . and what the beauty clearly offered.

His body remained unmoved.

The woman abovestairs had ruined him completely.

"Just ale," he said.

The woman pouted but poured a tankard and sauntered off, on to the next patron.

As Alexandra would be on to another man.

His entire body recoiled, and tension shot through him, leaving every muscle in his being tense and taut.

Do not think about it. Do not think about her with Wingrave.

Dallin stared into the contents, swirling the amber brew in a slow, smooth circle.

Think about her marrying for wealth and power.

Because the alternative—that she actually cared about Wingrave— left Dallin with an acrid, burnt taste on his tongue.

Tiredly, he dusted a hand over his face.

Dallin remained seated at his table, nursing the same drink until the merry music wound down and patron after patron trickled from the room.

His skin prickled with the sensation of being watched. Stiffening, Dallin glanced up.

The tall, gaunt innkeeper stared back. "Ye need something, my lord?"

Some of the tension went out of Dallin, and he looked around.

At some point, all the guests but for him had quit the taproom and made their way to either their rooms or cottages.

"No," he said, pushing his chair back. "Thank you for your hospitality." And most importantly, the brief escape from being alone with Alexandra in that room.

Handing the greedy innkeeper several coins more, Dallin headed abovestairs.

At least she'd be sleeping. At least he'd be spared from talking to her and learning more about this woman who would never be his.

He entered the dark room, closing the door and locking it behind him . . . and stopped.

What the hell?

Wide awake, her eyes pointed up at the ceiling, Alexandra lay on the bed with her arms folded on her flat belly. Only, it wasn't a bed by the way that beds went. At some point, she'd dragged the mattress into the corner—the corner he'd indicated would be his—and now rested on the ropes that formed a makeshift hammock.

"Dallin!" She turned her head, and nearly upset her precarious bedding in the process.

With a curse, Dallin strode across the room and steadied the swinging ropes. "What in hell do you think you are doing!" he fumed.

"Sleeping." She wrinkled her classically Grecian nose. "Or I've been trying to. I cannot sleep." She whispered that confession as if it were some grand secret she shared.

He snorted. "Because you're resting on damned ropes."

"That isn't why," she said. "Though I'm sure it isn't helping."

Dallin scooped her up, then promptly regretted not having thought through that action.

With only the thin slip of her nightshift between them, he felt every lush curve of her body. Possessed of a trim waist, she was also gloriously curved in all the places a woman should be.

Groaning, he set her down quickly and leapt back a step.

"You're mad at me," she incorrectly surmised.

She stared at him with hurt eyes.

I'm furious with myself for wanting what can never be. For wanting her, despite the fact she'd soon belong to another man.

It was too much.

Cursing, Dallin stormed across the room and hefted the surprisingly heavy mattress up from its place on the floor.

"You shouldn't have made a servant move this," he railed at her. Only, dressing her down didn't make him feel any better. It made him feel like the worst sort of bully.

"I didn't. I moved it myself."

Dignified, high-born Alexandra Bradbury had carried the heavy mattress herself. All so that Dallin could have it for himself.

He tossed the feather article down on those ropes she'd previously made her makeshift bed, and then made a quick dash for the corner.

Lying on the floor, Dallin rolled onto his side; giving her his back, he stared at the wall.

Time and time again, at every turn, she proved herself to be none of the things he desperately wished her to be. For if she were, in fact, nothing more than a rapacious miss, it would be altogether easier to let her go tomorrow morn.

Chapter 20

He hated her.

Climbing back onto the mattress, she stared at Dallin.

He lay there, tense and angry and staring at the wall, because he'd rather look anywhere else than in Alexandra's direction.

He despised her that much.

It was for the best. Tomorrow she'd retrieve her sister. They'd retrieve their family carriage and make the remainder of the journey back from Scotland. In less than a month's time, Alexandra would exchange vows with the Marquess of Wingrave. At which point her fate, her future, and her very happiness would be irrevocably linked to a cold, unfeeling man who'd not even deigned to meet her on the day the formal betrothal papers were signed.

There'd come a time in the not-so-distant future when a miserably married Alexandra would read about a certain Viscount C, set to marry some lucky woman who wasn't her.

And that lady wouldn't be one Dallin despised as he did Alexandra. It would be some woman whom he couldn't imagine his life without. A woman with whom he'd share the stories of the stars and journey to the places he longed to travel.

I want that. I want all that.

Another woman who wasn't Alexandra would discover the beauty of Dallin's embrace. He'd kiss another . . . and more . . . and wouldn't be repulsed, as Alexandra made him.

Jealousy, red and hot and throbbing, spread like a poisonous cancer within her for that nameless-for-now woman.

Alexandra sank her teeth into her lower lip and welcomed the sharp sting of pain.

How pitiable she was, longing for a man who held her in such clear disdain.

But he made it impossible for her to hate him.

Something warm and wet touched her cheek. She touched her fingers to that dampness and glanced up, scouring the ceiling for the place responsible for that leak. Only the white paint remained flawlessly untouched.

More of that moisture fell, and she drew a quick intake of breath as the realization threatened to bowl her over.

It is me. I'm crying.

All the tears she'd both wanted and been unable to shed for fear of them breaking her now came in a silent torrent.

And this time, she let them fall, unchecked.

Alexandra rolled onto her side so she lay with her back to Dallin's and silently wept.

She wept for all that would never be, and also for what would. She wept for the cold, empty future awaiting her with one man, while she was denied the one she truly wanted.

Dallin.

A man whom she'd fallen in love with atop a rooftop, and then these past days had fallen in love with all over again.

Alexandra shook; her body trembled violently, and she wrapped her arms about her middle.

And there was something so very cathartic and healing in this great weeping she'd denied herself.

The floorboards groaned, and she felt the moment Dallin's gaze touched on her across the darkened room.

"You're crying," he said gruffly, immediately crossing over.

She swiped at the tears on her cheeks. "I'm sorry if I'm k-keeping you a-awake." Only, it was as though speaking aloud had lent a new freedom to her tears, and she cried all the harder.

Dallin grunted. "You aren't keeping me awake."

"L-liar."

"I couldn't sleep."

"Because of my c-crying." She wiped her hand at her cheeks.

Reaching into his jacket, he fished around. As he withdrew a slip of fabric, a scrap of white fluttered in the darkness.

"Here," Dallin murmured, and touched that cloth to her cheeks, dusting away her tears.

Only, more tears took their place.

"Please don't cry," he implored.

"Because you hate crying."

"Because I hate seeing *you* cry."

That slight but revelatory emphasis only made her sob all the harder. For that meant he cared about her in some way.

Groaning, Dallin drew her into his arms and held her.

Alexandra buried her face against the fine fabric of his soft wool jacket. It felt so very wonderful, being held. Nay, not just that. It felt so very wonderful being held by *this* man.

Since the night her father died, Alexandra had been forced to be the rock in her broken and scared family. She'd been the one responsible for saving her mother and sisters. All along she'd known the minute she let herself collapse, she'd break apart and never be able to put herself back into any semblance of a person capable of being all they needed her to be.

Only, in Dallin's strong, warm embrace, she didn't feel weaker for crying.

As she wept, Dallin whispered soothing words against the top of her head, and Alexandra clung to him; she curled her fingers into his jacket and hung on to Dallin as the true lifeline he was in this moment. She held him tight, as she wished she could continue holding him forever, and cried.

She cried for what she wished she could have with him. And she cried for what would never be with him. She cried for the unfairness of being denied the future she yearned to know, all because of mistakes her father had made.

She cried until there were no tears left for her to shed, and the remnants of that release dissolved into a shuddery hiccup. When she'd finished, she remained resting there against Dallin's chest.

He did not set her away.

He continued to hold her in his strong, powerful arms and utter assurances in that calming way. Even after he fell silent, they stayed that way, locked in one another's arms.

I want to stay here forever. This is the only place I long to be . . .

And it was a testament to the manner of man Dallin McQuoid, Viscount Crichton, was. Despite his antipathy for her, he'd still offer her comfort and support.

Suddenly, it seemed very important that Dallin understood what drove her—not greed, not the dream of being a future duchess. But rather, Alexandra's love and devotion to her mother and sisters.

Alexandra sucked in a shaky breath, searched for a place to start, and found the easiest way to begin.

Even as she yearned to remain in his arms, she made herself edge away from him.

Concern filled Dallin's chocolate-brown eyes; those eyes, like the warmed chocolate that had once brought her comfort as a girl suffering some hurt or another, were the perfect shade for a man whose very presence soothed her. They also gave her the courage to speak.

"My bracelet," she began. "The one taken by the highwayman . . ." Her mouth went dry as she found the admission suddenly harder to speak than she'd anticipated.

Dallin tensed. "*That* is what you are worrying over." A muscle twitched at the corner of his left eye. "I'm sure Wingrave will purchase you another. One even finer and grander and more costly."

He made to pull away.

Alexandra took his hand, staying his movements.

"It was my mother's bracelet," she said softly.

The anger melted from his frame.

Understanding took the place of the earlier perplexity. "I trust your mother has scores of others," he said gently. "She would be far more upset with losing her daughter than a shiny bauble."

He didn't understand, after all.

"This one was different. The night I discovered I was to wed Lord Wingrave, my mother gave me that bracelet. It had been a gift from my father when they were betrothed. Theirs was also an arranged marriage, and she passed it to me so that I could have hope for my own union."

His eyes softened. "That is why you fought so desperately to keep the bracelet."

Alexandra nodded. "Please, just . . . let me say this." She wouldn't be able to do this unless she did it quickly.

Dallin fell silent.

And as there were no perfect words, only true ones, she just said it. "My family has no money."

Dallin cocked his head in confusion and stared back.

"Nix. Nowt. Naught." Alexandra turned her palms up. "Nothing."

"I . . . understand the meaning of the words. I just . . . don't understand. Your family—"

"Has lived a lie." She grimaced. "One that was so very well kept even my sisters and I remained unaware of the true nature of our circumstances." She paused. "They still have no idea." She murmured that last part more to herself.

"My father was miserable at managing his expenses and excellent at spending exorbitant sums of money. When he died, he left us in financial ruin with creditors breathing down our necks." And once she'd set the gates open, all the closely guarded secrets came tumbling out.

"The new marquess has prohibited us from selling any of the adornments. They all belong to him. And the pieces that do belong outright to us are not nearly enough to ensure our security or futures. We are completely and utterly financially ruined. There is not even a dowry."

"No . . . dowry."

She shook her head.

The secret of her family's circumstances had been one she'd been forced to guard closely. And just like the tears from before, it felt so very good to let free that pitiable truth with another person.

Dallin's mind existed in two competing states: his thoughts simultaneously raced and moved at an infinitely slow pace as he sought to process her admission. He sought to make sense of what she'd shared and came up *empty*.

Alexandra and her family were penniless. Nay, not only that. She had no dowry.

In a world where women were reliant upon their fathers and husbands, Alexandra's own sire had left her and her sisters and their mother *destitute*.

His chest ached. How much she'd faced this past year.

All the while, he'd judged her at every turn. He'd let himself believe she was an avaricious miss. Now he knew he'd done so only because that had been infinitely preferable to imagining the bright-eyed woman with a like fascination of the stars married to another.

What a bastard he'd been.

Suddenly, it became very hard to breathe past the weight bearing down on his chest. "Why didn't you tell me?"

"*Tell* you?" she repeated with a bitter-sounding laugh. "Tell *me*, Dallin. At what point have members of the *ton* spoken so freely about money or, worse, their lack thereof?"

Never. The answer to that was never.

"When should I have been so candid? *Hmm?* The night we were both attempting to interrupt our beloved family members from meeting one another? Or somewhere along the way of our journey to stop my sister and your cousin's wedding. We've only known one another a handful of days."

He started at that reminder.

For it was as though he'd known this woman forever, as though that long-ago night atop his family's terrace and under the stars their souls had become entwined.

"And Wingrave?" he asked quietly.

She turned her palms up and stared at her outstretched hands. "He met me but once, and only to look me over and determine whether I'd suit." Rancor spilled from every word that was a revelation of her impending marriage and feelings on that state she'd enter into with Lord Wingrave.

Fury filled him, a red-hot rage with the notorious scoundrel, so bright and potent it threatened to consume him whole.

Understanding set in. "That was the reason for your exchange with your mother."

Alexandra nodded. "Given your sister married the man the Duke of Talbert's daughter was to wed, he would never permit a match between any member of *my* family and a McQuoid. But when I . . . when I . . . m-marry Lord W-Wingrave . . ." She tripped and strangled on her words.

And Dallin commiserated, for thinking of her exchanging vows that would see her forever bound to that other man threatened to suffocate him.

"My sister will be able to wed your cousin, should she so wish."

"At that point, there will be nothing the duke or his son will be able to do to keep them apart."

But the cost would be Alexandra finding herself bound forever to the blackhearted Marquess of Wingrave.

He moved his gaze over her face. "I believed you didn't approve of a man who'd elope with her and put her reputation at risk."

"I believe a man so desperate to have her at any cost is a man who must truly love her."

Dallin's mind continued to spin.

Alexandra's features spasmed in a palpable grief and regret that threatened to rip him in two. "If only I'd shared the truth of our family's circumstances with Cora, then mayhap she would have understood. But I didn't even give her the chance," she said, her voice growing frenzied. "I've always been so determined to look after my sisters that I didn't think to include them in details directly impacting them and our lives, and . . ."

She sagged, as if the fight had gone out of her.

How much she'd taken on—the weight of the world entirely too great for one person to bear, let alone this woman, without any deserved control of her future.

Dallin drew her into his arms, and she went unresistingly. "Oh, Alexandra," he whispered against the top of her head. He held her that way for a long while, until the frustration and desperation at her situation became too much.

Needing to move, he stood, took a step, and then stopping in his tracks, he dragged a hand through his hair. "Why are you telling me this?"

Why now? Why, when papers had been signed and it was too late for them?

"I know you hate me and thought that mayhap if you know the real reason I'm marrying Lord Wingrave, then it would at least make sense."

A groan got stuck painfully in his chest. "I don't hate you," he said hoarsely.

Hope lit her eyes. "You don't?"

God, how could she not know?

Because you've been so wounded and miserable at the thought of her with another man that you've been nothing more than a crass bully.

"Your mother. Does she know how you feel?"

"She does and she wishes it could be different, but she is aware that our options are limited."

Alexandra spoke with the rote nature of one who'd heard those very words uttered by another.

Anger flared before his eyes. "And still, she'd have you marry Wingrave anyway."

A strained laugh burst from her lips. "What choice does she have? What choice do *I* have? I am a woman, living in a world that belongs in every way to men. I have no money. No land. Nothing that truly belongs to me worth any monetary value with which to help my sisters and mother. The only thing I have to offer that is of any value is myself."

Every word she spoke was a lash upon his heart.

Alexandra thumped a fist against her chest. "Do you think I do not *hate* that, Dallin? Do you think I do not resent, with every fiber of my being, that I must sell myself, no different from a prostitute, but with the benefit of a name, when I love another?"

Dallin stilled. "You . . . love me?" he whispered.

A pained laugh escaped her. "*Of course* I love you."

She loved him. His soul sang and his heart soared, and at last, he understood the magic that compelled men to draft sonnets. Only, as fast as he flew was as hard as he fell.

For papers had been signed, and a wedding awaited her upon their return.

"Why didn't you tell me about your family's situation?" he implored. "I would have . . ."

"What? Courted me?" An agonized sound, trapped somewhere between a sob and a laugh, spilled from her lips. "What should I have done, Dallin? Tell me. Go to you with my family's shame? You, who spoke so freely about the responsibilities thrust upon you and the longing you had to be free of those constraints so you might see the world, expected I should come to you and dump more new responsibilities upon your lap."

He'd never have viewed her in that light. "It would have been different. I wouldn't have seen it that way."

She scoffed. "Before that night, we knew each other not at all. You think I should have gone and humbled myself before you, asking you to give up your dream on the small chance that the one moment we had together under the stars meant the same to you that it did to me?"

Amidst the vise squeezing his heart, a lightness found its way in. "It did matter to me. It mattered very much." And now it was too late. Agony snuffed out that fleeting joy. "Being with you . . . marrying you, it would not have been me giving up a dream." He took a step toward her. "It would have been the birth of a new one."

A lone tear slipped down her cheek, and she swiped almost angrily at that crystal drop. Dallin caught the next crystalline bead with the pad of his thumb and brushed away the evidence of her misery. Even as that same sorrow and regret ate him up inside.

"My sister . . . your cousin, they met that same night, and then they *continued* to meet," she said in the tired tones of one who'd come to terms with her fate and future. "You and I didn't, Dallin. Neither of us tried, and we could both wonder how it might have been different . . . Wondering doesn't change what wasn't."

She could call it off with Wingrave.

Except as soon as the thought slipped in, he knew the reality of that possibility. He knew they lived in a world where that wasn't so very simple. Where contracts were signed and binding, and lives ruined were they to stand in breach.

Only, in this instant, he discovered he was as much of a dreamer as his sisters.

"I could marry you." Nay, that wasn't correct. "I *want* to marry you."

Her lips formed a stunned little moue.

Of happiness? Surprise?

Then, sadness brought those corners down into a heartrending grin. "And here I thought you hated me."

"Hated you? *Hated* you? God, Alexandra. A woman with your strength of spirit and courage? A woman who treats servants as equals? You're the manner of woman who is loyal and loving to her sisters and would do anything for her family." Dallin held her gaze. "How could I ever hate one such as you? That day at Lord and Lady Brookhaven's . . . I just let myself see something different, because it was easier than facing the truth—that you could never be mine."

"You want to see the world," she reminded him with a pleading in her tone. "You've already told me of the great journey you'll take when you return."

"Take it with me," he said, stepping toward her.

Her eyes glimmered, and she was luminescent in her hope. As quick as that light had been born, it flickered out.

"I can't."

When he made to protest, she spoke over him. "It isn't just my family Talbert would see ruined. He'll come for your family, too. Your cousin's business ventures. His siblings." She paused. "Your sisters. You know he will, Dallin."

Yes, he did.

And it ate him alive inside.

Dallin cupped her cheek.

Alexandra's eyes closed, and she leaned into his touch.

It wasn't enough.

Needing her closer, Dallin drew her into his arms, and she went unprotestingly. Fitting herself against his chest, Alexandra burrowed into him like a contented kitten.

Dallin pressed a kiss against the top of her silken hair, still slightly damp from the bath she'd taken.

They stayed that way, wrapped in one another's arms. Time ceased to matter. Moments, minutes, or a millennium may well have passed, and it was all the same.

"Alexandra," he said, his voice strained and pained, "if there's anything I can do for you . . ." Fetch her a star from the skies, even. He'd do it. "If there's anything at all, just tell me."

Alexandra edged out of his arms, and he cursed himself for having spoken, which inadvertently wrought that separation.

"There is . . . one thing," she said tentatively.

He nodded. "Anything."

"Will you make love to me?"

Dallin went absolutely motionless.

His ears played a game of trickery on him. That's all it was. For surely the request she'd put to Dallin was merely the stuff of his own longings.

Alexandra dampened her mouth in that endearing way he'd come to recognize signaled her nervousness.

"Forgive me," she said on a rush. "I've disgusted you."

"Disgusted me?" he choked out. "Alexandra, never. From the moment I caught you hiding on my terrace, I was completely and utterly captivated by you."

"But you will not make love to me," she said, her tone peculiarly flat.

She stiffened and turned, giving him her back, and if he were a gentleman, he'd allow her that thoroughly erroneous conclusion.

"It is not out of lack of want on my part," he said into the quiet. Alexandra stilled, and then faced him. Like one searching for the truth with her own eyes, she moved her gaze over his face. "I want you, Alexandra," he confessed, his voice thick with desire and yearning. "I want you more than I've ever wanted a woman." And more than he'd ever want any woman after her.

She took a step toward him. "Then, why—"

"Because you don't know what you're asking!"

"I *do* know, Dallin. I do. In fourteen days, I will be forced to bind myself to a stranger, a heartless gentleman with a reputation for being a rogue and scoundrel, set only on his own pleasures. I'll be forced to give myself to him."

Her voice became a muffled hum in his ears, as an insidious thought slithered forward: Of her in Wingrave's arms. Of Dallin coming over her and entering her and making her moan with her release and cry in surrender. His breath grew ragged as that mental imagery ravaged his very soul.

Alexandra slipped her hand into Dallin's, and the sound of her voice came whirring back into clear focus.

"I may have no choice but to . . . do this thing my family needs me to do," she murmured, blessedly sparing Dallin from the explicit visual of what she'd be made to do. "But I would have a choice in who I give myself to." Taking his hand, she guided it to rest upon her breast.

His palm curled reflexively around that soft, supple flesh. Her white cotton nightshift proved little barrier between them.

Alexandra's nipple pebbled against the nearly translucent garment, and riveted, Dallin stroked that peak with the same thumb that had previously brushed away her tears. Back and forth, he continued to graze his finger over her nipple.

She moaned softly.

Or mayhap that was him?

Everything had become all jumbled up in his mind.

As much as it cost him, Dallin managed to speak the last words he'd ever want to speak.

"Alexandra," he said hoarsely. "We shouldn't do this."

"Do you want this?"

How steady her voice was. How sure, when he couldn't make heads or tails of what was up or down.

Indecision flared in her previously only passion-filled eyes.

Alexandra wavered.

Let her believe you don't. Let her think you don't long for her the same way she longs for you. And get out. Get the hell out of this room and put that door between you until tomorrow comes and your time together comes to its inevitable conclusion.

She stepped out of his embrace. "I'm sorry," she said, avoiding his gaze.

Alexandra made to turn.

"I want you," he acknowledged aloud. "I want you . . . in every way, Alexandra. And I want to know what it is to make love to you. But I fear you will come to regret—"

She rushed back into his arms.

Their mouths instantly found one another.

They kissed like they were drowning and only this meeting of their lips could save them.

They kissed as two people who wanted only one another, but whom fate was determined to keep apart.

Over and over again, he slanted his lips over hers until she moaned, parting those remarkably soft and pliable lips, and he swept inside to taste of her.

Their kiss took on a sense of urgency as they lashed their tongues against one another, lovers who sought to brand the other, imprinting this kiss upon one another's soul.

Dallin filled his hands of her generous buttocks and drew her close. He pressed his aching shaft against the flat of her belly, and she reflexively, instinctually moved her hips in return.

"Dallin," she moaned, and the sound of his name falling from her lips threatened to drive him mad with wanting.

They moved in tandem, finding their way over to the bed. As they did, Dallin divested her of her nightshift, baring her completely so he could freely worship her with his gaze.

He paused and drank in the sight of her naked before him. Soft and rounded in all the places a woman should be, she possessed a slim, graceful body that would have sent the sculptors of old clamoring for their chisels and hammers.

Her taut, swollen nipples were a shy pink. At the apex of her long, shapely legs, a golden thatch of curls beckoned.

And through his extended, deliberate scrutiny, she stood before him, as proud as any goddess who'd been memorialized in stone.

Wordlessly, she opened her arms to him.

Yanking at his jacket, Dallin wrestled the garment free. The pop and clink of a button hitting the floor melded with the sounds of his and Alexandra's rapid, raggedly drawn breaths.

He added his shirt to that growing pile of clothes around them.

Then with a deliberate slowness, he held Alexandra's eyes and proceeded to unfasten his trousers.

When he'd kicked those aside and stood as naked as Adam before her, she looked down with an unabashed boldness and curiosity, and it was his undoing.

They found their way back to one another's arms. Their mouths instantly met in a kiss that would remain seared into his mind, soul, and heart for the rest of his days.

Dallin guided her down onto the mattress, and not breaking their violently hungry kiss, he stretched his body over hers.

He trailed his fingers along her collarbone and reacquainted himself with her breasts, and then slid his touch ever lower.

The moment he pressed his palm between her legs, a hiss exploded from between her teeth, and Alexandra arched up and into that touch.

He teased those moist curls, and then in a bid to drive her as mad as she made him, he slipped a finger inside her wet channel. She moaned and pushed herself against his touch.

He continued to stroke her, easing his finger in and out, over and over, making love to her with that lone digit.

Panting, Alexandra lifted her hips frantically, her undulations growing increasingly frenzied.

Dallin moved his mouth from hers, and she cried out. She attempted to bring him back to that kiss. Dallin, however, shifted his attention elsewhere. Closing his lips around a turgid nipple, he drew that flesh deep into his mouth and sucked. All the while, he continued to tease the nub between her legs.

His breathing came hard and fast and ragged and joined with her like frantic respirations; a symphony of their lovemaking played in his mind.

Dallin moved, lying between her legs, and then stopped. His chest rose and fell quickly from the effort it took to break from doing what he really wished and plunging himself deep inside her.

Alexandra forced open her long, heavy-looking lashes. A question blazed from those azure depths, one that questioned why he had stopped and also silently begged him to continue.

He'd not have her unspoken surrender, however.

"Do you truly want this, Alexandra? Because once you do, there will be no going back for you."

In response, she took his hand and returned it to her breast. "I want you," she said firmly, unshakingly. "I want to make love with you, Dallin."

It was all he needed.

They met once more in a kiss, and as he settled himself between her curved, sensuous thighs, Alexandra splayed them wider. Where she'd previously welcomed him with her words, now she did with her body, too.

Dallin further readied her, playing with the sensitive nub that sent her head flailing back and forth and incoherent ramblings tumbling from her lips and his mouth.

Dallin switched places with his fingers and brought the tip of his shaft against her sodden center, and then slowly entered.

He gritted his teeth. "You are so tight," he rasped as he slid inch by agonizing inch inside her.

"Is that a bad thing?"

A hoarse laugh escaped him, bringing his shaft deeper in her still. His pained mirth faded to a groan. "It is a good thing. A very good thing."

Sweat beading at his brow, Dallin paused so that she could adjust to the size and feel of him inside her.

Propped on his elbows, with his arms framing Alexandra's face, Dallin worked his gaze over her long, lustrous lashes. Her high, elegant cheeks, flushed and rosy and gleaming with the faintest shine.

I want to remember this moment forever. I want to stay in it so that we can be joined in ways that the rules of our rigid society deny us.

Alexandra's lashes fluttered open. A question filled her guileless blue-green eyes. "What is it?"

"I never want to forget this," he said quietly.

She reached up and twined her hands about his neck. "Let us only live in this moment," she implored.

As if she needed to beg him for anything. As if he wouldn't give her anything and everything she wished.

Dallin swept his mouth down.

This time the kiss between them contained an urgency that bordered on violence.

He sucked at her lush lower lip and nipped lightly at that flesh, wanting to mark her as his, and she returned the kiss in kind.

And then he entered her all the way. The feel of her, warm and wet and tight, was like a benediction.

Alexandra briefly stiffened.

Dallin stopped and drew back a fraction. Balancing himself on one elbow, he stroked a shaking hand over her face. "I'm so sorry," he said hoarsely. "I would never want to hurt you."

Alexandra reached a finger up and pressed that long digit against his mouth. "It doesn't hurt. It feels . . . different." Then she lifted her hips, as if experimentally. "And I do very much . . . like it," she added that last part, bashfully dipping her gaze.

And that admission freed him. Dallin began to move. They began to move. Their bodies rose and fell with a beautiful harmony.

Time melted away. The future, tomorrow's eventual parting, ceased to exist in this, his and Alexandra's joining.

I want her. I want her now and forever.

And yet . . . that wasn't to be.

Alexandra stiffened in his arms, and then her eyes went wide and her exquisite features tensed.

She let out a scream of surrender; her channel gripped and ungripped him as she lifted herself into his thrusts, over and over.

He gritted his teeth, continuing to stroke her, restraining himself.

Only after she crumpled onto the mattress and wore a sated smile from her own release did Dallin withdraw and spend himself over the side of the bed and onto the floor.

His entire body shuddered, and with a groan, he collapsed onto his side beside Alexandra.

Wordlessly, he drew her against him, folding an arm around her soft, heated body, and she borrowed of his warmth.

Neither he nor Alexandra sought to fill the silence. For there was no void when they were together.

Long after she'd begun to softly snore, Dallin stared up at the ceiling and fought his body on sleep.

Alexandra had offered him all that she could—her body and her complete surrender.

This would be enough. It would have to be. Only, holding her slumbering form against his side, why did it feel as though Dallin lied to himself?

Chapter 21

Alexandra had the most glorious dream. In it, she and Dallin had made love, and afterward they'd lain entwined in one another's arms.

In her dream, there'd been words of love and no formal betrothal of Alexandra and another standing between them.

A feather-soft kiss brushed against Alexandra's mouth, and she forced her heavy lashes up.

"Good morning, *mon étoile*."

Mon étoile. My star.

Apparently, dreams did come true. Or at least some of them did.

Smiling dreamily, Alexandra stretched.

She didn't know what she'd expected from Dallin when she'd awakened: Awkwardness. Regret.

Not . . . *this*. This tender warmth and affection with endearments falling from his lips was immensely better.

One part of her dream had proven true. Refusing to allow Lord Wingrave to intrude on this moment—one of the final ones she'd ever share with Dallin—she smiled dreamily up at him and stretched again.

"Morning," she returned, her voice thick from sleep.

Through the sluggishness of slumber, she registered her body, still bare under the sheets. Dallin, however, sat at the edge of the bed, fully clothed, shaved, and wide awake.

Then reality set back in—Cora. Her sister's elopement.

"I'm late!" She scrambled upright.

At that sudden movement, a sharp discomfort immediately twinged between her legs.

"You're not. We're not. I opted to let you sleep longer, but we are still not due to leave just yet." Dallin smoothed a palm over her cheek. "Are you sore?"

Suddenly shy, when she'd never been with him or around him, Alexandra drew the coverlet up to her chin. "I'm fine," she assured him.

At least, in the way he asked.

Dallin moved his gaze over her face. Sadness flickered to life in his keen brown eyes, and with an almost reluctance to his movements, he stood. "I've arranged for a meal to be brought and a maid to come help you while I see to the day's travel arrangements."

He turned to go.

Alexandra scrambled to her feet, dragging the sheet with her and nearly tripping over the white cotton fabric. "You're leaving?" she blurted, and then promptly curled her toes so sharply into the hardwood floor the arches of her feet ached.

"That is . . . you should eat, too. We both should." *Together.*

Anything so they had more time alone with one another.

"I've already broken my fast," he said.

"Oh."

Dallin reached inside his jacket . . . as if to check the time on a watch fob that was no longer there.

Because of me. Had he not returned for me, he'd still have that piece his brother gave him.

"Dallin," she said, taking a step toward him. "I . . ."

"Yes?" He stared at her, a question in his eyes.

I will miss you. I want you. I love you.

Alexandra froze, her breath trapped in her lungs, which had ceased to function.

266

How am I going to be able to walk away from him? I thought one night would be enough. But I'll never be able to let go.

Agony threatened to choke her.

"Alexandra," Dallin ventured quietly.

Startled, she jumped.

He stared at her with a question in his veiled eyes.

She cleared her throat. "I . . . just . . . I . . ."

Dallin took a step nearer. "Yes?"

"I just want to thank you for all you've done," she finished weakly.

Something flickered in his eyes, and then was gone. "Of course."

And with that, he took his leave.

Several minutes later, the same serving girl who'd helped Alexandra with her ablutions last evening reappeared.

With a quiet word of thanks, Alexandra accepted the young woman's help as she changed into a pale-blue riding gown.

After the girl had drawn Alexandra's hair into a serviceable chignon, she dipped a curtsy and took her leave, closing the door behind her with a soft, sad little click.

Alexandra stood fixed to the floor, unable to move, unable to breathe. For when she took so much as a step, she'd propel herself and time forward to a place she didn't wish to be—into a future that didn't include Dallin.

There came strong but quiet footfalls, footfalls she'd come to recognize so very well over these past four days.

KnockKnockKnock.

How had it been less than a handful of days they'd spent together? How could she feel like the other half of her soul was being cleaved in two at having to be apart from him?

KnockKnockKnock.

Alexandra bit the inside of her lower lip hard enough to draw blood, and she welcomed that sting and the metallic taste, the tangible evidence of her misery.

Giving her head a clearing shake, Alexandra had just started across the room when, from the corner of her eye, she detected a flash of white.

With a frown, she headed over to the small piece of paper. Dropping to her heels, she picked the scrap up and opened it.

And froze.

"Perseus and Andromeda were madly in love with one another after meeting each other a few hours earlier. They traveled, seeing the world . . ."

Heart racing, Alexandra drew the door open.

Dallin stood with his fist poised in its unfinished strike upon the door panel. "Is everything all . . . ?"

"What is this?" she asked breathlessly.

He looked to the paper held in her fingers.

A dull flush filled his cheeks. "Nothing." He reached for the note.

Alexandra edged backward, out of his reach. "When did you write this?"

He hesitated. "A year ago."

Her heart thumped slowly. "Why?" she whispered.

Dallin hesitated a moment later. "I'd discovered the answer to your question and thought to present it to you." He directed that admission to some point just over the top of her head.

"Why didn't you?"

Had he sought her out at some point, at any point prior to her betrothal, there could have been a relationship which could have proven he cared, and she would have shared about her family, and there would have been no betrothal to Wingrave.

When he didn't answer, Alexandra took a step forward. "Why didn't you?" she asked again.

"I intended to share it with you when we had the first of those two sets we'd discussed having." At last, Dallin met her gaze, and so much pain blazed from their depths it threatened to bowl her over. "As you know, those dances never happened."

They'd never had those dances because it had been too late. She'd already been promised to the marquess, and the promise of anything more with Dallin had ended in a quick death before there'd ever been a chance for something to begin. Or continue . . .

"Dallin," she whispered, stretching a hand toward him.

He edged away quickly, effectively preventing her touch. "I will wait outside while you have a moment to gather anything else you may need."

Alexandra watched miserably as he grabbed her valise and let himself out.

Gather anything else? She didn't have anything. She didn't want anything except more time with him.

The moment he shut the door behind him with a quick, decisive click, she let her eyes close.

Misery ravaged her insides. How very close she and Dallin had come to having . . .

What? A courtship? A marriage? A future together?

Wingrave had offered a hefty sum for the right to possess her. A sum that included enough money to care for her sisters and mother. And Dallin? He'd been clear that night when he'd shared with her just how much he chafed at all the responsibilities that fell to him as the responsible heir.

There'd never been a hope for her and Dallin. Not even if they'd had all the same stolen meetings Cora had known with Smith.

All she and Dallin had was the rest of their trip to Scotland.

With quaking fingers, Alexandra donned her cloak and fastened the clasp at her throat.

A tear fell, and she brushed her fingers under her eyes.

Do not cry. Do not cry.

Because the moment she started, unlike last night, she'd never be able to stop.

At least they had this last time together. It would be enough. It had to be.

Alexandra reached for the door handle, and then stopped.

She looked over her shoulder to that rumpled mattress where she and Dallin had made love, where he'd held her, keeping her safe and warm and secure in his arms.

I want to remember every part of that one night we had together. She wanted to keep each detail of that memory fresh, so that when she returned to London and traded that happiness for a lifetime of misery, she could relive over and over the one night she'd had everything she wanted in this world.

Releasing a shuddery breath, Alexandra pulled her hood up into place and forced her focus forward.

She pressed the handle, and the door gave far too easily, cruelly surrendering her to her future.

Together, she and Dallin made their way belowstairs to the quiet taproom. They didn't speak another word between them. And unlike all the previous silences they'd known which had been warm and comfortable, this proved cold and empty.

And Alexandra wanted to cry all over again.

They reached the establishment's front entrance, and unlike Alexandra's earlier struggle upstairs, without hesitating, Dallin drew the panel open on the end of their time together.

Wordlessly, he motioned for her to exit before him.

I can't. I don't want to. That voice silently screamed inside her head.

She stole one last look over her shoulder at the stairs leading up to that room where Dallin had made love to her so tenderly and beautifully. How would that one night they'd spent together ever be enough? It wouldn't. Just as she wanted him in her life and in her future, she wanted to share every part of her heart and body with him.

"Alexandra?"

That cry, spoken in an all-too-familiar lyrical voice, broke across her reverie of regrets.

Alexandra spun so quickly she knocked the hood back from her head as she found the owner of that stunned greeting.

A like shock knocked Alexandra back on her heels. From across the taproom, cloaked sister stared at cloaked sister. It couldn't be.

Cora?

Her younger sister gave an excited, happy nod, confirming Alexandra had spoken aloud.

They took flight at the same time and were instantly in one another's arms.

Alexandra clung to her sister. "Cora," she whispered against the side of the smaller young woman's head.

These past days, she'd not allowed herself to think of the danger her sister faced out on her own. She'd silently reassured herself that as Dallin's cousin, Brone Smith, even though he'd eloped with Cora, possessed some sliver of the honor and strength and capability Dallin did.

Now, with her sister safe in her arms, she welcomed the rush of relief that came in having her here and seeing for herself that her sister was unhurt.

Except . . . hadn't Alexandra already learned herself that the greatest pain was that which was invisible to the human eye?

Stiffening, she drew back a fraction. "Are you . . . ?"

"Oh, I'm just fine." Her sister laughed happily. "Better than fine." She dropped her voice to a faint whisper. "Brone and I eloped," she confided. "We encountered a highwayman. He took kindness upon us when he learned about our plans to wed and let us retain our coins and belongings. And then it stormed, and the rains were fierce and slowed our journey. One of our mounts was injured, and we were forced to stop our travels when we met *him*."

Him?

Alexandra opened her mouth to quiz her sister but could not get in a word edgewise over Cora's cheer-filled ramblings. "I expected he'd be most angry about me marrying Brone, given the enmity between their families, but he was anything but."

"Who, Cora?"

"He was most kind and tolerant and understanding and arrived with a maid to act as a companion, and he vowed his servants are only the most discreet and my secret was safe, and would remain so, but that I should return to London, where I might have a real wedding with Brone. And you are just so very lucky."

"Who?" Alexandra repeated.

Cora laughed. "You are correct. *We* are just both so very lucky," the always gay girl amended.

"No . . . who is it that *helped* you?"

Understanding lit Cora's eyes, and then she giggled. "Silly sister. *Him.*"

Alexandra followed her sister's gesture across the room and took note of the details her earlier surprise had obscured.

The young, unfamiliar maid in a somehow familiar uniform who sat at a nearby table. Mr. Brone Smith, who stood patiently in wait, smiling.

And then Alexandra's gaze went to the tall, dark, menacing-looking man she'd caught but a brief look at earlier in the Season, the only unsmiling member of their party.

Her heart knocked to a painful stop against her ribs, and her stomach muscles clenched. He stared back with hard, cold eyes of blue so dark they were nearly black.

Alexandra's betrothed.

Lord Wingrave.

Lord Wingrave, whose gaze strayed just beyond Alexandra's shoulder.

She stiffened, knowing precisely where he stared, where he looked. Who he saw.

She detected the flash of surprise, and then a peculiarly amused glint formed in the man's impossibly granitelike eyes.

And then the dark-haired stranger who would be her husband started toward Alexandra.

Nay, not toward her.

He continued walking right past Alexandra and stopped before Dallin.

Both men sized one another up. The marquess had several inches and several stone on Dallin and was heavily muscled where Dallin possessed a wiry strength. Still Dallin managed to exude a far greater aura of power.

He was the other man's superior in every way.

And yet, wanting him as she did, longing for him, did nothing to change the fact that ultimately Alexandra would and did belong to the forbidding figure beside him.

The marquess smirked. "Crichton," he greeted in frosty tones perfectly suited to one whose every unyielding feature was chiseled of ice.

A muscle ticked at the corner of Dallin's mouth. "Wingrave," he said flatly.

The marquess's lips curved up a fraction more in icy mirth. "Imagine us arriving at this *very* inn, at the exact same time." He inclined his head, and then angling his shoulder, he dismissed Dallin. "My lady," her betrothed at last greeted her, and he did so without a hint of warmth and with a wealth of warning.

She wasn't to acknowledge Dallin.

To do so would also be an acknowledgment of the fact Alexandra and Dallin had been together.

Not that she believed for a moment the shrewd Marquess of Wingrave hadn't taken one glimpse at her and Dallin and ascertained that there'd been far more than a mere chance meeting between them.

And what did it say about Alexandra that she didn't care what the marquess thought or felt about it? That the only thing she cared about was the fact that in mere moments Dallin would be gone from her life, forever.

Please, don't leave me. Look at me, Dallin, she silently pleaded. *To hell with the marquess and my betrothal. Just look at me. Do something. Say something. Anything.*

Without so much as another glance at the marquess, Dallin collected the door handle in his gloved fingers.

Misery lanced the heart that beat only for him.

Dallin paused, and hope reared its head in Alexandra like the glorious rainbow after the storm.

He cast a look back at her, and in his eyes, she saw reflected all her own yearning and regrets, and then, with that . . . he was gone.

Numb, Alexandra stood staring at the panel he'd closed with nothing more than a quiet click.

He was gone.

He'd left.

What would you have him do? Declare his love and say to hell with the rules of society which govern us and the contracts signed?

And yet as he walked out, having stolen nothing more than that last defiant glance her way, she accepted the truth: that was precisely what she'd wanted.

———— ✦ ————

Alexandra found herself back abovestairs of the old inn, this time in a different room—her sister's from the night prior.

While Cora prattled on, filling in the details about just how she and Brone Smith had come to be in the company of the Marquess of Wingrave and a maid, Alexandra sat in silence, taking it all in.

The Marquess of Wingrave had happened upon Cora and Mr. Smith after one of their horses had come up lame.

The marquess had learned Cora had eloped with Mr. Smith and didn't wish to stand in their way. Rather, he'd brought along a chaperone and encouraged them to return to London, where, following his and Alexandra's wedding, they would be free to marry in a public ceremony which would mark an end to the enmity between the McQuoids and Wingraves.

The marquess had been most kind.

The marquess was most generous.

The marquess would be a wonderful husband to Alexandra.

On and on her sister went, singing the lionized marquess's praises, until it became too much.

Alexandra slapped her hands over her ears. *"Enough!"*

She didn't want to hear about how wonderful the marquess had been.

Cora stopped. "I'm sorry," she said softly. "I didn't think—"

"No, you didn't," Alexandra interrupted, and all the frustration with and resentment of her responsibilities broke her. "That's just it, Cora. You didn't think about how your actions could have hurt your sisters and mother. You didn't think about the danger you put yourself in or any of the awful things that could have befallen you. You didn't think about the fact that I, Mama, and Daphne would not be with you on your special day. You thought only of yourself and your own happiness." While that was the last thing Alexandra could do or have.

Her sister stared back with wide, wounded eyes.

Alexandra made herself stop.

God, what was she doing? Yes, her sister had been foolhardy in her flight, but Alexandra's reaction now stemmed from her own resentments, none of which had anything to do with Cora and everything to do with their family's circumstances and the responsibility which fell to her.

Alexandra scrubbed a hand over her face.

"Forgive me, C-Cora," she said, her voice catching. She opened her arms and her younger sister flung herself into them.

Cora wept against Alexandra's chest, dampening the front of her gown with her tears. "I'm so sorry," she said in between great, heaving sobs.

Alexandra's own tears built and fell, too. "N-no. I'm sorry."

Sorry she'd taken her frustrations out on her younger sister. Sorry for resenting Cora for things as much beyond her control as they were Alexandra's.

They remained that way, holding one another.

"I love you, Cora," she murmured against the top of her sister's head.

"I love you, too, Alex," Cora whispered, using that nickname she'd called Alexandra by when they were small girls and Cora had been too young and unable to speak Alexandra's entire name.

There came a knock at the door. This wasn't a soft, thoughtful one like Dallin's earlier rapping. But brusque, impatient, and bold.

As one, Alexandra and Cora turned their heads.

"I expect it is the marquess," Cora said.

Alexandra's stomach churned. "Yes." She feared it was.

And in the ultimate reversal of roles, Cora took charge of the moment. Wiping at her cheeks, she crossed the room, opened the door, and swept out into the hall. "Lord Wingrave!" she greeted as happily as if they were old friends.

"Lady Cora," he said in those same steely tones Cora seemed wholly unaffected by. Directing his words over at Alexandra, he continued, "I've come to suggest we resume our journey."

Cora nodded. "Of course," she said.

When Alexandra didn't immediately follow, Cora stopped and cast a questioning look her way. "Will you not join me?"

"I'll be along shortly," Alexandra assured.

Cora nodded and then hastened off, leaving Alexandra alone with Lord Wingrave.

Reluctantly, Alexandra made herself leave the sanctuary of these small rooms and join her betrothed in the corridor.

The moment she did, he offered her nothing but a chilling silence.

How strange, finding herself alone for the first time with the man she was set to soon wed. Since she'd become betrothed to the marquess, she'd viewed him as a heartless monster. And yet he'd gone after Cora and promised to see her wed to the man she loved, despite his father's enmity for the McQuoids. As such, he couldn't be all bad.

"I want to begin by thanking you, my lord," she said softly. "I'm not sure how you learned about Cora's intentions, but I'm grateful to you for coming to her rescue, and also for your understanding of where her heart's affections lie."

Another thought, one that sent terror clamoring through her, gave her pause. "Have others discovered . . . ?"

"Your family's secrets are your own. And mine, of course. As for your gratitude? Do not make anything more of my actions than there is," he said frostily, effectively killing the brief moment of hope she'd had in the manner of man he was. "I know *everything*." Did she imagine a double meaning behind that slightly overemphasized word? "The duke does not take kindly to public humiliations. The last one served him, compliments of a different McQuoid, resulted in my betrothal to *you*."

Well.

"Now, I'd speak with you a moment, my lady," Lord Wingrave said curtly.

She dampened her lips. "Aren't we already speaking?"

He narrowed his midnight-black lashes. "Don't be coy."

Of course he'd have questions for her. She'd just hoped she'd be spared from answering them until London.

Lord Wingrave motioned to the room behind them.

Alexandra followed that gesture. "It wouldn't be—"

"Proper?" That and his wintry chuckle brought an end to the remainder of her words.

The marquess leaned close. "Given the fact you, my *betrothed*, have been traveling alone with another gentleman, I daresay having a discussion with the *actual* man you're *supposed* to marry would be far more permissible."

He knew she'd joined Dallin?

Alexandra felt the blood drain from her face, and she stared dumbly at Lord Wingrave.

How did he know that?

She'd not, however, be cowed by this man.

She lifted her chin and matched his iciness with a haughty disdain of her own. "You go too far with your assumptions, my lord."

"Do you think I am stupid, my lady?" he asked frostily. "Do you think I didn't see the way Crichton had a hand at the small of your back? That I didn't see the way you looked at him?" A mocking grin curled his hard lips. "That I don't know you likely gave yourself to him numerous times during your flight together?"

Heat slapped her cheeks. How callous. How cruel. How direct. "We didn't leave together," she said, finding her voice. "I was in a carriage accident and found myself stranded. He came to my rescue."

"How gallant," he said in deadened tones. "It does not, however, escape my notice that you didn't deny his bedding you."

Alexandra curled her toes reflexively in her shoes. "He didn't—"

He took a quick step toward her, silencing the remainder of that lie on her lips. "And do you think," he whispered, "that I'll not know the moment I have you under me that you aren't a virgin?"

She instantly closed her mouth. Her entire being burnt several degrees hotter with embarrassment . . . and shame.

Nay, not shame. She'd forever hold regrets, but not a single one of them would be about any of the time she'd shared with Dallin McQuoid or the things they'd done when they were together.

"Now," he went on as casually as if he'd spoken about Alexandra dancing with Dallin and not having made love with him. "May I suggest we continue the remainder of this discussion in private? That is . . . unless you'd rather risk other guests hearing—"

She entered the room before he'd finished that thought.

The moment he stepped inside, he drew the door shut behind them, and between the marquess's size and the fury emanating from his menacingly big frame, the previously comfortable, spacious room seemed suddenly very small.

She quickly became aware of the fact she'd locked herself in a room alone with the forbidding man. Alexandra hurriedly put a sizable distance between them.

He eyed her retreat with the closest she'd wager this man came to amusement. "Such *modesty* from my betrothed," he drawled.

Tired of his toying with her like a cat did its prey, instead of retreating farther, Alexandra forced herself to hold her ground. "If you intend to sever our arrangement, then get on with it," she snapped.

Lord Wingrave chuckled. "You'd like that, wouldn't you?"

"You . . . *don't* intend to end our betrothal, then?"

He rejoined with a question of his own. "Do you truly believe I care if you bedded Crichton or any man?"

Given her sister's ill-thought flight to Gretna Green and his having discovered not only that Alexandra had traveled alone with Dallin but that they'd been intimate, Alexandra should have been relieved that her marriage to the marquess would still go off.

His icy indifference, however, left her bereft. It left her longing all the more for a man who'd spoken of her traveling the world with him.

"Let me be clear, my lady." Lord Wingrave tugged off his gloves and slapped them together a moment before stuffing them inside his black wool jacket. "After we marry, you can bed whomever you wish, whenever you wish, as long as you do so with some discretion. Until then, I'd ask you to keep your skirts lowered."

With that crass request, he left.

Alexandra stared after him.

This was the man she was to wed? One who didn't care if she remained faithful to him? A vise wrapped about her heart and threatened blood flow to that vital organ, and she welcomed it, because the pain of that death would be preferable to the long, cold marriage that awaited her at the end of her ride home.

Chapter 22

A fortnight later
London, England

Resplendent in a silver satin wedding gown studded with sparkling crystals and pearls, Alexandra stared out her bedroom window at the adjacent townhouse . . . and that rooftop where she'd dared to dream and hope and love.

It felt remarkably like she'd come full circle.

I wish I could go back. I wish I could move back the hands of time to a night when there was no Lord Wingrave, but only Dallin and me and a secret meeting spied on by only the millions of stars twinkling up in the night sky.

Closing her eyes, Alexandra pressed her brow against the windowpane and borrowed warmth from that heated surface.

It did little to ease the chill that had invaded her very person.

There came a slight knock at the door and the rapid flurry of footfalls as her maid rushed to admit the person on the other side.

Too tired to even look back, Alexandra continued to peer intently at that roof.

One last glimpse. That's all I want. That's all I need.

There'd been so many times these past days where she'd stood just so, looking out for him.

McQuoid man after McQuoid man had gone onto that rooftop. But never Dallin.

The only glimpses she'd caught of him were fleeting mentions in the gossip pages, about the Viscount of C's impending plans to tour the Continent.

Alexandra knew the gossips had it both wrong and right. He'd travel. But rather, he'd set sail for those distant seas where the stars shone brightest.

"Oh, Alexandra," her mother said from behind her.

Alexandra stiffened but did not look back at her last living parent. Instead, she met her gaze in the clear, crystal panes.

She registered the quiet click of the door closing as her maid let herself out.

"You look beautiful," her mother murmured when they found themselves alone.

I look beautiful for a man I've no wish to marry. A man who neither likes me nor dislikes me, but who, worse, feels absolutely nothing for me.

A hand touched her shoulder, and lost as she'd been in those tortured musings, Alexandra stiffened.

"I know you are nervous, Alexandra. I know you have regrets, but in time, His Lordship will come to love you."

A man so callous and deadened he didn't care who she bedded?

"No, he won't, Mama," she said tiredly, without inflection but also determined to disabuse her mother of such hopes. His Lordship wasn't capable of the sentiment.

"Your father—"

"He is not Papa and I'm not you," she said, directing that truth to Dallin's rooftop.

"I know you *think* that—"

"Please stop," she implored, at last making herself look away from the household of the only man she'd ever love and the one man she truly wished to marry. "Isn't it enough that I'm marrying him?"

Her mother stared at her with stricken eyes. "If there was absolutely any other way . . ."

The marchioness at least had the wherewithal to let that thought go unfinished.

For there wasn't any other way. They were both aware of that.

Alexandra looked away first, returning her gaze to the McQuoid residence.

At some point, Dallin's married sisters had arrived on their husbands' arms.

Propriety dictated Alexandra step away from the window, lest she be caught staring at the ladies and their gentlemen. Those couples, however, were far too engrossed in one another to ever notice her standing there. The way they laughed and smiled as they made the walk from their carriages to the front steps bespoke affection and love and—

I cannot bear this. Her mother and youngest sister would be cared for, but in sacrificing herself at the marital altar, Alexandra would face the worst sort of death.

Of their own volition, her eyes slid closed.

Her mother gave her shoulder a light squeeze. "Alexandra," she murmured. "We should be going, but . . . you may take a minute. Ready yourself."

Ready herself? She would never be ready for this. Incapable of words but thankful for any reprieve, Alexandra managed a slight nod.

The windowpanes reflected her mother's retreating figure and then the door closing until Alexandra was at last alone.

Alone for the last time as a Bradbury. For the moment she stepped out of this room and into the hall, she'd never again belong solely to herself. She'd have no say or determination in her future. Not even her dreams would be her own. All would rest squarely with the man she'd bind herself to this day. And where marriage to the wrong gentleman was the equivalent of a prison, with the right man, with Dallin, it could have, it would have, been so much more.

The lady fortunate enough to be his wife would find herself a partner and not property. Beloved and not belittled.

And until her dying day, Alexandra would hate that lucky woman with every fiber of her envy-filled soul. Even as she'd pray the owner of his affections proved loving and loyal and deserving of him.

"I can marry you . . . I want to marry you . . ."

That promise he'd uttered whispered around her mind, as real as when he'd spoken it.

Some movement caught her eye, a slight flicker; Alexandra tensed. *Click.*

It is time. I'm not ready. I need more.

"I said I'll be along in a moment, Ma—" Her words trailed off as, in the window, she caught a glimpse of her sister standing at the entryway, more somber than Alexandra ever recalled seeing her. "Cora."

Cora closed the door and pressed her back against the prettily painted white panel. "I've spent a lot of time thinking about what you shared with me . . . regarding our family's finances." Cora's gaze grew wistful. "Do you know, when I met Brone, I thought there was nothing more that I wanted in the world than to be his wife."

And she'd eventually have that. Alexandra bit hard on the inside of her lower lip. While her heart sang for her sister's happiness, she yearned for such a future with Dallin.

Her sister wandered away from the door. "Each time we met, I fell more and more in love with him. Nothing was more important than him." Cora stopped in front of Alexandra. "It wasn't until we returned home from our . . . travels . . ." She sagely, and with a caution she'd not displayed before her elopement, substituted the scandalous words of where they'd truly been. "I realized I was wrong."

Alexandra stared at her in confusion. "You do not love him?" she whispered.

"Oh, no," her sister said. "I love him and will forever love him." Cora took Alexandra's hands in her own. "But I love *you* more. Your happiness, your future—they mean more to me than my own."

Tears filled Alexandra's eyes, blurring her sister's visage. "Cora, you do not understand—"

"Now that you've finally confided everything about our circumstances, I understand everything with even more clarity." Her younger sister steeled her features. "It is how I know I cannot and will *not* see you sacrifice your very self for me."

"I must d—"

"I heard him," Cora interjected. "At the inn."

Alexandra's mind raced. When . . . ? How . . . ?

"I remained in the stairwell, first to ensure you had your privacy, and heard enough to know I intended to hear every other word he had to say to you." Cora's eyes hardened. "I heard how he spoke to you and what he said to you, and these past days, Alexandra, I have not wanted to interfere. I have waited for you to have your say until this morn, when I realized you never intended to. Well, I am. Do not marry him," she said.

Oh, Cora.

Alexandra sank her teeth into her trembling lower lip.

Cora took the last step toward her. "I said, do not marry him, Alex. Brone and I, we have already talked . . . something that this family could begin doing some more of," she added under her breath. "Brone has enough means to see us cared for. Oh, it won't be the extravagant life you and I grew up with, but I don't want that. He is enough, and we will weather whatever comes our way, and that includes the wrath of the duke."

Her sister was still innocent enough to believe in happily-ever-afters. "Cora—"

"You are in love with another, Alex."

She started.

"Do you think I'm so self-absorbed and buffle-headed to not know when my sister is in love?" Cora flicked her nose. "I've seen the way you stare at that roof these past days, Alex."

"I always stared at that roof," Alexandra pointed out. It was what had brought her together with Dallin.

"Fine, but I saw the way you looked at Lord Crichton at the inn, and it's the same look."

How much her sister truly saw. Now, Alexandra wished Cora were the oblivious girl she'd taken her for.

"You cannot marry the marquess when you love the viscount," her sister said earnestly.

"Ladies do not have the luxury of marrying for love."

"I am."

"That is different."

"Only because *you* are the one making the sacrifice. Well, I'll not trade your happiness for my own. End it with him."

On the day of her wedding? It would be the scandal of the century. "It is too late."

"It isn't."

"I'd be in breach of contract. We would never survive. And there'd be absolutely no hope for you, Daphne, or Mama."

The door exploded open, and they looked over.

Their youngest sister slammed the door behind her.

Her cheeks fired red to match the fury in her eyes, Daphne charged over, her white, ruffled skirts flying about her. "I'll not have you marry Losegrave, even if it means I have to paddle naked through the Thames and drink the water when I make my way across."

"Wingrave," Alexandra automatically corrected, her lips twitching at that inadvertent slip.

"Oh, I *know* his name," Daphne said. "*Lose*grave is what we shall call him because that is what you need to do. Lose him."

Cora nodded. "That is what I told her."

"Do you think I want you marrying that Friday-faced fellow?" her youngest sister demanded.

She didn't have a choice. And she knew her sisters knew as much, just as she knew.

Alexandra drew her sisters into her arms and clung to them. "I love you both so very much."

"Please," Daphne pleaded. "Don't do this."

Remaining silent, Alexandra hugged her sisters more tightly.

For them, she could do anything.

She would have to.

Chapter 23

On the day she was to marry, Lady Alexandra Bradbury shone bright as the Diamond she would have been had fate and her father permitted her first London Season.

She and the glorious satin gown she wore glittered like the bracelet now held in Dallin's fingers.

Motionless, he stood at the edge of the roof and watched her as she walked like the ethereal queen she was to the gold lacquer carriage embossed with the Duke of Talbert's seal.

He'd vowed he wasn't going to look for Alexandra or so much as glance in the general direction of her family's household—a lofty goal, considering the Bradburys' mammoth residence was poised directly across the way from the McQuoids'.

Even with that, however, since Dallin's return from the English countryside, he'd managed to keep that silent pledge he'd made to himself.

When he left the household to finalize the arrangements for his upcoming travel, he took a carriage and kept his head down, buried in the papers *about* his upcoming travel arrangements.

When the McQuoid men gathered upon the rooftop terrace to drink and study the stars, for the first time in his life, Dallin bowed out of joining them in his once favorite spot.

Only, that once favorite spot would remain just that to Dallin . . . not because of his love of astronomy but rather because it was the place where he and Alexandra had met.

When he went riding in the early hours of the morn, he kept his gaze forward and steered his mount in the opposite direction, trying not to think of her.

And even when riding, with only his horse for company, thoughts of her existed and intruded, and they'd forever be there, reminding Dallin of her: of Alexandra hanging out the window in the midst of a rainstorm and calling for him to join her.

I wish I'd done so. I wished I'd said to hell with propriety long before she forced our journey to a stop, asking me to ride with her.

Dallin, however, had been so very adamant that they follow decorum—as best as such circumstances permitted.

He'd been determined to keep his distance from her so that he didn't fall any further under her spell.

But now he tortured himself with the look he'd fought so hard to keep from taking and accepted the undeniable truth—no amount of distance he could have put between them would have been enough to accomplish that futile goal.

He was madly, truly, deeply, and forever hopelessly in love with her.

"Of course I love you . . ."

Alexandra reached the carriage.

The conveyance that would bear her onward to her bridegroom. A carriage that, henceforth, she'd ride in as the Marchioness of Wingrave.

I will not survive this . . . I do not want to survive this. The immediacy of death was preferable to a world in which she belonged to another man, a world where she'd make love with another. Give him children.

I want those babes with her. I want a daughter with her spirit and strength. And a son with her smile . . .

She stopped.

And for a moment, he thought she heard his silent pleas, because of course, they'd always moved with a beautiful symmetry.

Mayhap she'd not get inside that carriage. Maybe she'd not do this thing. Maybe she'd realize that his life was forfeit without her.

Maybe. Maybe. So many maybes.

Two elaborately uniformed servants, in gold to match the duke's carriage and with crimson epaulets upon their shoulders, each held forth a hand to Alexandra.

Do not take it. Take me. Let us run away to that place where the skies were biggest and the stars most plentiful.

Maybe she would. Maybe she wanted that, too, and enough for her to risk the Duke of Talbert's wrath.

But then she climbed inside that carriage with her mother and sisters following solemnly after her.

So many maybes, and only one certainty: she was lost to him.

Dallin dragged a shaky hand through his unkempt hair, and it would never not hurt; the agony of this loss threatened to cleave him in two, and he longed for it. Because mayhap then the pain would be broken down into something that didn't hurt every corner of his body and soul.

"For someone about to take his first voyage, I'd expected you'd be a good deal more gleeful," a voice called from over his shoulder.

Arran.

Dallin stiffened, and hurriedly stuffed the bracelet inside his pocket. "What do you want?"

"Why, hello to you, *too*, big brother," Arran drawled, stopping beside him.

They stood shoulder to shoulder, staring down at the streets below.

"It is a big day," Arran murmured, his earlier teasing tone gone.

A big day? Or an agonizing one?

Dallin stiffened. His brother knew that? He—

"Your ship sets sail at two o'clock, does it not?"

His ship? What ship? What was to set sail? What was his brother talking about? The only thing that mattered about this day was *her*, Alexandra.

Then it hit him. Arran took Dallin's melancholy for unease about his impending travels.

After all, Arran didn't know about Alexandra. No one did. Everything Dallin and Alexandra shared had existed in secret, and a secret it would forever remain.

"Are you having second thoughts?" Arran asked.

"Second, third, fourth, and fifth ones," he muttered. None of which pertained to his upcoming trip.

His younger brother chuckled and slapped him on the back. "If it is any consolation, I had doubts when I first set out on the seas. The feeling is normal."

If Dallin could have laughed at just how off the mark his brother was in terms of the conclusion he'd come to about Dallin's doleful state, he would have. As it was, he'd never laugh again. Or smile. There'd never again be a reason for it.

Arran looked over Dallin's shoulder. "We've company."

Splendid. Dallin followed his younger brother's attention to the pair bearing down on them—Myrtle and Cassia.

"I've tried to lift his spirits," Arran said. "Perhaps you two can try."

"Try and succeed," Myrtle muttered under her breath as Arran quit the rooftop and left Dallin alone with their sisters.

Coward.

"If you've come to discuss my travels," he said tiredly, "I'm not inclined."

"Oh, no worries there," Cassia piped in in her usual cheerful tones. "I've been on enough journeys of my own, where I certainly haven't come to discuss all *that* with you."

Once, that had grated. Though the eldest, he'd seen less than his younger brother. Even Dallin's younger *sister* had seen the world.

Granted, she'd sneaked off and boarded the incorrect ship. Yet in so doing, she'd met and married the love of her life, a sea captain whom she now traveled with regularly.

How had he once believed leaving London and having freedom from responsibilities was the life he wanted? How, when all along it had been Alexandra?

"Aren't you going to ask what we've come to talk about?" Myrtle's query cut in but did nothing to ease the misery threatening to suck him under.

"No," he said, praying his brusqueness would spare him from whatever business had brought them here.

Alas, each sister tugged off her gloves, indicating they intended to settle in. Not in the mood to indulge anyone, including his beloved—though vexing—sisters, Dallin disabused them of the idea he was in any mood for company.

"I said I'm not—"

"Inclined," Myrtle interrupted, waving one of her kidskin gloves as she spoke. "Yes, yes. We know all of that. Worry not, we've not come to discuss anything with you."

Then, what—

Myrtle slapped a glove against his cheek.

Dallin started. "What the—*oww!*" His question gave way to a shout.

He glared at his two sisters. "What the hell was—*oww*," he exclaimed as Cassia's palm connected with his cheek.

"You shouldn't curse in the presence of ladies," Cassia said pertly, like a prim governess delivering etiquette lessons.

His scowl deepened. "Yes, well, *ladies* shouldn't go about slapping men for no good reason, and yet here we are."

"Oh, we've plenty of good reasons," Myrtle said, and before he could retreat, she brought her glove sharply across his cheek again.

This time, he managed to cover the opposite one in time to mute Cassia's follow-up blow.

"That is what sisters are for."

"Based on today's visit, I thought sisters were for abusing their brothers," he muttered.

"Saving," Myrtle corrected.

Dallin stared incredulously at his younger sibling. "I hardly think a full-on assault constitutes sisterly affection," he said dryly.

"It does when said full-on assault is necessary to save you," Myrtle shot back.

"Save me?" Dallin glanced between his two sisters, who, with the black glowers they shot his way, may as well have been the ones slapped and not the other way around. "Save me from what, exactly?"

"Yourself."

"And a lifetime of misery," Cassia added.

"A—"

"You are in love," Myrtle said quietly, killing the rest of that question on Dallin's lips.

He stared blankly at her. As wrong as Arran had been, his sister had proven right. How did she know that?

Her eyes softened, as if he'd uttered that query aloud. "You have all the makings of a person who is in love," she said gently. "You've been doing a lot of pining."

"I've not—" Only this time, he stopped himself from completing that lie. For he was pining. "You don't understand."

"That you are in love with Alexandra Bradbury?"

He started.

"It appears we *do* understand," Cassia said smugly, giving a little toss of her head.

Myrtle touched a hand to his shoulder, drawing his gaze to her. "It didn't take much to put the pieces together. Why, the night our family

293

gathered to discuss Brone's elopement, you were nearly incandescent with rage."

"And it was *rage* that clued you in to the fact that I'm in love?" he asked dryly.

"Aha!" Cassia jabbed a finger under his nose and waggled it. "You don't deny it."

His neck went hot, and he fiddled at the place his cravat should be . . . if he weren't in such a state of dishevelment. "I deny it," he said belatedly, and also, by the triumphant looks his vexing sisters shot his way, ineffectually.

"At *first*," Cassia went on, "we feared you had also fallen in love with Cora Bradbury."

"But *that* didn't make sense, as Brone had been seeing the lady for a year before she even made her debut, whereas your first interaction with the lady was when you attempted to interrupt her meeting with our cousin."

He flared his brows. "You knew all that?"

Both sisters rolled their eyes. "Of course."

The fight went out of him, and Dallin sat down hard on a nearby stone bench. "I love her," he finally brought himself to confess, and oddly he felt better for having shared that with someone.

"Oh, Dallin," Myrtle said softly.

His sisters instantly sank down on either side of him; each rested a head against his shoulder, much the way they'd done as small girls who'd wanted to rise early and join him fishing at dawn, but who'd invariably tired and fallen asleep while they sat beside the loch of their family's Scottish estate.

"A woman who doesn't love you isn't one deserving of your heart, Dallin," Myrtle said.

"You love me . . . ?"

"Of course I love you."

"She loves me," he said, his voice catching.

His sisters instantly scrambled away from him. Both appeared thunderstruck.

"*What?*"

"Then . . . why in thunderation is she marrying *Lord Wingrave?*"

Cassia volunteered an answer to Myrtle's question. "Perhaps she loves him but is more in love with the idea of being a duchess."

"That isn't it!" That denial burst from him. "She . . . she . . ."

"Yes?" they asked in unison.

Alexandra's family was in financial ruins, and she found herself and her sisters and mother without the benefit of anyone to care for them.

He couldn't say as much.

"There are reasons which are her own," he settled for. "And they aren't mine to share. She belongs to another."

Oh, God.

As soon as those words left him, he wanted to bend over and twist and writhe to escape the pain.

He'd not survive this.

He—

"*Ow!*"

Dallin looked at the spot where Myrtle had punched him. "What the—" He edged out of reach and modified his words before Cassia could land the fist she'd already curled. "What was that for?"

"Women do not belong to people, Dallin," Myrtle said, drawing his focus her way.

It proved an imprudent action on his part.

Cassia landed the blow she'd been holding back. "We most certainly do not belong to men."

"That isn't what I meant. I meant . . ."

They stared expectantly at him and spoke in unison. "Yes?"

He exploded to his feet. "She's marrying another! Papers have been signed, and she's wedding Wingrave."

As if to both taunt and torment Dallin with that truth, somewhere in the distance a tower clock chimed the hour.

The fight went out of him, and this time he sank to the floor, brought his knees up, and buried his face in them. "And there is nothing I can do about it," he whispered.

Only silence met—

"Oomph."

He glared up at his sisters. "Did one of you kick me?"

Cassia shot her slippered foot out, catching him in his lower back. "Now *both* of us kicked you. Why haven't you already gone to her?"

"McQuoids love fiercely, and they fight for those they love," Myrtle said angrily. "We don't . . . wallow in pity and say, 'Woe is me.'"

"I didn't say, 'Woe is me.'"

"You may as well have," she snapped.

Another bell chimed.

What was he doing? Yes, she'd said she loved him and he'd offered to marry her, but he'd not fought for her. He'd not promised to stand beside her family through the darkest times and greatest challenges that would come from her breaking off her betrothal. He'd not reminded her that together they could face anything so long as they had one another. And he'd not done so because he couldn't give the assurances that he'd be able to care for her family in quite the same way Wingrave would. His own sense of inferiority had blinded him to the ultimate truth—that as long as he had Alexandra in his life, they could and would confront any challenge, together.

Only to have realized . . . too late.

She'd already left for the church. A long while ago.

"What have I done?" he whispered. "The wedding is no doubt underway."

"Yes, which is why you must be quick." Cassia clapped her hands once. "Your horse awaits. Nathaniel and Val were so good as to see that your mount is readied."

He looked at his smiling sisters. They'd had his horse saddled before they'd even spoken with him? "But before you said she didn't deserve me."

"That was when we didn't know she in fact loves you," Myrtle explained. "On the small chance that she did, however, we wanted to be prepared. Now, we can stand here all day celebrating the brilliance of your sisters or break off a wedd—"

Dallin was already taking flight. His heart hammering, he burst through the doors and raced down the stairs. As he descended landing after landing, he cursed himself for having been on the roof, of all places. That roof where he'd met Alexandra Bradbury and fallen in love.

Breathing hard and fast, he raced down the foyer steps.

The family butler, Hanes, already stood in wait with the double doors opened. A footman came forward with Dallin's hat.

Calling out his thanks, Dallin took that offering, and as he shot outside, he slammed the article atop his head.

Dallin sprinted the remaining way to where his brothers-in-law held Pegasus's reins. "Took you long enough," Winfield drawled.

"Good luck," Aragon said in his usual growl.

Luck. Luck was what he needed.

Dallin wheeled his mount onward to St. James's Church and set Pegasus into an all-out gallop.

As other riders and drivers shouted profanities his way, Dallin stayed low over his mount's neck.

Why did I wait so long? What if I'm too late? Don't be too late. Please, don't be too late.

It was a litany that became a prayer he uttered over and over to God above.

The lord, however, must have had some grievances with Dallin this day.

St. James's Street grew increasingly clogged with carriages and riders, all brought to a standstill. No doubt the many distinguished guests gathered for the preeminent wedding of the Season. *Alexandra's* celebrated wedding to another man, one who wasn't Dallin.

He'd never make it. He'd not get there in time.

Why had he waited so long? Why had he waited at all?

Panic threatened to take him down, and Dallin brought his mount to a stop.

Doing a quick circle, he searched for help. God had already failed him this day.

"Guv'nor, ya need sumfin?"

Dallin wheeled about, finding the tiny owner of that even tinier voice. A small street urchin with dirt-smudged cheeks, a cap entirely too big for his little head, stared up.

It appeared help had come after all, in the form of a child.

Dallin scrambled to tug a purse from inside his jacket. Only, he'd forgotten his jacket. Why had he left without his coat? Why hadn't he donned his coat?

He reached for his timepiece. Only, he'd lost that, too.

"Money," he vowed. "I promise there will be a sum. Riches, and a post in my household should you so wish it."

"Gor, sir," the boy said with a gap-toothed grin. "'Course I do."

Giving him instructions to his family's residence, Dallin took off running.

The world existed in a chaotic hum of sound. Wheels turning. Horses neighing. Passersby yelling. Dallin's breathing. Harsh and hard and fast.

Do not marry him.

Marry me, instead.

Please. Please. Please.

The back entrance from Jermyn Street would be the best, most proper way to enter a ceremony underway.

But then, was there a respectable way to interrupt those same proceedings?

She was his, as he was hers. Their souls had been forged as the other half of each other's.

At last, Dallin reached the Piccadilly entrance of St. James's Church. Gasping and fighting for breath from his flight, from his fear, Dallin grappled with the door handle. He wrenched the carved panel open so hard and fast the effusive wreath of pink and cream English roses toppled to the ground.

Stepping on all those wedding flowers, crushing them under his feet, Dallin stumbled into the church.

Every guest's head swung to the entrance, to him. Lords and ladies gawked. The vicar gaped. Everyone gasped. Someone swooned.

His lungs burnt, and still he forced out something, anything to stop this from happening, to keep her from wedding Wingrave. "Stop!"

It was an unnecessary command. Everything and everyone within the room had already gone completely still the moment he barged inside.

Alexandra's bridegroom stared back with flinty, almost bored eyes.

Dismissing him, needing to see just one person, to speak with only one woman in this room, Dallin kept walking to the pale figure, celestial in her beauty, unrivaled by the stars.

The gathering of guests found their voices.

Through his long march down the aisle, Alexandra stared at Dallin with tragic eyes. Tragic because the ceremony had already been completed and there truly was no hope for them? If so, he'd whisk her off, and they could journey unto the end of forever, to a place where no one existed but them and their love of one another.

As he strode forward purposefully, the flurry of whispers grew and grew until they filled the sanctuary like a hive of a million honeybees swarming.

Dallin reached the altar and stopped.

"Dallin," Alexandra whispered, and the chattering ceased.

Silence won.

Of course, because she, this queen of his heart and queen of all, could slay a simple quiet.

"What is the meaning of this?" a voice boomed from somewhere behind them.

Talbert? The king?

Either way, it didn't matter. Only Alexandra did.

The gaunt vicar snapped his book of prayer shut. "I really must insist that you excuse yourself at once," he demanded in nasally tones.

Dallin held out a bracelet.

Alexandra went absolutely still.

He placed that beloved piece in her palm. "I returned to London with the intention of preparing for my journey at sea, but instead, I found myself searching for and at last finding this."

Alexandra looked at her mother's bracelet, then lifted tear-filled eyes to his. "*This* is why you're here?"

"I came so I could reunite you with a keepsake so precious to you," he said. "And also to tell you how much I love you." Gasps went up. "How desperately I want you." More gasps filled the church.

Dallin cupped her cheek, and her golden lashes fluttered.

He worked his gaze over her beloved face. "But more, how desperately I want to spend the rest of my days making you smile and laugh."

"I want that, too," Alexandra whispered in tones so hushed, so very faint, he may have merely conjured them from his own yearnings.

Someone clapped. Two people, rather. So there were two in the church who didn't wish him dead. He glanced briefly to his supporters.

Alexandra's beaming sisters lifted their joined fists and shook them Dallin's way.

The girls' mother instantly lowered their hands and whispered furiously to them.

Whatever stern rebuke she'd doled out, it did nothing to diminish their happy smiles.

Dallin returned his attention to Alexandra. "Do not marry him, Alexandra," he said quietly.

Her gaze slipped over to a still-bored-looking Wingrave. Wingrave, who actually wore a faint air of amusement, tipped his chin up at Alexandra, as if daring her to end their wedding.

"Remove this upstart at once," the Duke of Talbert thundered.

No one made a move.

But then, fortunately, guards and constables and burly servants weren't generally guests at weddings between powerful families.

Talbert's cheeks grew florid. "I will see you ruined. And if she walks away, I'll see the both of you ruined. Her entire family."

"He'll try," Dallin murmured, and Alexandra slid her gaze back to him. "He will try, but we will have one another, and we will have the support and love of each other and our families. And that will be enough."

With her gaze, she found her mother.

"So sorry," the marchioness clearly mouthed. "Be happy." And then in a loud, clear voice, she called out, "We will weather this. It will be all right."

"The hell it will," Talbert bellowed.

"Please," the man's wife entreated. "You are making an even bigger scene, Your Grace."

"Bigger than *this*, you stupid woman?" the duke shouted, gesturing to the altar.

Dallin angled his body so he could block that blustering nobleman. "You see, Alexandra, I thought I wanted to travel. I thought I'd wished to shuck my responsibilities, if even for just a bit, and explore some of what the world had to offer. And then, once you were gone from my life"—he spoke in hushed tones for her ears alone—"it occurred to me."

"What?" she whispered.

"I didn't want those things more than you. Rather, you were all I wanted. The stars, the seas, the sunsets . . . None of them matter as long as you aren't in my life."

A little sob escaped her, and she buried that sound in her fist.

"Be my partner in life and life's journeys, Alexandra. Our love will strengthen us. Whatever trials and tribulations come, let us face them together."

"Oh, Dallin," she said achingly. "I cannot do that."

His heart forgot its function. It turned to hard, immovable stone in his chest, cutting off his life's blood flow and paralyzing him.

"You cannot," he repeated in deadened tones.

Alexandra shook her head.

From somewhere behind them, through the fog of his own misery and despair, he registered the pleased grunt belonging to the Duke of Talbert.

Dallin's arm fell uselessly to his side.

Oh, God.

I'll not survive this.

He turned to go. Or tried to.

Alexandra caught his hand, keeping him there, and he was so very desperate for even a fleeting feel of her that he clung to her and this moment.

"That is," she said softly, "I cannot let you abandon your dream of seeing the stars and the world. I'd only ask that we take that journey together."

A strangled laugh and cry escaped the both of them.

Dallin caught her in his arms and covered her mouth with his. "I love you," he rasped in between that kiss.

Simultaneously laughing and weeping, Alexandra cupped his face in her hands. "I love you, Dallin McQuoid."

And amidst swells of applause from the congregants, together, hand in hand, Dallin and Alexandra made their way down the opposite end of the aisle, and to their future, *together.*

About the Author

Christi Caldwell is the *USA Today* bestselling author of *The Duke Alone*, *The Heiress at Sea*, and numerous series, including Wantons of Waverton, Lost Lords of London, Sinful Brides, Wicked Wallflowers, and Heart of a Duke. She blames novelist Judith McNaught for luring her into the world of historical romance. When Christi was at the University of Connecticut, she began writing her own tales of love—ones where even the most perfect heroes and heroines had imperfections. She learned to enjoy torturing her couples before they earned their well-deserved happily ever after. Christi lives in the Piedmont region of North Carolina, where she spends her time writing and baking with her twin girls and courageous son. Fans who want to keep up with the latest news and information can sign up for her newsletter at www.christicaldwell.com.